LORD OF MATHURA

Ashok K. Banker is the author of the internationally acclaimed Ramayana Series® and other books. His books have been published in fifty-seven countries, a dozen languages, and have seen several hundred reprint editions with over 1.4 million copies currently in print.

He lives in Mumbai with his family. Visit him online at www.ashokbanker.com

BOOKS BY ASHOK K. BANKER

Lord of Mathura

KRISHNA CORIOLIS — BOOK IV

Ashok K. Banker

HARPER

First published in India in 2012 by Harper
An imprint of HarperCollins *Publishers*
a joint venture with
The India Today Group

Copyright © Ashok K. Banker 2012

ISBN: 978-93-5029-316-4

2 4 6 8 10 9 7 5 3 1

Ashok K. Banker asserts the moral right
to be identified as the author of this work.

HarperCollins *Publishers*
A-53, Sector 57, Noida 201301, India
77-85 Fulham Palace Road, London W6 8JB, United Kingdom
Hazelton Lanes, 55 Avenue Road, Suite 2900, Toronto, Ontario M5R 3L2
and 1995 Markham Road, Scarborough, Ontario M1B 5M8, Canada
25 Ryde Road, Pymble, Sydney, NSW 2073, Australia
31 View Road, Glenfield, Auckland 10, New Zealand
10 East 53rd Street, New York NY 10022, USA

Typeset in 11.5/ 14.2 Adobe Jenson Pro
InoSoft Systems Noida

Printed and bound at
Thomson Press (India) Ltd.

For V.K. Karthika:
Editor, Publisher, Fellow Book Lover.
For hearing Krishna's flute and understanding that the song
belongs to those who listen.
For continuing to show epic faith in me and my work.

All you faithful readers
who understand
that these tales
are not about being Hindu
or even about being Indian.
They're simply about being.

In that spirit,
I dedicate this gita-govinda
to the krishnachild in all of us.
For, under these countless
separate skins, there beats
a single eternal heart.

preface

If it takes a community to raise a child, it surely takes a nation to build an epic.

The itihasa of the subcontinent belongs to no single person. The great epics of our culture – of any culture – may be told and retold infinite number of times by innumerable poets and writers; yet, no single version is the final one.

The wonderful adventures of the great Lord Krishna are greater than what any story, edition or retelling can possibly encompass. The lila of God Incarnate is beyond the complete comprehension of any one person. We may each perceive some aspects of His greatness, but, like the blind men and the elephant, none of us can ever see everything at once.

It matters not whether you are Hindu or non-Hindu, whether you believe Krishna to be God or just a great historical personage, whether you are Indian or not. The richness and wonder of these tales have outlived countless generations and will outlast many more to come.

My humble attempt here – within these pages and in the volumes to follow – is neither the best nor the last retelling of this great story. I have no extraordinary talent or ability, no special skill or knowledge, no inner sight or visionary gift. What I *do* have is a lifelong exposure to an itihasa so vast, a culture so rich, a nation so great, wise and ancient, that their influence – permeating into one like water through peat over millennia, filtering through from mind to mind, memory to memory, mother to child and to mother again – has suffused every cell of my being, every unit of my consciousness.

And when I use the word 'I', it is meant in the universal. You are 'I'. As I am she. And she is all of us. Krishna's tale lives through each and every one of us. It is yours to tell. His to tell. Hers to tell. Mine as well. For as long as this tale is told, and retold, it lives on.

I have devoted years to the telling, to the crafting of words, sentences, paragraphs, pages, chapters, kaands and volumes. I shall devote more years to come, decades even. Yet, all my effort is not mine alone. It is the fruition of a billion Indians, and the billions who have lived before us. For each person who has known this tale and kept it alive in his heart has been a teller, a reteller, a poet, and an author. I am merely the newest name in a long, endless line of names that has had the honour and distinction of being associated with this great story.

It is my good fortune to be the newest reteller of this ancient saga. It is a distinction I share with all who tell and retell this story: from the grandmother who whispers it as a lullaby to the drowsy child, to the scholar who pores over each syllable of every shloka in an attempt to find an insight that has eluded countless scholars before him.

It is a tale told by me in this version; yet, it is not my tale alone to tell. It is your story. Our story. Her story. His story.

Accept it in this spirit and with all humility and hope. Also know that I did not create this flame, nor did I light the torch that blazes. I merely bore the torch this far. Now I give it to you. Take it from my hand. Pass it on. As it has passed from hand to hand, mind to mind, voice to voice, for unknown millennia.

Turn the page. See the spark catch flame.

Watch Krishna come alive.

author's note

All my books are long in the gestation, some conceived as many as thirty-plus years earlier, none less than a decade. It takes me that long to be sure of a story's longevity and worth and to accumulate the details, notes, research, character development and other tools without which I can't put my fingers to the keyboard. This particular story, Krishna Coriolis, originated in the same 'Big Bang' that was responsible for the creation of my entire Epic India universe – a series of interlinked retellings of all the major myths, legends and itihasa of the Indian subcontinent, set against the backdrop of world history. I'm using the term 'Big Bang' but in fact it was more of a series of carefully controlled delayed-time explosions over the first fifteen to eighteen years of my life.

At that time, the Krishna story was a part of the Sword of Dharma section of the Epic India library, which retold the 'dashavatara' storyline with an unusual twist as well as an integral part of my massively ambitious retelling of the world's greatest epic, the Mahabharata or the Mba. I began work on my Mba immediately after I completed the Ramayana Series in 2004. After about five years of working on my Mba – a period in which most actual MBA students would be firmly established in their careers! – I realized that the series was too massive to be published as it was. I saw that the Krishna storyline, in particular his individual adventures, could stand on their own as a separate series. So I separated them into a parallel series which I titled Krishna Coriolis. Naturally, since the story now had to stand on its own, rather than be a part of the larger Mba story, I had to rewrite each book to make it stand on its own, with a reasonably complete beginning, middle and end. This process took another three years, and resulted finally in the form the series now takes. You're holding the fourth book of this parallel series in your hands now, titled *Lord of Mathura*.

Lord of Mathura is just the fourth part of the Krishna Coriolis, which is interlinked with the much larger Mba series, which itself is only one section of my whole Epic India library. To read the Mahabharata Series, start with the first book, *The Forest of Stories*, available in all good bookstores online and near you. Yet, I've laboured to make *Lord of Mathura* stand on its own and be a satisfying read. Naturally, it's not complete in the story, since that would require not just the full Krishna storyline but also the larger Mba story and the larger context behind that as well. In that sense, it's just a part of the big picture; but even the longest journey must start with a single step and if you permit, *Lord of Mathura* will take you on a short but eventful trip, one packed with action and magic, terror and adventure. The reason why the book, like the remaining books in the series, is so short, almost half of the length of my earlier Ramayana Series, is because that's the best way the structure works. By that I mean the individual parts of the story and the way in which they fit together. Sure, I could make it longer – or shorter. But this felt like the perfect length. In an ideal world, the entire series would be packaged together as one massive book and published at once – but that's not only impossible in terms of paper thickness and binding and cover price affordability, it's not the right structure for the story. Stories have been split into sections, or volumes, or, in our culture, into parvas, kaands, suras, mandalas and so on, since literature was first written. You might as well ask the same question of Krishna Dwaipayana-Vyasa – 'Sir, why did you split the Mahabharata into so many parvas and each parva into smaller sections and so on?' The fact is, a story needs to be structured and the story itself decides which structure works best. That was the case here and I am very pleased with the way *Lord of Mathura* and the other books in the series turned out.

The Sword of Dharma mini-series, as I call it now, is also written in first draft and tells us the experiences and adventures of Lord Vishnu in the heavenly realms. It is a direct sequel to the Ramayana Series as well as a bridge story to the Krishna Coriolis and Mahabharata Series. And since it deals with other-worldly events, it exists outside of 'normal' time as we know it, which means it is also a sequel to the Krishna Coriolis and also a prequel to the Ramayana Series. I won't confuse you further: once you read Sword of Dharma, you will understand what I mean because the story itself is an action-packed adventure story where questions like 'when is this taking place?' and 'so is this happening before or after such-and-such?' become less important than seeing the curtain parted and the world beyond the curtain revealed in its full glorious detail. No matter how much I may show you in the Ramayana Series, Krishna Coriolis and Mahabharata Series, all these 'mortal' tales are ultimately being affected and altered by events taking place at the 'immortal' level, and only by seeing that story-beyond-the-story can we fully comprehend the epic saga of gods and demons that forms the basis of Hindu mythology in our puranas.

In *Flute of Vrindavan*, we saw Swayam Bhagwan (as the Bhagawatham calls him) grow in strength and maturity to despatch all the asura assassins sent by Kamsa, risking his own immortality time and again to keep his adoptive tribe of Vrishnis safe in their exile. In *Lord of Mathura*, we proceed at breakneck pace towards the final clash between God Incarnate and his nemesis. Finally, in this book, the Krishna–Kamsa conflict concludes with an epic one-on-one fight on the wrestling field as the fifteen-year-old Slayer lives up to his name and fulfils the prophecy. But that is not the end of Krishna's woes. *Rage of Jarasandha*: Krishna Coriolis Book 5 picks up the story immediately after *Lord of Mathura* and brings another enemy to the fore. The dreaded Magadhan himself, father-in-law of Kamsa and a far more powerful being, Jarasandha makes his true intentions regarding Mathura clear at last, besieging the city with a force so superior, everyone wonders if even Krishna and Balarama can defeat it.

The Kamsa threat is only the first major crisis that confronts the young adult Krishna. His epic journey in human form has only just begun. And that too is only part of the much, much larger tale of Krishna, which itself is part of the larger tale of Lord Vishnu, which is only part of the far greater saga of gods and demons. It's an epic saga, but the beauty of it is that each portion is delicious and fulfilling in itself!

Enjoy!

	yadricchaya chopapannah	
	svargadvaram apavritam	
	sukhinah kshatriya partha	
	labhante yuddhamidrisham	

Blessed are the warriors
Who are chosen to fight justly;
For the doors to heaven
Shall be opened unto them.

Prarambh

one

The song of the flute filled the hamlet of Vrindavan.
Its sweet, mournful melody carried to the remotest eaves and highest treetops and no creature that heard it failed to be moved.

Its presence brought comfort and strength to the denizens of that secluded valley, assuring them that they were safe in this secluded retreat away from the world at large, that someone powerful and benevolent was watching over them, and that any threat would be dealt with at once. But there was another message the flute imparted – one embodied by the sweet sadness of its song – that life and all its pleasures were finite and would end some day, and one must make the best of the time one has, for it will not last. It mourned the lost brothers and sisters of the Vrishnis who were in Vrindavan in voluntary exile from their beloved homeland; it mourned the tragedy that had befallen the Yadava nation; it shared the grief of love and loss, death and failure, war and vengeance.

The flute sang of things that could not be expressed, things that were felt but left unsaid, things that had happened before and would happen again, inevitably, but not now, not just yet. The flute song was the pause between battles, the respite between wars, the rare moment of peace between the violence of yesterday and the madness of tomorrow. The melody was what kept the Vrishnis sane and whole and nourished them with the nectar of hope each fine day in Vrindavan. The flute was their reason for going on, for facing each day with confidence.

When the song was done, the hand that played the flute lowered the instrument. The player wiped the wooden reed on his brightly coloured anga-vastra before tucking it securely into his waistband sash. Even now, despite all that had gone before, he was still just a boy.

Yet there was a serenity about him that belied his years. His dark face could be sombre and brooding like a monsoon cloud. Yet, when he smiled, his white teeth flashed in that dark space – like lightning against a pitch-black sky. His hot brown eyes gleamed with life, danced with intelligence. His smile tended to crease one cheek more than the other, giving him a sly rascally look that portended mischief. Unconcerned about his appearance and grooming, he nevertheless managed to always look fetching, almost girlishly handsome. In contrast to his brother's fair-skinned bullish bulk, he was a slender dark calf.

Already, the mother gopis gossiped about what a handsome young man he would turn out to be and how some young gopi would be very lucky to have him as her mate. Child marriage was common among Yadavas but not compulsory. Nanda Maharaja's sons, by virtue of being born to the clan chief, could choose their mates when they pleased, provided the girls like them too. The Vrishnis, even more than other Yadavas, appreciated the finer emotions and the heart played as important a part in that choice as other factors such as clan, tribe, gotra and family. In Krishna's case, he was already a prince among gopas and could have any gopi of his choice for a paramour and wife.

The younger gopis returning from the pastures, herding their calves in front of them, were proof of this adoration: every last one smiled and waved and greeted him as she passed by, praising his flute playing. He smiled enigmatically as he always did, saying nothing but acknowledging them all and somehow making each one feel as if it were *she* alone that he had smiled at so fetchingly. They ran giggling, happy, to pen their calves for the night.

The lazy summer was working its way slowly towards autumn and the cowherds of Vrindavan spent the evenings indulging in their favourite pastime – ras-lila. When the day's work was done, everyone looked forward to a few hours of companionship and respite. The cowherd's life was a simple one: hard work, but with no unendurable hardships or glamorous highs, merely an endless series of routine repetitions, day after day, season after season. After the first traumatic year of exile, the idyllic hamlet of Vrindavan now seemed like home to the Vrishnis and they had already come to love and enjoy its bounty.

Playing his flute, Krishna wandered down the dales and glens, pastures and pens, hills and dips, lakesides and wooded areas. At the meadow where the community played ras-lila, every gopi waited and hoped to see him appear. More than one dreamt romantic dreams of herself with Yashoda's dark-hued son. But today Krishna was not in the mood to play. Today he felt his heart ache with a peculiar sadness – the dusky languidness of evening and the satisfaction of a long day's hard work commingling with the certainty that this season of peace and calm would not last, that it was but the lull before the coming storm, and when that storm came, it would be terrible in rage.

He was not feeling anxious, exactly, for despite his mortal form, he was Himself incarnate and as such immune to the weaknesses and injuries of flesh and mortality. But he had come to care deeply about the people amongst whom he lived and he knew they would pay a price for sheltering him – were indeed already paying a price, for here they were in exile from their beloved home pastures.

Many mortals believed that to be able to see the future would be a wondrous gift, but those immortals who *did* see the future knew that it was no gift, nor wondrous. For the future, like the past, like life itself, contained not only good, wonderful things and events, but also many dark, terrible, painful things. What person would want to know all the bad that was to befall him? Mere knowledge of it alone would cast a backward shadow over the rest of that person's existence. And so, in Krishna's case, that shadow loomed long and large, for he could see all the way into Eternity.

In a manner of speaking, it was grief that Krishna was experiencing. For time could keep no secrets from him. And he saw the terrible wages of insubordination – death and suffering – that had been endured since his birth on this mortal plane, the anguish that was being borne at that very moment, and in the ones yet to come. And the burden of all that pain lay heavy upon his heart.

And so he wandered the hills of Vrindavan and played his flute, filling the world with the sweet–sad beauty of his song, trying to lighten his burden through music.

He was not wholly successful. But it helped. It helped a little.

And that was enough.

two

War was an art.
Kamsa was a master of the art.
He charged through the enemy ranks, flailing, pounding, battering, bludgeoning, hammering ...

Though he wielded swords and weapons when required, his new method of attack relied more on brute force than technique or finesse. Under Jarasandha's guidance, and aided by the Magadhan's Ayurvedic elixirs, his body had grown even harder and become more invulnerable than before. Finely honed Mithila steel would go blunt when it came in contact with his skin; a javelin thrown by a bull-strong giant would shatter without leaving the tiniest scratch on his body. Even arrows with special heads designed to punch through armour would splinter on impact with his impenetrable hide.

But more amazing than his ability to withstand damage was his ability to inflict it – as he was demonstrating so ably right now.

He was working his way through a throng of enemy foot soldiers. There had been perhaps four or five hundred when he had made first contact. Two score or more had been killed at that very instant, bodies crushed and smashed to bloody pulp like ripe berries under the impact of his weight and forward momentum. The huddled mass of the remainder, no doubt believing that by concentrating their strength they might resist him, swayed for a moment, then held their line like a hemp rope strung taut between trees. Perhaps half a score more were then crushed between their own comrades and Kamsa when he pushed forward.

He saw men wheeze bloody spray from their mouths and nostrils as their lungs collapsed or were punctured in the killing crush. He heard bodies crumple and lose their very shape as he exerted his strength. Others exploded like bulging wine bags bursting under an elephant's foot, spraying bloody remains everywhere.

He was coated in blood and guts and bone chips and offal.

His flaring nostrils could smell the sweet stink of victory.

He roared and heard his roar resonate, the increased density of his body somehow altering his voice, making it sound lower-pitched, guttural, hard enough to assault and cause physical pain to those unfortunate enough to be in close proximity to him. He saw men clutch at their ears and blood ooze from their auditory orifices.

He spread his arms, bent forward in a bull's charging stance, locked his knees and shoved forward with a mighty effort.

The ranks of enemy soldiers rippled like grass in a strong wind. At the back of the huddled ranks, men were thrown yards away, tumbling madly head over heels.

He heaved again, then pushed forward, feeling his feet sink into the hard-packed earth, the earth yielding beneath his weight and force.

The entire battalion of enemy soldiers was pushed backwards as if struck by a battering ram. The soldiers at the edges and rear went flying in all directions, their bodies flung through the air like scarecrows in a storm gale. Others were thrown onto their backs and trampled underfoot by their own comrades. Yet others pierced or penetrated by their comrades' weapons or armour.

Kamsa grasped hold of as many of the nearest unfortunates as he could get hold of – perhaps a score of enemy soldiers – picked the whole mass up bodily, and *shoved* them.

The soldiers whom he grasped and used as purchase got crushed like ripe grapes, their bodies and organs spattering in his iron grip. Their combined bulk served as a cudgel with which he bludgeoned the battalion itself. He shoved this way then that, pushing forward until the whole mass began to give way like a laden wagon once inertia is overcome; then he walked forward slowly, steadily, step by step, shoving a throng of five hundred men backwards.

It was a sight to behold.

Many of Kamsa's own men stopped to watch. Even the *enemy* stopped to watch the incredible sight.

It was a grape-press and Kamsa the vintner pressing living men into blood-wine.

By the time he had pushed ahead a hundred yards, every last man in the battalion was dead or dying from fatal wounds.

Finally, Kamsa stopped and let go of the men he had in his grasp. They fell like wet sacks to the bloodied ground. The gleaming, armour-clad gathering had been reduced to half a thousand pulped and mangled corpses.

He glanced back and saw the gory trail of his death walk: two score yards of the battlefield painted crimson, like a great mark of death upon the face of the enemy's ranks. It reminded him of a freshly ploughed field, the dark just-turned earth contrasting with the unploughed side. Except that what he had done here was better compared to reaping, not sowing.

He looked around the field. The battle was continuing on either side, but not a single enemy soldier approached him or dared to attack. If anything, the warriors had pushed back and away to stay clear of him. It was one thing being in front of him in battle and so being compelled to fight and quite another to witness the mayhem he caused and still wish to fight him.

He stood alone, alive, in a clearing of corpses within a forest of battle.

He grinned and thumped his chest twice to mark his victory. There was no need to issue the typical chauvinistic roar of triumph.

The sound of his chest thumping itself was louder than a full array of tom-toms. It resonated across the field – louder even than the mangled screams and clash of weaponry – like a giant drumbeat tolling the defeat of the enemy.

A movement caught his attention out of the corner of his eye. It was a single warrior, racing towards him on foot, sword held up like a javelin. It was a senapati of the enemy army, probably the commander of the battalion he had just threshed like bloody maize. The man must know that he stood no chance, yet he came straight at Kamsa, striking down diagonally as if dealing with a normal human opponent. Fool! To think he could attack Kamsa with a single sword.

To give credit to the fool, he was fast.

The sword raked Kamsa's waist, the blade crumpling like tinfoil, and with his other hand, the man tried to stab Kamsa with a dagger, aiming for his throat. Kamsa was impressed by the man's courage and folly and permitted him his attempt. When the blade point shattered and the blade itself gave way with each successive stab, the man was left with no weapon and no hope of success.

And yet he fought on, audaciously, hopelessly, pitifully.

He hammered at Kamsa's body with his fists, kicked out, jabbed and slapped Kamsa, breaking his own ankle, wrists and forearm, and dislocating both his shoulders out of sheer fury and desperation.

Kamsa grasped hold of him with a single hand, holding him up by the throat, the broken body still flailing desperately.

Kamsa was curious. 'Why did you throw your life away? You knew you could not best me.'

The man stared down at Kamsa with hate burning in his black pupils. 'You slaughtered my entire tribe today, Childslayer. What is a chieftain without a tribe? Kill me now and let me die with honour like my kith and kin!'

Kamsa cocked his head, glancing sideways at the grape-pressed bodies of the men he had killed. An entire tribe? Had he really done that? In just a short while, no more time than it might take him to eat a meal or defecate.

'Fight me now, Monster of Mathura!' the chieftain cried hoarsely. 'Fight me or die!'

Fight me or die? Kamsa almost smiled at that absurd threat.

Then, without even looking at the man, he closed his fist around the man's throat, feeling his fingers meet as the bones and tendons and flesh turned to mush in his fist. The flailing and threats ceased at once. Kamsa let the corpse drop to the ground heavily, blood spurting from the severed throat.

Though he had heard it often before and knew he would hear it again, he did not like that phrase. Not the first one: Childslayer. That one he did not mind for he had slayed children and enjoyed doing so. He didn't mind being called what he truly was, after all.

It was the second name he didn't care for.

Monster of Mathura.

He was no monster. He was Kamsa, king of the Yadava nation. *Lord* of Mathura.

When would the world accept him as such?

three

Jarasandha was pleased. Watching the battle from a high promontory, he viewed Kamsa's rout of the enemy with pride and pleasure.

His protégé had come a long way. Kamsa had done him proud.

His son-in-law's prowess on the battlefield today and in the preceding months had been nothing short of formidable.

No other fighter in his ranks matched the power and ferocity of Kamsa in battle. Certainly, none matched his tally of kills to date. The king of Mathura took lives like a force of nature, heaping up bodies like a whirlwind or monsoon typhoon.

Even Jarasandha sometimes found reason to marvel at his accomplishments. The sheer volume of casualty inflicted by his son-in-law was prodigious. Kamsa had already become a legend in the ranks of the Magadhan Army. Once written off as a mere stripling Yadava capable of being taken down by a handful of Mohini Fauj warriors, the son of Ugrasena and Padmavati had now earned the respect of even Jarasandha's most renowned champions. Almost all had come to accept and befriend him, some more closely than others. A few, very few indeed, had made the mistake of antagonizing or opposing him and had paid the price of their folly, mostly on the akhara – the wrestling field which was the only place where Jarasandha permitted his soldiers to resolve their internal differences. There, as on the battlefield, Kamsa fought with a ferocious single-mindedness that was unmatched, despatching those foolish enough to oppose him with mortal blows or crippling injuries. Those who played against him sportingly, he dismissed from the game with a mere broken limb or two.

From an immature boy unable to overcome his own base desires and lusts to a true warrior and leader of armies, Kamsa had come a long way.

Even his governance of Mathura had improved considerably. While the resentment remained and pockets of resistance continued to defy his claim to the throne, the overall situation had improved. No more open defiance and challenging of his authority. No more martyrdom and suicidal frontal assaults on his soldiers or himself. Political backbiting and character vilification were not things that troubled Jarasandha overmuch: they were a part of public life and he was aware how bitterly the people of his dominions spoke of him behind closed doors. So long as that bitterness was restricted to back-door gossip and mere talk, it did not bother him. If anything, it only proved that Kamsa was maturing as a politician and statesman: every successful ruler was bound to have people who resented him. It was only when that resentment boiled over into open sedition that it became a cause of concern.

Jarasandha had risen and come forward to gain a better view of Kamsa's triumph in battle. Now he regained his seat, gesturing to his lackeys to fetch him choice sweetmeats. He always enjoyed sampling the local specialities of each region he conquered. For some reason, eating their food made the conquest real and memorable. The fact that he literally ate choice portions of meat carved from the bodies of victims in each region, prepared by their own cooks in the style of the

region, lent a new meaning to the term 'sweetmeat'. It also added
to his awe-inspiring reputation as the 'eater of nations'.

As he snacked on some delicious spiced cuts taken from
the living body of the chief of chiefs of the region he had just
invaded and was in the process of conquering, Jarasandha
considered Kamsa again.

He knew that the change that had overcome his son-in-law
stemmed from diverting Kamsa's rakshasa predilection for
violence and lustful living into more manageable diversions.
Cooped up in Mathura all year long, Kamsa had taken to
unleashing his appetites on his own people. That was not an
advisable course of action for a monarch. The old Yadava who
had trained Kamsa in the use of his new-found abilities had
clearly understood this and had successfully showed Kamsa
how to divert his considerable power and strength into more
sporting pastimes.

Jarasandha had then taken Kamsa to the next level, turning
him into a yoddha in his own ranks and using him as a tool
of conquest and expansion, while providing Kamsa a natural
outlet for his aggression. Better that Kamsa batter the brains of
enemies in the battlefield than the heads of his own citizens in
the streets of Mathura. Jarasandha had encouraged and enabled
Kamsa to wrest the throne from Ugrasena for his own ends, but
a kingdom weakened by internal strife was not what he desired.
He wished Mathura to remain strong and resilient so that when
he ultimately sidelined Kamsa and effectively governed the
region, it would be a valuable part of his greater plan.

Thus far, the plan had succeeded magnificently. Kamsa had
performed brilliantly and Mathura had settled into the routine
of bureaucratic torpor that was the usual condition of most
capital city states. The bitter strife that had threatened to plunge

it into civil war only a decade earlier had settled into a series of disgruntled factions jockeying for positions of power and seeking to ingratiate themselves with Kamsa and his powerful father-in-law.

Only a few pockets of outright resistance remained, buoyed by their delusional faith in their supernatural saviour, the legendary 'Slayer of Kamsa'. But thus far, the Slayer hadn't so much as dared to harm a hair on Kamsa's handsome head. If and when the mythic Deliverer truly lived up to his name, he would be dealt with swiftly and firmly. Like most myths, the Slayer probably thrived on half-knowledge and shadowy rumour, and the instant he stepped out into the clear light of day, he would be vaporized like mist. The only danger, if one might perceive it even as that, was the growing cult of believers who regarded the mythic eighth child as some kind of avatar of Vishnu, or even, Jarasandha chuckled to himself softly, as God Incarnate! These foolish superstitious peasants! They would believe *anything* fed to them by their Brahmin oppressors.

In any case, Jarasandha had a plan for dealing with the so-called Deliverer. Supernaturally empowered or not, God or mere myth, the plan Jarasandha had in mind would put paid to him once and for all, both the child and the myth. He turned his thoughts back to the main topic that required his attention.

Jarasandha's main focus was on building Kamsa's strength and reputation, both as a yoddha in battle and as a king. Among the Yadavas, the two were always interdependent. While he enjoyed Kamsa's participation in his own ongoing campaign of conquest, he also ensured that Kamsa returned to Mathura regularly enough to establish his dominance and leave no doubt about his kingship. The day-to-day governance was ably handled by veterans like Pralamba and his own minions and hand-picked loyalists, but even though he was mostly a figurehead, it was still important for Kamsa to be *seen* governing. It was time now for Kamsa to return and be seen again as Lord of Mathura. That was what he had decided after viewing the battle: Kamsa had earned sufficient valour points these past weeks. Now he must be sent home.

He watched now as the familiar vahan wound its way up the hillside, bringing Kamsa to him.

Moments later, Kamsa stepped off the vahan and bowed to Jarasandha, grinning as he presented his father-in-law and emperor with the severed head of the chieftain he had just defeated. 'My emperor,' he said. 'A little something for your stew tonight!'

Jarasandha chuckled. 'Well done, my son. Come, sit with me. You have done well today.'

Kamsa inclined his head graciously. Along with other graces, he had come to accept his position vis-à-vis Jarasandha as well, a fact that pleased the Magadhan. It was tiresome to have to keep swatting down the younger man and remind him who was top dog in this pack. Better to accept one's position and enjoy the fruits of grace.

'By your grace, Father,' Kamsa said as if echoing this very sentiment.

Jarasandha smiled.

Yes. Kamsa had turned out quite well, after all.

four

Kamsa noted that Jarasandha had set up his observation post in front of the mouth of a cave. The interior of the cave was dark and forbidding, and he had heard rumours about the being that dwelled within. He was curious about it but this was not the time to ask Jarasandha. Perhaps later …

Jarasandha was silent for a while. Then he broached the subject that he had been waiting to discuss with Kamsa. The one problem that Kamsa and he had yet to conquer. Kamsa had been expecting him to bring it up and was not surprised when Jarasandha spoke.

'I wish to speak with you about the Deliverer. It is time we despatched that problem once and for all.'

Jarasandha's tone was casual, as if speaking of a troublesome chieftain of a tribe that refused to yield despite the rest of the nation surrendering. Just another gnat to swat.

Kamsa did not take the problem of the Slayer as lightly. He felt his own grin vanishing and his face hardening at the mention of the old nemesis.

'The first group of assassins led by Putana was defeated,' he replied. 'And the Vrishnis have gone into exile, taking refuge in a secret hamlet within the Vrindavan hills. Finding them is difficult enough, getting to the Deliverer virtually impossible. And killing him …'

Kamsa clenched his fist, crushing the goblet he had just drunk from without even realizing he was doing so. The metal crumpled in his fist, blood-red wine spilling between his fingers and dripping to the ground. 'If only I could face him once, myself. I would …'

'You would endanger us all,' Jarasandha said sharply. 'I have told you this before and I shall say it again, Kamsa. A wise general does not go running himself to face his arch enemy. He uses his army, his captains, his akshohini, strategy and tactics, ruses and wiles, to achieve his ends. You are no longer a mere warrior–prince. You are King Kamsa of Mathura. If this "Deliverer" comes to you, you will have the chance to crush him. But it is *not* your place to go looking in crannies and nooks for cowardly rebels.'

'Then what would you have me do?' Kamsa asked.

Jarasandha carefully selected an item from the platter beside him, a delicacy left almost raw. He inserted it into his mouth and chewed slowly, savouring the exotic flavour. A trickle of blood escaped from the corner of his mouth and wound its way down his chin. His tongue shot out, cleaning the trail, the tip of the extended organ lingering around his jaw and neck for a moment before retracting into his mouth with a slurping sound.

'Childslayer,' Jarasandha said.

Kamsa frowned.

'That is the name by which you are known, is it not?' Jarasandha asked. 'The name by which you became famous amongst your kinfolk?' He smiled slyly, the twin tips of his forked tongue slithering in and out between his lips. 'Or notorious, as some would say?'

Kamsa shrugged. He had long since become inured to

Jarasandha's attempts at provocation. Besides, he didn't mind that particular title. It was true, after all.

'You earned that name because of your fondness for slaughtering newborn babes, infants, the firstborn male child of every household. Is this not so?'

Kamsa nodded.

Jarasandha sucked on another delicacy, something wet and pinkish that prompted the Magadhan to make a slurping sound as he relished it. 'It is time to resurrect that reputation. To unleash the Childslayer once more.'

The ground beneath them began to shudder. The Mohinis stationed near the mouth of the cave appeared nervous and unsettled. Most of them moved away from the dark opening, leaving only their emperor's immediate bodyguards at their posts. The shuddering continued, growing steadily in intensity … as if something were approaching. Jarasandha himself appeared calm and unruffled. Kamsa took his cue from his father-in-law. He knew better than to show trepidation or nervousness in Jarasandha's presence. 'When with men, one must behave like a man,' Jarasandha always said.

'Unleash …?' Kamsa asked.

Jarasandha smiled slyly again, dabbing at the corners of his lips where pinkish juices were smeared. 'You sent Putana and Baka to assassinate the Deliverer. Their failure has upset Baka's brother asura greatly. He desires vengeance.'

Suddenly, Kamsa understood the meaning of the cave and the shuddering and the reason why the Mohinis – who never showed fear even in the face of certain death – seemed so afraid. 'Agha,' he said. 'I recall Putana mentioning him when she recommended Baka. He was unavailable at the time for some reason.'

Jarasandha chuckled. 'Unavailable. That would be one way of putting it. Yes, Putana assumed that she alone would be more than sufficient to deal with the eighth child. To have sent Agha would have been like sending a lightning bolt to kill an ant. But now we see that the purported Deliverer is not to be underestimated. Therefore, I have summoned Agha. He is eager to undertake this task in your name. To do the childslaying for you.'

The rumbling reached a crescendo. Kamsa could see something approaching from deep within the dark maw of the cave, as if some mighty creature were rushing up to the surface from deep within the bowels of the earth. It would arrive at any moment now.

Kamsa nodded. 'So Agha will go to slay the Deliverer.'

Jarasandha beamed. 'Not just the Deliverer. *All* the children of Vrajbhoomi. We have got information that the Deliverer has at least one sibling, empowered with supernatural abilities as well.'

The skin on the back of Kamsa's neck prickled but he said nothing. He had heard the rumours too. They made him uneasy. How many Slayers of Kamsa were there? What were these supernatural abilities? And what of the conviction – so deeply rooted in some of his citizenry that they would not renounce it even under extreme torture – that the Deliverer was in fact Vishnu Incarnate himself?

Jarasandha continued. 'It's best to be safe. Rather than chance killing one and sparing the other, Agha will wipe out the entire population of young male Vrishnis. As we already know, they have taken refuge in a secret hamlet in the Vrindavan hills. By travelling within the earth as only he can do, Agha will ensure that his identity and movements remain unknown. Then he will seek the clan out and slaughter the children. If he can kill the Deliverer too, well and good. If not, he will force him to emerge from hiding and confront you directly.'

Kamsa swallowed, his throat suddenly dry. 'Excellent.'

Suddenly, the cave collapsed, engulfing the Mohinis standing closest to it, even though they were at a distance of several yards from the entrance.

Kamsa watched as the roof fell upon the unfortunate Hijras, then drew back, shuddering. And then the entrance of the cave opened again, wider than before. Within it he saw the half-broken bodies of the Hijras, screaming in agony. Then the cave shuddered again, violently, and they were swallowed into its depths. Weapons drawn and ready, the remaining Mohinis had moved as far away from the entrance as possible. The mouth of the cave turned this way then that, seeking fresh victims, before it raised itself up to point and roared a deafening blast.

The cave was not a cave at all, Kamsa realized. It was an asura. A snake-like being as large as a small hillock, curled upon itself, with a maw as enormous as a cavern. Most unnerving of all was its effective camouflage that enabled it to lie so close to the Mohinis without giving them cause for suspicion.

'Agha,' Jarasandha said pleasantly, introducing their guest. 'Meet Kamsa, the Childslayer. It is at his bidding that you undertake this mission we entrust unto you. Go to Vrindavan, find the child avatar of Vishnu and eat him as well as all the young children around him.'

The stench of rotting flesh such as Kamsa had never smelt before wafted out of the asura, carrying the memory of a thousand carcasses consumed and half-digested within that gargantuan belly. A sound like a deep bass trumpeting filled the air, causing Kamsa's very bones to vibrate within their sockets. A deep redolent rumbling intonation that was closer to thunder than to any voice spoke then, at a pitch so low, dogs began barking and baying across the land in panic: 'EAT THE CHILDREN. IT SHALL BE DONE.'

Kamsa grinned at Jarasandha who smiled back.

All three of them laughed. Jarasandha, Kamsa and Agha.

The sound of their laughter echoed like distant thunder. It carried a long, long way.

Kaand I

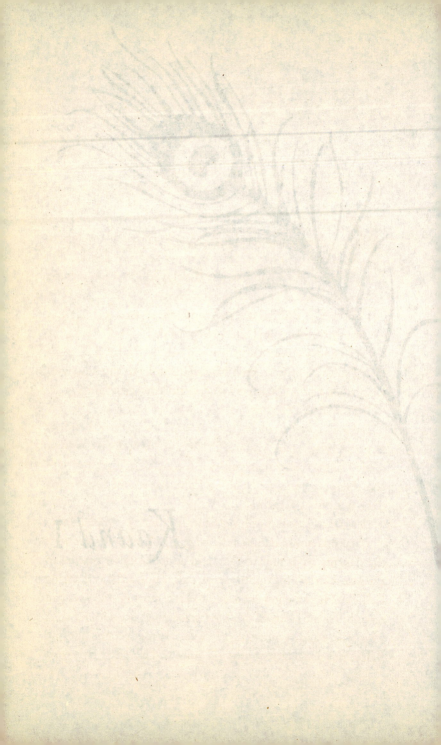

one

'Krishna!'

Balarama looked at Krishna and raised his eyebrows. Then he wiggled his eyebrows so they danced like caterpillars. It was a habit he had developed recently – mainly because he knew it annoyed Rohini-maata.

However, it didn't have the same effect on Krishna. His younger brother ignored him and continued walking, using the crook to nudge a calf that had lagged behind the herd. The calf lowed softly in protest, then trotted dutifully to catch up with its mother, its hindquarters swaying, little tail twitching.

'Krishna! Wait for me!'

Balarama began dancing from foot to foot, the way the gopas did while playing ras-garbha. But because of his bulky body, it looked funny rather than graceful. It took all of Krishna's self-control not to burst out laughing. Balarama would do anything to be noticed by Krishna!

'Krishna!' This last call was plaintive, almost complaining.

Balarama now combined the wiggling of the eyebrows with the dancing from foot to foot, and added another gesture to the mix – stretching out his arms, palms upwards, as if asking for help. He somehow managed to keep moving sideways and downhill while doing all this, almost keeping pace with Krishna who was walking normally. It was impressive, considering Balarama's usual lack of physical grace and his girth. Balarama began mouthing the word 'Krishna!' with an accompanying expression that imitated the caller who, from the sound of her voice, was fast catching up with them.

The total effect was hilarious, and had Krishna not been determined to keep from laughing, he would have been in splits, rolling on the ground. It was certainly one of Balarama's best performances in his teasing mode.

Krishna casually stuck out the crook and tripped Balarama up. His brother stumbled with an 'Uff!' and somersaulted downhill, rolling over and over several times before crashing into the trailing calf and its mother cow. Both raised angry moos and were joined by the rest of the herd. Balarama landed on his rear and sat up, grass on his face and hair, and more than a little cow dung all over. He spat out a mouthful of grass and glared up at his brother.

Krishna spread his hands apologetically and shrugged as if to say, 'What else to do, Bhaiya? You were being a pain!'

Balarama grinned and waggled his eyebrows again, looking at a point just behind Krishna.

Krishna sighed.

The sound of female feet padding across the grass approached and then little Radha's pretty face popped up beside him. 'Krishna, I've been following you for *yojanas*!' she said breathlessly.

Since the distance from the village to the pasture hills was barely three miles and a yojana meant a distance of roughly nine miles, it was unlikely she had actually run for even one yojana, but Radha always liked to exaggerate.

Krishna smiled indulgently at her. 'Why are you following us, Radha?'

'Not *us*, silly,' she said, still breathless. 'Just *you*. I want to keep you company while you graze the herds.'

He smiled, shaking his head. 'I have Balarama to keep me company. And aren't you supposed to be milking the cows and mixing curds and making buttermilk and things like that?'

She grinned impishly, a solitary dimple appearing in her right cheek as she turned her round face up to him. 'I won't tell if you won't tell!'

Krishna grinned. Despite her tendency to follow him around like a newborn calf, he had to admit he found Radha endearing. While all the Vrishni gopis could be as boisterous and rowdy as their male counterparts, Radha was bolder and more adventurous than most. She thought nothing of climbing trees or running races with the boys and was capable of winning at both! Even Balarama who was as instinctively chauvinistic as most Yadava males didn't protest too loudly. What he did do, as he had done just moments ago, was tease Krishna about Radha's obvious crush. More than once, Krishna had caught her gazing at him in frank adoration. And when he played his flute, no matter where she was or what chore she was engaged in, Radha would drop everything and come running to sit at his feet, rest her chin on her upturned palms, and listen in rapt admiration.

There was no doubt that she was a fan of his flute-playing, but it went beyond that. She would fetch and carry for him even when he requested her not to do so: Krishna didn't like having others do his work as he didn't believe in anyone being superior or inferior. But given a chance, Radha would act as his willing slave. It took several stern admonishments from Krishna for her to stop. Now she settled for following him around wherever he went. It had started to become a bit of a nuisance, especially when Balarama and he wanted to go off together in search of fresh pastures, or merely rove the wild unexplored backwoods behind the hamlet. Radha was always so excitable and noisy, there was no way to spend a quiet afternoon with her around.

And here she was again, hot on their heels, breathless and excited.

Krishna and she reached the bottom of the hill where Balarama was dusting off his clothes.

'Balarama-bhaiya,' she sang happily. 'I was calling and calling, didn't you hear me?'

Balarama glanced at Krishna with a look that suggested that his eyebrows might venture skywards at any moment. 'You never called out to me, Radha. You only called Krishna's name.'

Radha slapped her forehead. 'Of course! How silly of me! Next time, I'll make sure to shout your name just as loudly. Then you can make Krishna walk a little slower so I can catch up. I can barely *run* as fast as he can *walk*. Isn't he amazing?'

Since Radha was one of the fastest runners in Vrindavan and Krishna rarely moved faster than a leisurely stroll, playing his flute as he went, there was nothing Balarama could say without contradicting her. So he settled for a shrug and a non-committal grin. But the instant she looked away, he waggled his caterpillar eyebrows at Krishna again. Krishna sighed. It was going to be one of those days!

They walked along quietly for a few moments, the only sounds being the lowing of the cows and calves and the tweeting of birds on the treetops.

Radha sighed heavily. 'Great Vishnu in vaikuntha!' she said. 'It's so quiet and peaceful here. Not noisy and bustling like in the village.'

Krishna sensed Balarama turning his head and could almost hear his elder brother's unvoiced comment: 'The reason why the village is always noisy and bustling is because *you're* there!'

Wisely, Balarama didn't speak his thoughts aloud. They continued walking quietly for a while longer, and Krishna was just starting to think, *Why, this isn't so bad, after all. Maybe Radha can keep quiet for a bit. She may finally be growing some patience and good sense.*

As if to prove him wrong, Radha screeched.

The sound made Krishna and Balarama jump. Even the calves nearest to them jerked in response. Several cow mothers turned their heads, their otherwise constantly moving mouths pausing as they sought out the source of the distress signal. Their tails twitched in agitation.

When Radha screeched, the whole world paid attention. 'Look!' Radha cried excitedly, 'marigolds!'

And she was off, sprinting between the cows and calves, racing towards a patch of saffron-golden flowers about a hundred yards further on as if it were the finish line of the most important race of her life.

Krishna watched her heels kicking up dust as she sprinted away and finally permitted himself to look at Balarama. This time, both his brother's eyebrows were raised high and Balarama had one arm crooked, the fist resting on his waist, head tilted disapprovingly in a deliberate parody of disapproval.

Krishna sighed and nodded. 'She can be quite a handful.'

'You think?' Balarama replied.

They both burst out laughing, shaking their heads in despair.

'She's really not that bad,' Krishna began, 'She's sweet and well-meaning. If only she wasn't so loud …'

Radha screamed.

Balarama raised his eyebrows. 'You were saying, Bhai?'

Krishna grinned. 'She must have found lotus flowers this time.'

Radha screamed again. Then, plaintively, 'Krish-na! Come quick!'

Balarama said, 'You have been summoned by the princess.'

Krishna elbowed him affectionately.

Radha shouted, her voice tinged with genuine panic this time: 'Krishna! Balarama-bhaiya! Please come quickly. Something strange is happening here!'

Krishna and Balarama exchanged a sharp glance and began sprinting towards Radha.

two

Krishna stopped short and looked around, expecting the worst.

He could see nothing amiss.

Radha was standing in a bed of marigold flowers, clutching a few to herself and staring at the ground a few yards further away.

'What is it, Radha?' he asked.

She pointed. 'There.'

He looked. Balarama, who was a slower runner, came up beside him and looked as well. They exchanged a glance, frowning.

'I don't see anything,' Balarama said.

'There, silly!' Radha said impatiently. 'Use your eyes! It's right in front of you.'

They looked again.

'I see grass, a tree, flowers, earth …' Balarama shrugged. 'I have no idea what she means.'

Radha sighed loudly then came stamping up between them, pushing them aside. She leaned over and pointed at a plant growing between a clump of flowers.

'There. Don't you see *that*? That shouldn't be growing there.'

She was pointing at a perfectly ordinary looking plant.

Balarama turned his back to her, rolling his eyes at Krishna.

'Why shouldn't it be growing there, Radha?' Krishna asked as patiently as he could manage.

She put one hand on her hip. 'That plant doesn't belong there! It's just wrong.'

Krishna resisted the urge to sigh and roll his eyes. 'Well, I'm sure Bhoodevi had a good reason to make it sprout up in that spot.'

Now it was Radha who rolled her eyes. 'Bhoodevi? The spirit of the planet wouldn't make that plant grow there. She wouldn't make such a foolish mistake.'

She went on for a while about how the plant was poisonous and posed a danger to the cattle and how they would have to watch for more like it in case one of the calves happened to munch it. Krishna, more involved in helping Balarama steer the herd through the woods, listened with only half his attention. Radha chattered non-stop all the way, not helping one bit with the steering, rattling off the many different ways in which young calves' lives could be endangered by consuming the wrong fodder.

They emerged from the woods into a vista of such perfection that even she was momentarily silenced. The three of them stood at the top of a rise, staring out at rolling hills covered with lush kusa grass of emerald green. Even Krishna didn't know what to say at first. A gentle wind blew softly across the undulating slopes, the grass rippling like waves on the Yamuna in the wake of a ferry boat.

'It's the perfect pasture,' Radha said. 'It really is! Look at that grass. I have never seen anything like it before. I must go tell my father.' She bent down and pulled up a handful of the grass, taking care to uproot it with a little sod still clinging to the roots. 'I'll be back!' she cried, racing back the way they had come.

'Don't hurry,' Balarama muttered.

Krishna elbowed him affectionately.

Balarama pushed him back. Krishna almost lost his balance.

'It is a great pasture,' Balarama said.

'It's perfect,' Krishna admitted.

The herd seemed to think so too. The cows were mooing and lowing to one another happily, munching away, tails flicking rapidly. The pastures closer to the village had been used up and it had been hard to find fresh feed for the herds of late. The cattle of Gokuldham were used to roaming freely across the seas of grass in Vrajbhoomi, not being cooped into a bounded valley as was the case now in Vrindavan. The village elders had begun speaking of this more often at the meetings, wondering aloud how they would manage once the existing pastures were fully depleted.

Now, it seemed, there was a solution. Krishna and Balarama had found new pastures, better than any other in Vrindavan. Perhaps even better than any in Vrajbhoomi.

three

R adha ran back the way they had come, through the woods.

Passing the bed of marigolds she had spotted earlier, she slowed. She would break off a section of the plant she had seen earlier and take it back to show her mother; maatr would know what the plant was called and might be able to understand why it was growing away from its natural environment. Despite her confident banter, all Radha knew for sure was that the plant was of a type that grew underground or in caves, never on open sunlit ground. Her mother would know much more about it.

And both her parents, along with the rest of Vrindavan, would be thrilled to hear about the discovery of the new pasture. To a cowherd, fodder was one of the most important things in life. Finding it, maintaining a constant supply, growing more … much of the art of herding had to do with ensuring one's herds always had good fodder all year round, and when the creatures you cared for chewed constantly and needed to be fed every waking minute, that could prove to be a great challenge.

Radha smiled as she waded through the marigold bed, careful not to stamp on even a single flower. Like anyone who loved plants, she treated them with respect and affection. She would never dream of plucking a flower unless it was needed and even when she did so, she always took care not to damage the plant itself.

She stopped and looked around. This was the spot where they had halted earlier. She could see the clumsy footprints left by heavy-footed Balarama and Krishna's lighter-footed careful treads. The plant should have been right here. But it wasn't.

It was gone.

How was that possible?

She looked around, puzzled. It was shady and cool where she stood, the eaves of the overhanging branches providing considerable shade. Further away, the early morning sun streaming down through interwoven branches left dappled patterns on the trunks of fruit trees. She realized that there was very little birdsong audible, almost none, in fact. And she could neither spot nor hear too many squirrels or other little creatures. That was odd but not extraordinary. There was also a stench coming from somewhere that she could not place, a fetid odour, as of raw carcass. Perhaps some predator had killed nearby and the remains were upwind of where she stood. She glanced that way: the shade was so dense there, it was almost dark. Dusky, twilight dark.

She peered, wondering just how thick the trees were to be able to block out the sunlight that effectively, then shrugged. All that Bhoodevi did served a purpose. Perhaps the poisonous plant she had spotted earlier was the natural diet of some creature that lived in such shadowy wooded areas. Perhaps one such creature had come by and eaten it already. It was quite dark there in the shade between those two enormous trees, almost dark enough to be the entrance of a cave. The plant usually grew underground or in dark caves, so it wasn't completely unreasonable for it to grow here in the relatively shady spot.

She held up the handful of kusa grass she had uprooted and smiled. Her father would have the distinction of telling Nanda

Maharaja and the rest of the Vrishnis about the new spot. It would brighten everyone's day. There would be a feast tonight, she guessed. And dancing. Ras-garbha. She would have a chance to dance with Krishna! His lila was the best of all. Nobody else could play as gracefully as he.

Singing to herself, little Radha ran back towards the hamlet of Vrindavan with the good news.

Behind her, the shadowy darkness that she had peered into only moments earlier stirred and began moving sluggishly, preparing to consume its next meal.

four

Yashoda heard the excited shouts and came out of her house, using her elbow to open the door since her hands were covered with curds. She had been making lassi for the family for the day, a considerable chore considering the quantity Balarama and Krishna consumed. She saw Vinayaka and Sudipta's little girl Radha surrounded by a crowd of excited young gopas and gopis. Several older cowherds were gathered around as well, listening to the girl. Radha was describing something in great detail, spreading her arms wide and spinning around to indicate something vast and beautiful, as far as Yashoda could tell. Her pretty face was beaming with pleasure and from the reactions on the faces of those listening, it was apparent that they were enjoying listening to her ebullient description too. Yashoda smiled and brushed an errant hair off her forehead with the back of one hand, smearing a little curd on her face in the process but not minding it. She wondered what they were all talking about. Then she saw Rohini leave the group and come walking briskly to her.

'What is it?' she asked even before Rohini reached her doorstep.

'New pastures!' Rohini said, infected with the same enthusiasm that seemed to be spreading throughout the village. People were gathering around, converging from all over as the news spread. 'Our two little rascals have discovered new pastures beyond the north-eastern woods!'

'Really? That's wonderful. Are they big enough to feed all our herds for a while?'

Rohini gestured towards the crowd gathered around little Radha. It had grown fivefold already and was still expanding as the whole of Vrindavan's population rapidly converged on the bearer of the good news. 'If you believe Sudipta's daughter, they are big enough to feed all the herds in the whole Yadava nation for all eternity!'

They laughed. 'Little Radha has always had a tendency to say more than is needed,' Yashoda said. 'Especially when it involves our little Krishna.'

'Yes, she is quite besotted with him, isn't she?' Rohini smiled. 'In any case, even if one takes her exaggerations with a big pinch of salt, it still suggests these new pastures must be quite bountiful. Perhaps even enough to feed our herds for two or three seasons.'

'Which would give the present pastures time to replenish.' Yashoda beamed. 'That's wonderful news! I must find Nanda and tell him.'

'Oh, he already knows,' came the reply. 'He's gone to organize the gopas and get them to start moving the herds at once.'

'I want to go too,' Yashoda said, then remembered her half-stirred curds. 'But I have to finish this batch first before it settles.'

'I'll help you,' Rohini responded. 'Four hands will make the churning go faster than two. Then we'll go to see the new pastures together.'

Smiling happily, they went inside the house.

On the street outside, Radha finished repeating the description of the new pastures for the umpteenth time, then, as the gopas and gopis in the crowd turned to one another to discuss the implications of this exciting news, she looked up at her own parents.

Her father had already examined the sample of kusa grass and pronounced it eminently edible. He had even bitten off a straw and chewed it enthusiastically, drawing laughter and good-natured jesting. The mood in Vrindavan was happy today, happier than it had been in a long while. Now, her father had gone off with Nanda Maharaja and the other elder gopas to organize the migration of the herds, while her mother remained there, speaking with other gopis, many of whom were Radha's aunts.

'Maa,' she said, tugging at her mother's garment.

'Yes, Radhey?' Sudipta said, looking down at her daughter.

'Can I go back and show my friends the way to the new pastures? They want to take the rest of the calf herds there right away.'

Sudipta looked at her sisters, a questioning look on her face. A few gopas were around and they heard her query as well. Nobody had any objection to their children taking their calf herds to the new pastures. Everyone – man, woman, child, cow and calf – in the village was going there anyway.

'Go ahead, but don't get lost on the way,' she said with habitual motherly affection. 'Those woods are quite dense, I'm told.'

'*Dense*, Maa?' Radha repeated. 'They're dark as caves in places! But don't worry, I could find the way back even in the dark with a cloth around my eyes!'

She ran off to tell the younger cowherds that she had permission. They let out a series of whoops and cheers, each running off to fetch his or her own little herd of calves and nursing mother cows.

Shortly afterwards, as Rohini and Yashoda were finishing the last batch of buttermilk, a procession of young gopas and gopis passed through the centre of the village, leading all the young calves and cows with them. Sounds of tongues clicking, bells ringing and excited young voices shouting to one another filled the air.

The hustle and bustle was reminiscent of the way things had been back in Gokuldham before the Vrishnis had been forced to go into exile. There was a sense of hope and anticipation. Discovering new pastures was as big a miracle for cowherds as finding a new continent would be to an explorer. Perhaps their luck had changed at last. Perhaps the good lord Vishnu had seen it fit to grace them with happy days once again. The last few months had been dark, frightening times, with asuras assaulting their children and with the simple cowherds discovering that the Slayer had been born in their midst, thereby blessing them with the good fortune of living in close proximity to him as well as guaranteeing great hardship and struggle ahead. Today's news was a much-needed boost to their flagging morale and everyone intended to make the most of it.

The grown-up gopas and gopis, smiling and commenting on the exuberance of their children, watched as the young ones marched happily down the pathway. Little did they know that they would not be seeing them again that day and for many, many days to come.

five

The procession wound its way from Vrindavan to the north-eastern woods, singing and dancing merrily. There was a festive spirit in the air. A boy in front, a good friend of Krishna and Balarama, named Sridhara, played the horn, its sound carrying across the entire hamlet.

Most gopas and gopis played the flute, a musical instrument favoured by Vrishni cowherds for its ability to carry its melody long distances and remind herds of the presence of their watchers; the fact that they played (or attempted to play) melodies favoured by Krishna belied their musical ambitions. There was not a child in Vrindavan who did not look up to their youthful Saviour and Deliverer and adore him as a Vaishnavite adores Vishnu.

The less musically inclined carried slings which they used as they went, pausing to engage in contests of skill – 'I bet you couldn't hit that brown leaf on the top of that tree!' – then sprinted to catch up with the rest, an easy task considering the bovine progress of the herds. The prize for the victor was that he would get to run up to Krishna and touch him first, shouting as he did, 'I touched him first, I was first!'

Those who were not as proficient in sling-shooting would get upset at not getting to touch Krishna first and snatch the slingshots from the winners and throw them as far ahead as they could, even ahead of the herds in front. The winners would go running to retrieve them but the others who had lost would race them and reach first, throwing the slings even further. So it would turn into a race and the young calves, seeing their young masters and mistresses running ahead, would increase their pace, drawing moos of protest from their lactating mother cows.

One of the slings landed in a clump of trees. Unaccustomed to mammals in their environment, the cuckoos roosting there set off sharp calls, flying about in agitation. The gopas imitated the cuckoos and climbed the trees, passing the slings to each other to prevent the owners from retrieving them. The owners laughed good-naturedly and tried to chase down their slings.

Young monkeys screeched from the trees, leaping from branch to branch, upset at the hairless simians who had invaded their domain. The boys attempted to imitate them, hanging from branches and swinging while calling out in monkey voices. The herds caught up with them and trundled past as they continued their monkey-play. The gopis called the gopas monkeys and cuckoos as they went past, giggling at their antics. Then they dismounted from the trees and ran again to catch up with the herds.

When they reached a brook, they splashed through it, sending frogs leaping helter-skelter in startled panic. The boys imitated the frogs, leaping in the water till they were soaked from head to foot. Soaked, but at least clean at last, if only for the moment, as their mothers would have commented if they had seen them then!

In this manner, with even their herds sharing in the infectious elation, they made their way to the north-eastern woods, playing and shouting and engaged in tomfoolery. They barely noticed when the path grew darker and more shadowy, devoid of monkeys, cuckoos, frogs and other wildlife, or the fetid stench that filled the air in that particular neck of the woods.

The herd slowed down, sensing something amiss, but the children drove them on relentlessly, too impatient to be cautious. Those who commented on the denseness of that part of the woods and the fetid odour were told by their friends that there was probably a swamp nearby.

Radha had a moment of unease when she saw the calves and cows in front entering a place dark enough to be a cavern entrance, but then she recalled that it had been there earlier as well, and continued chatting with her gopi friends. The gopas were too excited and up to mischief to notice much except that it had become darker. They incorporated this change of environment into their play, pretending to be bats swooping this way and that, deliberately banging into each other or brushing gently against the mother cows and patting their rumps affectionately.

Slowly, the entire gang made its way into the open, waiting maw of Agha.

six

Krishna felt the rumble of distant thunder and stopped playing his flute.

He looked around.

Balarama had gone exploring the pastures, seeking to measure their full extent. A runner from the village had informed them that their father and the other elders were bringing the herds there and that Radha and the younger herders had already set off with the calf and mother herds. They would be reaching shortly.

The sky was bright blue, with fat, shapely clouds drifting lazily by, casting undulating shadows on the sea of kusa grass; the wind playing with the grass was a soothing accompaniment to his flute, and until a moment ago, Krishna had been as close to yoganidra as it was possible to get on this mortal plane. The rumbling was a harsh counterpoint to this placid quietude.

He realized he had *felt* the rumbling rather than simply *heard* it.

There it was again.

Like the rumbling of a stomach left too long unfed.

Exactly like that!

Except louder, much *much* louder.

The ground beneath his feet shuddered noticeably this time, like a minor earthquake. The calves nearest to him lifted their heads long enough to stop chewing and moo indignantly. Their mothers stopped chewing too. Several of them turned to look in his direction.

He raised a hand, calming them.

Where was Balarama?

Krishna cast his inner eye outwards, travelling at the speed of a bird across the top of the tall grass, over the hill and down the next valley, then up the next rise and down the next dip, until he located his brother who was still walking towards the far end of the pastures in a northerly direction.

Sensing his brother's questing consciousness, Balarama paused and turned to look back the way he had come. His fair broad features frowned, understanding that there was something wrong. Even as far away as he was, he could feel a vestige of the tremors that Krishna was experiencing.

Balarama turned and began running back to Krishna. The grass brushed against his pumping feet, staining his already grass-stained lower body greener. His muscular legs pounded the ground hard, bearing his bulk easily but not as swiftly as he would have liked at such a time.

'I'm coming, Bhai,' he said softly, knowing he would be heard even miles away.

Krishna turned back and looked in the direction of the woods. That was the only way to get to where he stood. To either side of the woods, the landscape was dangerously broken and undulating – steep rocky rises and abruptly plummeting wadis. Dangerous enough for humans, much too risky for cattle.

Krishna began running towards the woods. There was something intending harm to his friends and their herds in them. Unlike Balarama, he ran with great litheness and athletic grace. His slender form was built for speed. He raced through the tall grass like a humming bird speeding back towards her nest. The calves and mother cows he had been herding looked back in dismay, lowing to each other to lament Krishna leaving them.

He burst through the woods and came face-to-face with a monstrosity.

Something that resembled a gargantuan earthworm was shattering tree trunks and cracking branches as it undulated. The dust and soil falling from its body suggested that it had freshly emerged from beneath the surface of the earth. It bucked and shuddered, its enormous length shivering as it shifted from side to side. It touched a sala tree a yard thick at the base and the trunk cracked with a resounding sound, the tree toppling over to crash down heavily. Monkeys and birds and animals screamed and chittered elsewhere in the woods, but no animal or bird sounds were audible in the vicinity of the heaving demon.

Krishna understood that the creature must have emerged from the ground and insinuated itself into the woods slowly, gradually, moving perhaps a few feet at a time, then waiting for hours before moving again. Over the course of days, perhaps weeks, it had taken up position in the darkest areas of the woods, then lain still, waiting. Like a serpent, it had intertwined itself between trees, looping and twisting sinuously until it covered a considerable area. He could only imagine the length of the beast from mouth to tail: miles, certainly. Perhaps a whole yojana long! The bulk of its body was still inside the ground, he saw, and that was why it was moving so violently now. It was trying to retreat into its hole, to return underground where it could travel more easily through the subterranean caverns to which it was accustomed, to consume its meal at leisure.

He already knew what its meal consisted of: the calf herds and child cowherds. With the power of his inner eye, he could see little Radha and the other young gopas and gopis along with their calves and mother cows, all inside the belly of the beast. They had been startled when the ground had begun moving underfoot and the world around them began to shake. Now they were terrified, for they understood that this was no earthquake or tremor; they were inside some great creature's maw, about to be consumed.

Krishna could see them screaming and crying out plaintively, scared despite their inherent braveness, for how could they fight such a creature once they were *inside* its body? They could hardly guess at what it even looked like, and the fetid rank air as already choking and sickening the children as well as the cattle.

The question was why the creature had not consumed them already. All it had to do was gulp and swallow, and every last child old enough to mind the herds in Vrindavan would be digested alive, slowly, agonizingly. The most merciful death would be suffocation for lack of air; the most terrible, a slow acidic digesting over days.

'I will not let that happen,' Krishna said grimly. He raised his voice, raising his cowherd's crook and shaking it at the towering beast. 'I will not let you take them!'

At this, the beast ceased shuddering.

Suddenly, a section of its vast body rose up in the air, like the head of a snake rising to open its hood. Except that the segmented body resembled a worm more than a snake and when the head rose up, it did not widen into a hood, merely opened to reveal a great mouth, some fifty yards wide and perfectly round. Blind and lacking any other sense organs, its maw opened in sections to reveal interlocking and overlapping flaps of dusty, grimy, leathery hide that resembled an iris spiralling open. Within it, he saw an immense terrifying darkness, and several yards deep inside that darkness he saw his friends and their herds struggling to stay upright, leaning against each other or against the more sure-footed bovines, pale and very scared, crying with fear and incomprehension. Many were indignant or upset too: Krishna saw some of the bolder young gopas wield their slings, looking for a target. There was none. They could hardly fling stones about in the beast's mouth; they would only hit their own friends or cattle. They were eager but had no way to fight such a creature. Helpless and angry, they hollered to Krishna to do something.

'Release my friends!' Krishna shouted.

A deep rumbling awoke from inside the earth. It began from under the ground, and Krishna knew that it was coming from the part of the asura's body that was still beneath the surface, deep within the earth. By the time it travelled to its maw and burst from the open orifice, it emerged as a cruel imitation of laughter. Lacking a mouth, the creature spoke with a mentally projected sound that resembled boulders gnashing against each other in an avalanche.

'*I WILL EAT YOUR FRIENDS AND DIGEST THEM,* it said. *THEN, WHEN I AM DONE, I WILL EXUDE THEM AS OFFAL INTO THE BOWELS OF THE EARTH.*'

Krishna's eyes blazed deep blue, his dark skin exuding a glow that nullified the darkness of the worm's shadow in the woods.

'Who are you, demon?' Krishna demanded.

'*I AM AGHA. BAKA WAS MY BROTHER DEMON. PUTANA WAS AS A MOTHER TO SOME OF US, A SISTER TO OTHERS. I WILL AVENGE THEM AS WELL AS THE OTHERS YOU SLEW. I AM THE SHAPE OF YOUR VENGEANCE.*'

'You are a worm!' Krishna said. 'And I will crush you underfoot. I command you to release my friends at once. They had nothing to do with the deaths I caused. I killed your demon kin. I am the one at whom you should direct your vengeance!'

Agha's maw lolled this way then that for a moment, as if considering Krishna's words.

'MY MISSION WAS TO KILL THEM ALL. BUT I WOULD RATHER CONFRONT YOU AND EAT YOU, DELIVERER. YOU ARE THE TASTY MORSEL I SEEK. I HAVE NOT FEASTED IN MONTHS. YOU WILL MAKE A GOOD MEAL ... DEVA.'

'I will be your meal, or you mine. That is between us and we shall settle it ... once you release those innocents and set them back on the ground unscathed and alive.'

Agha's mouth lolled for another moment. Then the giant worm head swayed and lowered itself to the ground in a clearing created by its own retreat.

The instant its mouth touched the ground, Krishna shouted to his fellow gopas and gopis. 'Radha, Sridhara ... my brothers and sisters of Vrindavan! Flee! Take your herds and flee.'

An exodus began, as the frightened children and cattle emerged from the maw of the gargantuan demon worm, stepped once more upon solid earth, and backed away fearfully, gazing up at the great creature into whose mouth they had all trooped unsuspectingly. Many were coughing and choking, some even spewing the contents of their belly, sickened by the stench and filth of the creature's interior.

Balarama arrived just then, winded but spoiling for a fight. Speaking to Krishna with the mind-voice they had both used almost since birth to communicate with each other, he shouted silently: *Brother, I am here, shall we attack the creature together?*

No, Krishna said firmly. *You lead Radha and the others with their herds to safety. Take them back home. Keep the elders and others away from this part of Vrindavan. Get as far away* as *possible. This battle may range over a great distance. I do not want anyone injured.*

Balarama's face darkened upon sensing Krishna's words. But then he looked at the size and adjudged the length of the asura and knew that Krishna's suggestion was wise and necessary. His natural propensity for aggression was subsumed by his unquestioning devotion to his brother. His anger subsided and was sublimated instantly into energy, the energy he would need to do as Krishna bade him.

He nodded and began herding the children and cattle away. They disappeared into the woods and Krishna sensed them making their way back to the village as quickly as they could possibly go. This time, they traversed the same route sombrely, many in tears, others angry and furious with the demon; there was no singing or playing or frolicking.

Krishna resented the asura for that more than anything else; it might not have harmed any of them, but had nevertheless instilled terror into the hearts of the innocent. For that alone, he would make this creature pay dearly.

'Come, Aghasura,' he said, stepping forward. 'You said you wanted to eat me alive, did you not? Go ahead, then. Here I am. Eat me!'

Agha issued a coughing sound that might have been a peal of delighted laughter.

Then the worm beast turned its maw towards Krishna, raising a cloud of dust.

Krishna stepped into the giant cave-like orifice. The instant he set foot inside, the overlapping flaps closed shut.

The asura's body shuddered as it began to swallow its prey, moving him forcibly down the length of its body to digest him.

seven

Nanda heard the beast before he saw it.

He was leading the main body of the clan's herds over a hilltop when a deep coughing sound issued from somewhere ahead. The cattle shied momentarily, lowing in puzzlement. The sound was loud, louder than any animal living in these parts could possibly make, and utterly alien in its deep, rasping tone. It was accompanied by a deep rumbling sensation as the earth itself quivered underfoot. This upset the cattle further, causing some to bolt downhill. Gopas sprinted to head them off and the situation was well under control, but Nanda's heart ran cold as he understood that it was yet another asura attack. What else could it be? Things had been so peaceful these past weeks, Yashoda and he had even begun to hope that the worst was over. Despite all that Gargacharya had said, as parents, their hearts longed for their Krishna to have a chance at a normal life, playing and gambolling like any young gopa.

But now, here was yet another reminder that the devas had a very different fate in store for his child.

And that is the instant he saw the beast.

It rose up in a cloud of dust, towering above the tops of the trees in the wooded area to the north-east of Vrindavan where his people seldom ventured. Nanda had explored these parts himself when they first came to dwell here and had written the region off as being inhospitable and uninhabitable. He had had no idea that beyond those dense woods lay several lush green pastures. It had sounded like a miracle when he received news that Krishna and Balarama had found those pastures. But now, looking at the creature that rose from the woods, he wondered if it had been a curse.

Shedding dust and earth and stones from its grimy body, the creature resembled an earthworm freshly emerged from the ground. It was enormous, the size of a hundred sala tree trunks clumped together. Rearing up, it ponderously swayed from side to side, like any subterranean creature unfamiliar with the world above the surface. It appeared to be blind, he noted, for he could see no eyes or any other discernible organs. Its maw opened then, wide enough to accommodate the entire herd that roved in front of Nanda – several thousand heads and more. Its whole length stirred sluggishly between the trees, cracking trunks and shaking entire fruit groves till they shed their ripe loads, and he saw that its winding body stretched for miles. Hardly able to comprehend the existence of such a beast, let alone imagine his little Krishna confronting it, he clutched his crook tightly. His breath caught in his throat at the very thought. What new threat was this?

Then the beast's maw turned towards the hilltop on which Nanda stood, and for a moment he could see into that gigantic oral orifice – and in it he saw the tiny dark form of his beloved Krishna, inside the mouth of the beast!

The father in him wanted to cry out and run to his son's aid. But even in that brief glimpse, he saw Krishna's stance, as steady and balanced as if standing on solid ground, playing his flute. He saw also the deep glow of powerful blue light that exuded from Krishna's body, spreading outwards to illuminate the dark mouth which was attempting to consume him. Nanda was reminded that this was not merely his adoptive son, it was Vishnu Incarnate.

Then the giant worm swayed and crashed down to the earth once more, then plunged underground, the entire hillside and countryside shuddering as it burrowed its way through the ground, seeking to bury itself deep within its natural habitat. Trees were uprooted and knocked off, trunks split, the air filled with debris. Cattle lowed and reared and turned their heads in alarm, and it was only the efforts of his expert gopas and gopis that prevented a stampede.

In a moment, the entire thicket ahead was concealed from view by the billowing cloud of dust. The earth continued to tremble mightily and from somewhere deep inside, the sounds of the beast could still be heard, making that peculiar trumpet-like sound of distress or rage, or both.

Yashoda came up beside Nanda, breathless from running too fast. He glanced back and saw her sisters and the rest of their clan approaching as fast as they could. His wife put a hand on his arm, clutching it tightly and, knowing her every gesture well enough to read her heart's innermost secrets without her having to say a word, read the fear and anxiety in her clasp.

Not saying a word, she read him as easily, and stared at the enormous cloud of dust drifting slowly in their direction. He was glad she had missed seeing the beast itself. Yashoda was strong but the sight of that creature was enough to give any grown Vrishni nightmares for the rest of their life.

All around them, the other gopas and gopis were pointing and staring and talking in hushed, anxious voices.

Finally, Yashoda spoke, putting into words the inevitable question. 'Krishna?' she asked, her tone suggesting she already knew the answer but had to ask anyway.

He gestured towards the cloud. There was no need to say more.

He felt her grip tighten around his arm, squeezing hard enough to choke off circulation. He let it stay, saying nothing.

They stood like that, watching, for a long while. There was nothing they could do except wait. And pray.

eight

From the sensations rippling through the demon's body, Krishna understood that it was attempting to burrow deep inside the earth. Its intention was plain. Burrow into the ground, swallow and digest him. Any human would suffocate from the lack of air. Even if he survived, he would be crushed by the grinding maw, then have his flesh dissolved by the beast's powerful intestinal acids.

But of course Krishna was no normal being.

He felt Aghasura's body breaking through packed earth, shattering stone and igneous formations as it burrowed. He felt also the vibrations of the segmented body underfoot as it shifted its flesh and tissue, carrying him deeper into its innards, like a moving floor. From all around him he became aware of the fetid odour of rank juices. The ground underfoot grew squishy and squamous, the air rancorous, and he felt himself spattered from all sides with disgusting fluids.

Like any worm, the demon was basically one long digestive tract, its entire being devoted to the act of feeding and processing food. The first part of the process was to shower the prey with stomach acids to break it down into its constituent parts, all the while pushing the food further down the length of its body. Like any large creature, it probably needed to feed constantly. Krishna wondered how Aghasura found sufficient nourishment.

That answer came soon enough. Krishna heard and felt the worm demon slowing in its downward progress, then the distinctive sound caused by the unwinding of its gigantic maw as it opened up, followed by peculiar animal sounds of protest and outrage. The mouth closed again and he felt the presence of other living creatures nearby. He willed his crook to glow and issue blue light, and saw a pair of blind slug-like beings squirming restlessly as they came to terms with their fate. He saw as well as heard and smelt a fresh barrage of digestive juices splash the new arrivals, and heard their low grunting as the acids began to eat through their hides and flesh.

Krishna willed his crook to dim again, eliminating the nightmarish glimpse. Evidently, Aghasura had not been content with swallowing him alive and had decided to pause and consume some more food, some manner of subterranean fauna, the existence of which was neither known nor imagined above ground.

Soon, the grunts of the new prey subsided as they began to succumb to the assault.

Krishna decided it was time to turn the tables on his new tormentor.

He willed his own body to exude light, brilliant glowing blue light produced by the cells of his body using the energy of Brahman. He increased the glow steadily, lighting himself until he glowed as brightly as a small sun. The two unfortunates wallowing in their predator's tract saw the glow of Brahman shakti exuding from their fellow prey and emitted sounds of alarm at this blinding effulgence.

Other creatures clinging to the sides and top of the underground caverns also observed the brilliant glow bursting out of the giant worm as it rolled past. Blue light exploded outwards, like a firefly's light visible through gaps in the fingers of its holder.

Krishna continued to increase the intensity of his radiance, bathing the worm demon's insides with the heat of his divine energies until he felt the darkness around him dispelled by his own brightness. The effect was immediate: Aghasura's progress slowed as the worm demon began to feel the scorching heat of God Incarnate's wrath.

nine

Balarama and the other children paused and looked back. The dust cloud still hung in the air above the woods. They were some miles away from that place now and Balarama judged them to be safe from immediate threat.

He had done as Krishna had instructed, without question or complaint. But he still resented having to leave his brother to battle this new menace alone. His *younger* brother. It went against every cell of his being. Why else had he been put upon this mortal plane if not to protect and help his younger sibling?

True, he was doing so as Krishna wanted him to and herding the children to safety. But it was not the same thing. Besides, Balarama was a fighter, a warrior, a yoddha. Until he matched strength and arms and wits with an opponent, he was not complete. His frustration was not directed towards Krishna, who had had no choice but to ask Balarama to lead the children to safety. He was annoyed with the circumstances: he longed to be the one doing the fighting as he had been when the calf demon had attacked.

As if sensing his conflicting emotions, Radha spoke up beside him. 'He will triumph, will he not?'

Balarama answered without doubt, 'Krishna always triumphs.' But he clenched his fists in frustration, wishing he were there in the thick of the fight, alongside Krishna.

Radha glanced at him. 'You would rather be with him, fighting by his side.'

He nodded.

'He is your younger brother, you wish to protect him.'

Balarama sighed. 'Krishna does not need protection. He protects us all. All worlds are in his shadow. He is the Protector of all Creation.'

'And yet you are his older brother and would fight for him.'

'To the death,' he agreed.

She was silent for a moment. 'It must be strange to have a younger brother who is so powerful a god, the great Protector Vishnu himself made incarnate in human form.'

Balarama shrugged. 'He is what he is. He is Krishna.'

Radha nodded at the wisdom of this simple statement. 'He is Krishna.'

They fell silent as a new rumbling filled their inner ears, sensed rather than heard. The ground trembled as something immense approached. Then, with an explosion of assorted waste, Aghasura breached the surface of the earth again, in a spot about two miles from the place where he had attacked the children. The watching children exclaimed in horror as they viewed the sheer size and scale of the gargantuan being.

Aghasura's body was blazing with a blue light that originated from a spot somewhere to the fore of his length. It was blindingly intense, visible even in the bright sunlight, and shone out with such potency that it seemed to be tearing its way out of the worm's body, bursting forth. The holes appeared all along the beast's hide, starting as small pinpricks through which the blue glow leaked at first, then expanding steadily to larger and larger wounds, until the creature was bleeding and oozing life from a hundred different places.

It was clear that the blue light was causing the worm considerable pain, for it thrashed and squirmed in the air, thudding to the ground with earth-shaking impact again and again, in a futile attempt to squash the source of the light. Its body convulsed and quivered, undulating and twisting. Yet all its struggles were of no avail.

From the hilltop overlooking the woods, Nanda, Yashoda and the adult gopas and gopis watched, keeping their precious herds in check to avoid a stampede. From the pastures, the children of Vrindavan and their calf herds and mother cattle watched as well. All Vrindavan watched. Even the birds in the sky hovered and stared down, eyes round with amazement at the sight of a worm so enormous struggling and suffering for its life. A few of the larger ones opened their beaks and longed for a taste of such a worm, imagining how rich and dense its flesh must be, packed with nutrients. How early would a bird have to rise to catch such a worm? None dared attempt to find out!

Slowly, with great heart-rending sounds of agony, the worm demon began to die. In great torment, it thrashed and tossed several times, finally slapping down on the grass one last time, shattering more trees and sending splinters of fresh timber flying hundreds of yards away as its great length came to rest near one of the many subterranean holes made by its own passage. Here its body quivered and trembled in its death throes, life slipping away from its tortured flesh as the power of Brahman exuded from a thousand places on its body. It bled blue light that illuminated the dark woods, and which was visible from yojanas away.

Balarama started running almost as soon as the worm subsided. Radha and the other children followed, eager to see for themselves that Krishna was safe and well. It was one thing to know that he was God Incarnate and would always triumph, but quite another to see for themselves that their friend and playmate was unharmed and well.

With swathes of earth layers ripped up and piled helter-skelter, and raw dark earth from a hundred yards down mixed with topsoil and flora and vegetation, the ground was torn up. Trees lay scattered like fallen warriors after a battle, flower beds crushed to smidgens of colour. Radha recognized the bed of marigolds she had spotted earlier and pointed it out to Balarama as they ran past it. Closer to the spot where Aghasura had fallen, the earth was ruffled and brindled like a wild dog's fur. The children had to pick their way carefully to avoid falling or breaking their feet. The calf herd had been left behind in the pasture for the time being. The calves would be safe enough there: they were too afraid to move away and the mother cows would ensure the calves stayed together.

Finally, the children reached the site of the fallen asura. Even in death, the demon worm was a terrifying sight: enormous as a hillock turned on its side, maw gaping open, oozing putrid purple unguent, its seemingly endless body winding in labyrinthine coils across the countryside before finally disappearing into the ground where it continued for who knew how many more miles. It was hard to believe such a creature could exist in the same world as ordinary mortals. Yet here it was, proof that demons lived among us freely once and many still did, albeit in secret now.

Krishna stood facing the creature, his body glowing with the blue light they had seen exuding from Aghasura towards the end. As Radha and Balarama approached, Krishna raised his arms and incanted a mantra they could not hear – in fact, it was not intended to be heard by human ears, not then and not ever – and the result was incredible.

Aghasura's corpse began to burn with the same blue light, aflame with tongues of blue fire that rippled down the creature's length at the speed of wind. In seconds, the yojanas-long body of the asura blazed, then crackled sharply in the noonday sun, then sizzled and scorched and spit relentless blue fire, turning the enormous winding body into ash. A breeze sprang up out of nowhere and bore the flakes of ash away into the sky and beyond the limits of vision.

ten

Nanda and Yashoda stared down into the abyss. It was hard to believe that a living creature could have burrowed so deep into the ground. Had they not seen Aghasura with their own eyes, they would not have believed it possible for such a being to exist. Apparently, the demon worm, in its last desperate thrashing, had broken the surface of the ground hard enough to leave a crack in the ground that descended several hundred yards and was over two score yards wide. The tunnelling of its passage must have come close to some crevice below, breaking through that underground cavern to leave this great ditch which cut across the only access to the woods – and to the pastures beyond.

Nanda wondered if perhaps the demon had *intended* to do this and had managed to wreak this last act of vengeance upon the people whom his Slayer protected. He dismissed the thought as moot. The demon itself was dead, slain by their little Krishna in a magnificent display of his supreme powers. What did it matter how or why the ravine had been produced: its existence made it impossible for the Vrishnis to take their herds to the new pastures.

He looked around at the others. They had already ascertained for themselves the lay of the land. Nothing needed to be said. Their faces were sombre. He knew that none of them was concerned any longer about fresh feed for the cattle. Right now there was only one question on their minds.

'How will our children return home across this abyss, Nanda Maharaja?' asked a gopa.

Nanda looked at Yashoda who was staring up at him, round-eyed, her anxious face asking the same question.

He looked around. Everyone was looking to him for leadership.

'Krishna will bring them home,' he said, sounding more confident than he felt.

'But how?'

He spread his hands. 'He will find a way. He defeated that great beast. We all saw him do it. What is crossing a mere abyss after accomplishing such a feat?'

'Even so, we are worried. Krishna is superhuman, he is invulnerable. He can battle asuras and leap mountains. But our children are merely mortal. What if harm befalls them? Who knows what other asuras lurk in those woods?'

'Yes!' echoed another gopi. 'We want our children home safe with us.'

'Right now!'

Yashoda looked at her husband, then turned to the crowd of agitated Vrishnis and raised her hands. 'My husband has answered you already. Krishna will bring them home safe, somehow.'

'But *how*?' asked a gopi, her eyes glinting with emotion. 'How can we simply take your word for it? The lives of our children are at stake.'

Yashoda gestured at the devastation left after the battle with Aghasura. 'Did he not just save your children today? Did you mean to stop him midway and demand to know how he was saving them? Does it even matter?'

There was an embarrassed silence in which she heard several

whispers and caught more than a few sharply exchanged glances.

'Krishna will bring our children home,' she said firmly. 'All we need do is have faith in him.'

Many heads nodded approvingly. After a moment's thought, even the gopi who had demanded to know 'how' nodded, looking a little shamefaced at her outburst. Nanda did not take offence at any of this: when it came to their children, parents could resort to any words or means.

Nanda cleared his throat, glancing at Yashoda with a telling glance to indicate his appreciation for her stepping in at the right time. She squeezed his arm as he spoke. 'It would be pointless standing around here. I suggest we return to the village with our herds and return to our day's chores as usual, until Krishna's return with the children and the calf herds.'

Everybody agreed and turned to go, starting the laborious process of getting the herd turned around and moving back homewards.

As Nanda glanced back at the devastation wrought by Aghasura, he had a brief moment of misgiving, the very doubt that had delayed his response when confronted by the angry parents of the stranded children. He had not wanted them to see his uncertainty, hence had not replied at the time. Fortunately, Yashoda had not shared his lack of confidence and had reassured their troubled minds.

What if Krishna is unable to bring them home safely? What if he cannot bring them home at all?

That was a possibility too terrible to contemplate.

He put the thought aside and followed his wife and clansmen home, trying not to think about it further.

Krishna will find a way.

He must.

eleven

Krishna and Balarama stepped aside from the main group of children. Radha and the other young gopas and gopis were still jubilant, celebrating their near-death experience and subsequent survival as a result of Krishna's heroism by chanting harvest songs. Even the cattle seemed relaxed, chewing the fresh green grass with lazy ease. They had stopped briefly in the woods at Krishna's request, one he had made after seeing Balarama's face when he returned from scouting out the way ahead.

'What is it, Bhaiya?' Krishna asked, speaking softly in order to avoid being heard by the others. It was evident from Balarama's face that something was amiss. 'Where are our parents?'

Balarama spoke softly as well, keeping his face turned towards Krishna and away from the others. 'They must have returned home. There is no way for them to cross over to us. The demon created a great rift before dying. It is impossible to cross such a great abyss.'

Krishna looked into Balarama's eyes, then shut his own, accessing Balarama's visual memory of the rift. He saw the yawning ravine, the darkness deep below, the devastation wrought by the dying worm, the ragged sheer cliff-like sides of the drop, and accepted the impossibility of anyone making such a crossing, leave alone young children with calves and mother cows in tow. He continued to view the surrounding area through

Balarama's eyes and saw that there was no other way across. With the abyss too wide to bridge by any natural or man-made method, or to cross via rope or sling or anything else, they were effectively cut off from the village.

'What shall we do now?' Balarama asked.

Krishna was silent for a moment, contemplating the larger meaning of this occurrence.

'If we both used our strength, maybe we could throw rocks into the crevice to fill it up,' Balarama suggested.

Krishna shook his head, still silent. He saw that action being taken in his mind's eye, saw every last detail of it vividly: Balarama and he heaving great boulders and rocks and flinging them down into the abyss, working for days, weeks, then months, without success. The gulf was deep beyond measure. It would take more than a year to fill it and even then it might not be safe to cross. The crevice was so deep, it had opened up veins in the earth's crust that exuded dangerous vapours that were toxic to breathe in.

Besides, the upheaval created by such a great landfill would endanger the children and calf herds. After all, this was pasture land. To fill such a great crevice would mean tearing up miles of pasture fields and could well provoke further seismic unsettling.

Balarama nodded, reaching the same conclusion that his brother had drawn through their shared spiritual link.

'What if we build a bridge using tree trunks?' Balarama said. 'That way we would only have to cover the gap, not fill in the whole crevice.'

Krishna envisaged that course of action too: the vapours rising from the crevice would rot the trunks before the bridge was completed, rendering the bridge unstable and even more dangerous than a rock fill-in. And the danger from the vapours themselves would still remain. He shook his head again.

'Then maybe we can each take hold of a child or calf in each arm and leap the divide?' Balarama asked, his face crinkling as he realized the folly of such a suggestion even before he finished giving it.

Krishna almost smiled as he envisaged this option: Balarama taking hold of calves and cows and children and leaping across. No, it was much too dangerous, apart from the fact that the mere act of leaping such a dangerous abyss might permanently disturb the mother cows or calves. The same went for the children, even without taking the vapours into consideration. If they had not been facing such a dire crisis, he would have smiled at the image. However, he settled for another regretful shake of his head.

'Or we leave the herd behind and take our friends across somehow?'

Krishna shook his head at once this time. He didn't even have to think about it. The herds could not be left behind. They would pine for their keepers, for their fellow cattle, and most of all, for Krishna himself. He knew, as did everyone in Vrindavan, that his flute playing soothed and eased the herds, kept them healthy and safe from sickness and disease, and caused them to give rich nourishing milk that kept the denizens of the hamlet healthy and strong.

No.

Leaving the calf herd and mother cows behind was tantamount to slow suicide for the Vrishni clan. They were gopas and gopis. The herds were as much part of their lives as their own beloved families. They would literally pine to death without their calves and mother cows.

They bandied about numerous ideas and options, some ludicrous, others desperate, all quite impossible to implement successfully. Each time, Krishna was able to envisage all possible outcomes with his mind's eye and prevent him and his brother from making unnecessary and dangerous efforts.

'Well then what *shall* we do?' Balarama blurted at last. He was impatient and tired.

The children were growing restless too. They wanted to be home with their parents and families. Only the calves and mother cows were content to munch on the delicious grass all day, so long as Krishna was near.

'We have to do *something*, Krishna!' Balarama said impatiently.

'No,' Krishna said. 'We cannot do anything. We must simply wait.'

'*Wait?*' Balarama asked, then frowned. 'For how long?'

Krishna thought for a moment. 'For one full year.'

Balarama stared at him, aghast. 'One full year? What do you mean?'

Krishna placed his hands on his brother's forehead, showing him the vision he had seen in his mind's eye. Balarama stiffened momentarily as his mind began to be commandeered by Krishna, then relaxed and saw the images his brother intended him to see. Together, they viewed the earth deep within the abyss shift and change position, great plates of rock and igneous formations shifting slowly, grinding with enormous force against each other, constantly moving this way then that, great rivers of lava flowing far beneath, and great explosions and tectonic movements rippling through the body of Bhoodevi, the mother deity of the mortal realm. They saw how, over the course of the next four seasons, the abyss closed of its own accord, suppressing the deadly vapours and bridging the gap to make that narrow ridge of land perfectly safe to cross or walk or stand on for millennia to come.

Krishna removed his hands from Balarama's head.

Balarama stared at his brother. 'You mean ... We are to stay here in these pastures until ...'

'Until a year has passed.'

'But why? How could this come to pass?' Balarama began to say something more, then hesitated.

Krishna nodded, urging him to go on.

'How could you *let* this come to pass?' Balarama asked.

Krishna shrugged. 'I did not. It was meant to be. Our stay here serves some larger purpose that even I do not fathom right now. All I can say with surety is that we, the children of Vrindavan, the calf herd and the mother cows, are meant to stay here in these new pastures until a full year has passed. After that time, we will be free to go home once again.'

'But how ...' Balarama began, then stopped. 'So you do not know the whys and wherefores of this event?'

Krishna shook his head a final time. 'There are some things even I must accept as given. This is the nature of the universe. Every being or event is governed by other beings and events. All things are interrelated. Not every mountain can be climbed, not every abyss bridged, not every problem resolved to one's satisfaction. Sometimes, one must simply wait.'

Balarama nodded slowly, almost sadly. 'Then we wait.'

But there was no joy in his voice.

twelve

Thewas low in the evening sky. The cattle had been
returned to their pens but were restless, missing their
calves and the mother cows. The adult gopas and gopis
of Vrindavan missed their children too, more so because of
the attack of the asura that morning. They worried that some
harm might have befallen their children despite Krishna's best
efforts. Even if their children were safe and sound, they longed
to have them in their presence, to see for themselves, to touch,
hold, embrace, kiss.

The members of the families usually ate their evening meals
together and it was almost time to eat, so they worried that
their children would be hungry, thirsty and tired. Every adult
in the village was out of doors or standing on the threshold of
his or her house, waiting and watching. Their eyes kept straying
towards the dirt road that wound its way out of the village and
over the hills that led to the north woods, expecting to see those
familiar exuberant faces come bobbing over the last rise, hear
those playful voices shouting and calling out boisterously.

Dogs – whose loyal eyes gleamed as they followed their
little lords and ladies about all day long – lay listless, waiting
for their little masters and mistresses and not touching their
own food, for they were habituated to eating scraps at the
feet of their young owners, gobbling each morsel proudly and
tilting their heads to listen intently to the laughter and teasing

of the children. Now, they could not understand why the day's routine had changed, why the young brats had not returned home as usual.

Nanda, Yashoda and Rohini waited together, along with the rest of their extended family. All eyes were anxiously fixed on the road, all hearts heavy with concern, all stomachs empty, for none had eaten a morsel all day long, nor would they eat until their little precious gems were safely back in their treasure troves.

Nanda's parents Parjanya Maharaja and Variyasi-devi in particular were very anxious, kneading their palms and cracking their knuckles repeatedly. An air of tense anticipation hung over the entire village. Nobody was taking care of the evening chores, nor were there any preparations for the festivities all had spoken of earlier. After all, when the children had not yet returned safely, how could their return be celebrated?

The sun slipped lower; sunset was imminent. Birds began to fly back to their nesting places. Long shadows crept across the land, and the cattle began to low uneasily, sensing the unhappiness of their caregivers. The usually happy hamlet was deathly quiet. A pallor of anxiety hung over every house and field.

Suddenly, a gopa sitting on a high forked branch of a tree shouted excitedly. 'They are coming!'

At once, the entire tableau came to life. People began bustling about, cook-fires were relit in haste, the dogs leapt up from their supine positions and began barking and running about in excitement, cattle stopped lowing and craned their heads to catch a glimpse of the children.

And then, like a mirage resolving into reality, came the children, over the rise of the hill, down the last winding road and into the village. Parents ran, shouting, and embraced their little gopas and gopis. The children screamed in joy and sprinted to hug their parents, squeezing until their arm sockets ached. Dogs barked and leapt about joyfully. The calves trundling behind the children raised their tired heads and mooed as loudly as their little voices would allow, announcing their happiness at being home again. The mother cows settled for lowing sonorously, then rubbing foreheads with their mates and fellow cows.

Soon, the tense atmosphere was completely dispelled and life seemed normal again. One by one, each family went indoors, settling down to eat its evening meal. Someone mentioned the planned celebration, but as the evening progressed, it was decided that everyone was too tired and needed a good night's rest, so Nanda Maharaja declared that the next day would be a day of feasting.

'But cows will still need to be milked and sick calves still need to be nursed,' he reminded everyone as he went about informing them. He always repeated the same words of caution, smiling broadly as he did so, reminding his clansmen that for those who lived off the land, there were no holidays, but that did not mean they could not celebrate.

Vrindavan went to sleep peacefully that night, relieved and content, and Nanda and Yashoda and the rest of their family took special pride and care in feeding the evening meal to their little Krishna and Balarama. For once, even Yashoda did not question how much dahi they consumed – and the quantity was prodigious even by their healthy standards!

Back in the pastureland, across the unbreachable rift, the young gopas and gopis had accepted Krishna's explanation that they would be staying there for a while longer in order to let their herd graze and nourish themselves on the rich new feed.

But at sunset, they began to long for their families. The younger ones were on the verge of crying for their parents, the older ones for their siblings, and some even cried for their dogs and their homes. One young boy cried for a sparrow with a broken wing he had nursed back to health, thinking that the sparrow's eggs were to hatch that very day and that he might have missed seeing them hatch. A mood of gloom and misery descended along with dusk.

Then, to their surprise, their parents appeared, bearing bundles of food and gifts. Their dogs came bounding over the pastures, leaping through the tall grass, their tongues lolling joyfully.

The parents of the boy who had nursed the sparrow even brought the entire sparrow nest, complete with eggs and mother bird. The eggs hatched as he watched in rapt amazement. It had been his dream to see baby birds hatching, and that dream was fulfilled that evening. All the little ones were content by evening's end, all their day's desires fulfilled, every single family reunited. It hardly mattered that it was in the pasture fields and not at home. To the Vrishnis, the fields *were* home in a sense.

As night fell, the parents set up camp in the pastures and made their children comfortable for the night, singing lullabies and putting them to sleep with affection. They regretted having to go away, but promised to be back the next day and every day, as long as the children stayed in the fresh pastures. They also explained, as Krishna had, how the calf herds and mother cows would benefit from feeding continually on the lush grass and, by degrees, the children were soothed and lulled to sleep.

They slept peacefully and happily that night, regarding the stay in the pastures now as a great adventure and responsibility, believing that they had to stay there for the sake of the herds, for it was true that the distance from the hamlet to the pastures was too great to cover easily each day and the herds would benefit from a few days of rest.

Only Balarama knew what they did not even suspect: it was Krishna who had partitioned his essence and taken the forms of all the grown gopas and gopis, even the forms of the dogs and other creatures, in order to placate the children.

He had done the same in the village, presenting himself as the children and the calf herds and the mother cows, so that the parents would be at peace, believing their children to be home safe, and the cattle would be relieved to have their mother cows and calves back safely as well.

Krishna had promised he would bring the children home safe, *somehow*.

He had kept his promise.

And he kept it every day for the next year.

Kaand II

When the year was over, almost to the day, the crevice was fully closed and the surface of the ground restored to its earlier appearance. It was difficult to believe that such a great abyss had existed there at all. Krishna and Balarama led a joyful procession of young gopas and gopis and their herd homewards at last. Balarama looked around at the ground that had been blighted only a few weeks earlier and wondered aloud at how such a thing could have come to pass.

'Everything serves a purpose, my brother,' Krishna said cheerfully, as if they had only been out for a day trip and were returning home at the end of the day.

'What possible purpose could have been served by keeping us away from our families for a year?'

Krishna shrugged. 'I do not know. And in the end, it hardly matters why. All that matters is the how. How we endure each new crisis and overcome it. For the only thing certain in life is that there shall always be crises.'

Balarama was not content by that response. But he accepted it.

Radha was almost sad to part with Krishna. Her house came before Krishna's and Balarama's and she seemed loathe to go in, waiting by her threshold and waving to them until they were out of sight. Then she went in, seeming less happy to see her family again than to have spent the time with Krishna. Of course, she thought, as did all the other children, that they had seen their families only the previous evening!

Yashoda was surprised when Krishna came running into the house and hugged her. 'Arrey!' she exclaimed, smiling with maternal pleasure. 'What happened? You act as if you have not seen me in months!'

'One full year, mother,' Krishna said. 'I have missed you dearly.'

Yashoda swatted him playfully. 'What nonsense are you talking? You went in the morning and came home in the evening! Only one day has passed.'

Krishna looked up at his mother with unadulterated love in his eyes. 'Mother, one day apart from you is like a year to me.'

Yashoda looked down and saw something in his eyes, something that she had not seen in the Krishna who had bid goodbye to her that morning. Something she could not quite define. It was the same Krishna, yet different.

She did not know how that could be possible, but knew that with Krishna, *anything* was possible. She felt her heart reciprocate the great outrush of emotion brimming in his eyes, and clasped him to her breast, embracing him tightly. She kissed his face all over, rubbing his arms and legs, then took him by the hand into the other room and fed him the best meal of his life.

Watching him eat, she felt fulfilled and sated herself. While he ate food that nourished his body, being with her child nourished her soul.

two

There was a shortage of fruit in Vrindavan. The elders were concerned as all the fruit trees had been yielding rotten or poor produce. Their concern did not have to do with taste or luxury. Fruit was essential for good health – their own and of their cattle. They had to find a new source of fresh fruit quickly. Yet they must do so without leaving Vrindavan. How was this to be accomplished?

Sridama had a suggestion which he offered to the younger gopas as they were discussing the matter while watching the calf herds. 'I know a place where there is plenty of fruit. It's like a heaven of fruit, with the most juicy, tasty fruits you ever imagined, all growing in one place.'

The boys exclaimed, some of them licking their lips. Every Vrishni loved fruit. Even some of the dogs sitting around their masters looked up, twitching their tails hopefully at the prospect of fruity treats.

'Take us there,' they said. 'Let us go now!' It had been so long since any of them had tasted fresh fruit, they could barely wait.

Sridama looked around, his smile fading. 'I cannot.'

'Why not?' someone asked.

'Nobody is supposed to go there,' Sridama replied.

'Where?' Balarama – who took every such statement as a direct challenge – asked at once. To say in Balarama's presence 'nobody dares do this' or 'nobody can do that' was like pointing a finger at him and challenging him to do it himself. 'Tell us how to get to this heaven of fruit.'

Sridama looked around nervously. 'I'm not supposed to say.'

Balarama stepped forward, elbowing the other boys aside without any malice. 'Tell me, Sridama.'

Sridama looked at Krishna, whom he revered. 'My father made me promise not to tell anyone ...'

He paused significantly, looking directly at Krishna.

Krishna glanced at Balarama. They understood what Sridama meant: Krishna hardly fell in the category of 'anyone'.

'You can tell me, Sridama,' Krishna said to his friend.

Sridama shook his head. 'A promise is a promise. I cannot tell.'

The other gopas all voiced their protest.

Krishna thought for a moment, then said, 'He made you promise not to tell anyone the location, is that right?'

Sridama nodded vigorously.

Krishna grinned. 'But he didn't make you promise not to *show* anyone, did he?'

Sridama thought for a moment, then slowly shook his head, a smile appearing on his thin, long face.

Krishna rose to his feet. 'Well, then, you won't disobey your father if you show us the way. Come on, let's go find this fabulous fruit grove!'

A chorus of cheers exploded as everyone followed after Krishna and Balarama.

Balarama tugged at Krishna's elbow as they started off down the pathway. Krishna glanced curiously at his brother.

'Bhraatr,' Balarama said in a voice that suggested he did not want an argument. 'You promised me last time that next time it would be my turn to deal with any threat that befell us.'

Krishna nodded. 'So I did.'

Balarama jerked his head ahead, indicating the way they were headed. 'In case anything should happen today, remember that. *I'll* do the fighting this time.'

Krishna grinned. 'Very well, Bhaiya. But in case you need any help, I'll be there, right behind you.'

Balarama snorted. 'Me? Need help? Never in an entire aeon. I can handle any asura that makes the mistake of showing me its ugly face.'

Krishna shrugged. 'So be it, Bhaiya. The next asura that threatens us will have you to deal with.'

'And you won't interfere, even if I'm in trouble,' Balarama warned.

Krishna nodded. 'Not unless you ask me for help.'

Balarama thought for a moment, then his features broke out into a wide grin. 'That's fine. That's quite fine. Thank you, Bhraatr! I won't let you down.'

Krishna slapped his brother on his back. 'I know you won't, Bhaiya.'

Balarama glanced one last time at Krishna, to check if there was any double entendre or hidden meaning to Krishna's words. But for once his brother seemed completely sincere. Balarama grinned. Finally, he would get a chance to fight!

He didn't notice the sly, mischievous grin on his brother's face.

three

'There. Up ahead through that gap, then up a little way, then down again, and you will find yourself in the palmyra grove.' Sridama mimed.

'Palmyra grove?' one of the other boys said. 'Here? In Vrindavan?'

'It must be a trick by the asuras to lure Krishna in,' said Krishna's cousin, the son of his uncle Upananda. 'We should go back and report this to Nanda Maharaja. He will know what to do.'

Sridama shook his head woefully. 'He knows about this grove. It was discovered some time ago by my own father and me.'

Balarama and Krishna exchanged a glance. *Father knew about this fruit grove? Then why didn't he ask everyone take fruit from here?*

Sridama looked around fearfully. 'Because a demon resides in the grove.'

The boys reacted at once, some opening their eyes wide, others exclaiming.

Only Balarama was intrigued, excited even. 'What sort of demon?' he asked, trying to appear nonchalant.

Sridama looked sheepish. 'You will laugh if I tell you, but it's a very dangerous demon. It killed three men even before we came to Vrindavan to live.'

Balarama looked at Krishna, holding his gaze. Krishna sighed and tilted his head as if having second thoughts about something. Balarama kept his gaze steady, as if demanding something. Finally, Krishna sighed again and nodded, relenting. The rest of the gang exchanged glances, wondering what that was about, but said nothing. They were used to Krishna and Balarama communicating in mysterious ways.

Balarama let out a whoop of satisfaction and started up the path. The other boys called after him, alarmed.

'Balarama-bhaiya, the demon!' one said.

Sridama looked at Krishna. 'He's going inside the grove, isn't he?'

Krishna shrugged.

'To find the demon and fight it himself, yes?'

Krishna shrugged again.

Sridama covered his face with his hands. 'My father will kill me if anything happens to Balarama! He'll say it was my fault!'

Krishna put his arm around Sridama's shoulders. 'Nothing will happen to Balarama. I'll make sure of that.'

And Krishna went up the path too, following behind his brother.

The other boys looked at each other, scared witless and wondering what to do.

There was nothing to do really, except wait.

four

The brothers looked around, astonished.

'There's enough fruit here to feed all of us for a year!' Balarama said.

And there was. The palmyra grove was an idyllic place: fruit trees of every description grew all around. It was impossible for such a diverse variety of fruits to grow together in one place; many required different kinds of soil or sunlight or water, yet here they were, clustered together like an enormous tribe, growing side by side, shoulder to shoulder. The sweet aroma of fresh fruit was everywhere, sometimes pungent, sometimes sweet, sometimes mingled, as various trees exuded their scents.

Krishna plucked an orange from a low-hanging branch. He tore a piece of the peel off and juice squirted out, almost hitting Balarama's eye.

'Ow!' Balarama exclaimed, rubbing the juice from his eye, the eye watering at once. 'You did that on purpose!'

'Sorry, Bhaiya,' Krishna said innocently. 'Here, have some of the fruit. It's delicious!'

Balarama took a quarter of the orange and popped it into his mouth. Tangy nectar exploded on his tongue. He blinked and chewed. 'It really is, Bhraatr! This is the best orange I've ever eaten!' He crunched a seed by mistake and made a face. 'And I don't even like oranges!'

Krishna pointed. Growing close beside the orange tree was a jackfruit one, enormously tall and massive and ancient-looking. 'Look. That's impossible. Orange and jackfruit never grow together.' He turned around, pointing this way then that. 'Nor do banana and strawberry. Or jamun and sweet lemon!'

Balarama shrugged. 'There must be magic at work here. Maybe the demon who lives here loves fruit. Maybe he used his magic to make these trees grow here.'

Balarama stopped and looked around.

'What is it?' Krishna asked, finishing the last of the orange.

'Listen. What do you hear?'

Krishna listened. 'Nothing. Not a sound.'

'Exactly. That's impossible too. In a grove like this, there should be any number of birds, animals, insects, all consuming the fruit openly or secretly, and they would make *some* noise. But I don't hear so much as an ant nibbling on an orange peel.'

Krishna didn't need to point out that ants didn't make much sound nibbling: Balarama was merely trying to make a point. He nodded, looking sombre. 'You're right, Bhaiya, somehow, this demon has scared off every living creature in the vicinity.'

'Yes,' Balarama said, bending low to the ground and sniffing. 'He must be very powerful to keep this beautiful trove of ripe fruit all to himself.'

'And very dangerous,' Krishna added.

'I don't care,' Balarama said at once, spinning around. He pointed a finger at Krishna. 'This time, I'm going to face the demon, Krishna. You owe me this one. You promised!'

Krishna grinned. 'And I intend to keep my promise, Bhaiya!'

Balarama narrowed his wide eyes suspiciously. 'You mean it?'

'Of course,' Krishna said, spreading his arms in invitation. 'Be my guest, Bhaiya. This demon is all yours to deal with.'

'And you won't interfere if the fight gets rough? You promise to let me deal with him on my own? Entirely?'

'Well, I can always come to assist you if you need me,' Krishna said.

Balarama bristled. 'I don't need any assistance! I can handle any asura on my own.'

Krishna raised his hands in surrender. 'Okay, okay. Let me go look around. You start shaking the trees so we can collect the fruits that fall.'

'And if you hear anything or spot the demon, shout out and call to me,' Balarama warned. 'Don't engage him yourself. Agreed?'

'Agreed,' Krishna called back over his shoulder. He smiled a secret smile as he left.

Balarama went up to an apple tree, grabbed hold of the trunk and shook it hard. Scores of apples rained down, most of them on his head and shoulders. He grimaced and kept his eyes shut, peering out when the deluge was over. One errant apple thudded down on his head and bounced off. He caught it in mid-air and examined it. It looked beautifully ripe, red, and luscious. He wiped it on his anga-vastra till it shone. Then he took a bite. The crunching sound it made was delicious in itself; the juicy pulp that he bit into was sugar sweet and of the perfect consistency. It had been a while since Balarama had eaten an apple at all, let alone one this tasty. He chewed his way through the whole apple in moments, then picked up another one, bigger and juicier-looking than the first. He bit into this one too, sweet sticky juice spattering his cheeks. He wiped it away as he demolished the second apple.

So absorbed was he in biting into the crunchy apple that he failed to notice the beast approaching him from behind until it was upon him. The first inkling he had was a mighty blow to his back. It felt as if two giant hammers had pounded on his back, driving him forward. He fell against the apple tree hard enough for the trunk to crack and the few remaining apples to plop to the ground.

Balarama turned around and looked at the creature that stood before him, rearing up on its hind legs and revealing a mouthful of large jagged teeth. Its eyes glowed red and it stank of a peculiar sweetish odour that he could not place at first.

'A donkey?' he said, unable to believe the evidence of his sight. That was what the demon looked like, a donkey!

The creature reared up and lunged forward in a manoeuvre no mere donkey was capable of executing. Balarama rolled aside just in time. The donkey's forepaws struck the apple tree with enough force to split the wood into splinters. The tree crashed to the ground. Then the donkey demon flipped over and swung around with an agility and peculiarity of movement that was impossible for any four-footed animal. No doubt about it: this was an asura.

In case Balarama still had any doubts, the creature opened its mouth and instead of the usual braying donkey sound, let off a series of deep menacing growls befitting a lion or a tiger. Then it reared up again, preparing to launch forward in that peculiar way, somehow able to leap forward only on its hind legs while attacking with its forelegs. Balarama saw that its forepaws had sharp talons in place of the usual cloven feet and if he had any reservations left about harming a mere donkey, they were dispelled at once by the sight of those deadly talons.

'Come on, then,' Balarama muttered. 'Let's see what you have.'

The donkey demon flew at Balarama with a speed that was astonishing – and unexpected. It took Balarama by surprise, and he barely got time to dodge the attack. Even so, the left forepaw nicked his shoulder, tearing the muscle there and drawing a splatter of blood that stained the strewn apples on the ground, matching their ripe red colour.

Balarama roared with displeasure. 'Now you've sealed your fate!' he yelled.

He charged at the donkey just as the demon reared up again, flashing its deadly teeth and hammer-strong paws.

Boy and donkey clashed with a resounding thud.

Krishna heard the unmistakable sounds of a fight and ran back to the spot where he had left Balarama.

He arrived just in time to see Balarama grappling with a being that resembled a donkey but was clearly demoniac in nature.

Krishna grinned and watched as Balarama took hold of the demon's hind legs and swung the beast around. The beast issued a resounding roar of outrage.

His upper body heaving with the effort and legs planted firmly on the apple-strewn ground, Balarama swung the donkey demon around over his head. Then he let go.

This time, the donkey asura screamed in terror, the unmistakeable cry of a creature that faces certain death. It flew several dozen yards high in the air before falling back to earth.

Moments after landing, it lay still, its body grotesquely sprawled in a manner that left no doubt about its state.

Krishna approached Balarama, still carrying the armful of fruit he had found.

Balarama dusted off his anga-vastra and arms. The wound on his shoulder was gaping, the skin torn and hanging by a flap, the flesh visible and bloody. Krishna gestured at it with his eyes and Balarama shrugged and slapped at it casually as if to say it was nothing, but he did wince a little, belying his bravado.

'Nice fruit,' Balarama said, pointing his chin at the armload Krishna was carrying.

'Nice fight,' Krishna said, jerking his head in the direction of the dead donkey. 'Who was that?'

Balarama shook his head. 'Just some donkey!'

They burst out laughing.

Just then the other boys entered the clearing – eyes wild and ready to do battle, but terrified at the prospect of facing another Aghasura or Putana-like demon – carrying sticks and slings and stones in their hands.

'Krishna! Balarama!' they cried. 'Where is the demon? We will stand with you against it.'

The brothers exchanged a glance. Then, as one, they rolled their heads and pointed at the dead donkey.

'There. Be careful. It may only be pretending to be hurt.'

The boys turned to stare wide-eyed at the broken body of the asura. As recognition of its form flooded their scared minds, their mouths opened and tongues lolled.

'But … but … it's only a donkey!' cried one of them.

Krishna winked. 'Takes one to know one! Balarama fought it all by himself. I never lifted a finger. Right, Bhaiya?'

Balarama rolled his eyes but nodded. 'Right, Bhraatr.'

Krishna burst out laughing as Balarama glared at him hotly. After a moment, Balarama's temper subsided.

'You knew all along,' he said accusingly. 'You knew the next demon would be an ass, not a real demon like Agha or Baka or Putana. That's why you let me fight it alone.'

Krishna chuckled. 'But it was a real demon, Bhaiya. You even have the wound to prove it. Besides, you made an ass out of it in the end.'

Balarama glared at him again, then shook his head and started chuckling, despite himself.

In moments, both Krishna and he were laughing together.

The other boys joined in.

six

Once the blighted land had healed itself, the new pastures were quite safe to travel to and back. Between the new pastures and the magical fruit grove, the Vrishnis had ample nourishment. The lush supply of fodder and fruit energized the herds as well as the carers.

For once, the Vrishnis were well fed, safe and relatively content. News from the outside world came rarely, but what little of it trickled in suggested that the Usurper had finally reduced his campaign of terror against the Vrishnis and other clans still loyal to Ugrasena. Not quite a truce, but a political detente seemed to have emerged. A season of calm between storms. Nobody believed it would last or that the Usurper genuinely desired peace and prosperity for the Yadava nations, but they needed to rebuild their strength and prepare themselves for the final assault. Akrur and his associates send word across the land that everyone should lie low and bide their time.

Busy with his endless wrestling tournaments in various corners of the Magadhan Empire, Kamsa himself seemed to be away from Mathura more often than present on the Yadava throne. Even when he was at court in Mathura, Magadhan ambassadors hovered around every district of Mathura, never in official positions but always watching over the shoulders of the Yadavas who governed or administered the various governmental functions.

In this manner, Jarasandha was controlling his interests in Mathura without overtly seizing power. It was a frustrating time, for the Yadavas were neither wholly free from tyranny nor being oppressed sufficiently to warrant an open rebellion.

This was the genius of Jarasandha at work, Gargamuni said, to keep the Yadavas under his thumb yet never give them any justification to openly rise up and shed the blood of their tyrannical king.

At such a time, the Vrishnis and other loyalists had no choice but to wait things out. Rising up or resorting to violence would only seem churlish and spiteful on their part. The only thing to do was bide time and await their moment.

As cowherds accustomed to spending days simply waiting and watching over their flocks, waiting was something the Vrishnis were good at doing. So they waited. And watched. And rebuilt their strength.

One day, the opportune moment would come and they would rise and follow their deliverer to freedom from tyranny.

seven

Krishna was playing his flute sitting on the hillside overlooking the lake near the new pastures.

It was a day of feasting for the clan and everyone was gathered by the lake in their festive colours. Families sat and ate under the trees or on the meadows. The herds grazed freely in the new pastures, permitted to eat their fill, for that was how they would feast. Children played in the lake, splashing and swimming, the smallest ones riding their father's shoulders. The older children swung from a rope tied to the overhanging branch of a great banyan tree and let go to fall into the lake.

Radha sat near Krishna, listening enraptured to his playing.

She seemed to change a little more each passing day, growing before his very eyes. Since the time in the pastures, all the children of Vrindavan had grown closer to Krishna than ever before, but of them all, none more than Radha. She followed him wherever he went, often to his exasperation. Sometimes, when Balarama and he wanted to play rough games with the boys, she would insist on joining in, and the other boys would object vociferously, unwilling to be as rough with a girl as with each other. Krishna didn't mind as much as Balarama did. Radha could outrun any boy or girl in the village and she could hold her own in virtually every game as well.

Besides, he liked having Radha around. Ever since they had returned from the enforced exile, she had changed almost overnight. Before, she chattered constantly, driving Balarama crazy. But now she had a quietude that he found comforting. She never demanded that they talk and was content simply to sit and stare at the clouds or watch the birds or fish or cattle.

Krishna felt immensely contented simply being one with nature. There was something about the rhythm of the world that he found very soothing, whether it was rain falling on eaves, wind weaving through pastures of tall grass, koels calling out to each other from high branches or simply the sight and fragrance of flowers swaying in the breeze and surrendering their pollen to flitting bees, he could watch and listen to it for hours on end. It made him feel connected to the earth, to Bhoodevi herself.

After all, it was at her behest that he was here on this mortal plane, helping her save her children from the tyranny of asuras. So, like any child, he was content to simply lie in Mother Earth's cradle and watch her go about her work through infinite forms and means. And the new Radha seemed to enjoy it just as much as he did. Far from chattering the hours away, she could find contentment in simply lying or sitting near him and immersing herself in the sounds of nature just as he did, lost in the infinite song of the earth.

He lowered his flute at last. He loved the way the sounds of the world seeped back into his consciousness after a long session of flute playing. Seeing the colours seeping into things and the earth become animate once again was like watching a new day dawn over the world.

He heard the voices and laughter of the people in the meadow below, the splashing of the children in the lake, the satisfied lowing of the herds in the pastures ... it was a beautiful day, overcast with gentle clouds that obscured the sunlight enough for one to lie on one's back and stare at the powdery blue sky. The water in the lake appeared lighter hued than usual. Birds flitted through the branches of trees overlooking the lake. A pair of woodpeckers were at work on one immensely tall tree nearby on the hill, working steadily at pecking a hole large enough to accommodate their family. The rat-a-tat was pleasing in its own way. Even nature's stenches were just smells, her noises part of the music of life, and Krishna embraced it all, the loud with the soft, the roar with the whisper, the humming with the growling, the swamps as well as the orchids.

'That was your best ever,' Radha said. She was looking down the hill, at the lake, yet Krishna knew that her eyes were shining in response to his playing. He had sensed the changes brimming within Radha, had understood what they meant and what they implied; he knew what they would lead to over time, and it made him sad at times, for what she desired could never come to pass, what she felt could never be reciprocated. Yet she had every right to feel, to desire, to be what she chose to be, and he would not deny her that experience, even if it led to sadness.

'I was trying to imitate the song of the earth on a summer's day,' he said. 'A day like this.' He fell silent again, still listening to the music of Bhoodevi all around them. 'I didn't succeed.'

She turned to look at him, startled. 'You succeeded so well! Your music is ethereal. Even apsaras in swargaloka can't play music like you can, Krishna. Your flute speaks a language all its own. All eternity stops to listen.'

He was surprised. The new Radha rarely spoke much, this eloquent and passionate speech was unusual coming from her. Apparently her loquaciousness hadn't vanished completely; it had merely been sublimated into a more elegant avatar.

'The song belongs to those who listen,' he said gracefully, acknowledging her praise and accepting the compliment. 'Without the right listener, that woodpecker's hammering is just noise. But to me …'

'It's music. As it is to me,' she said.

He smiled. She *did* understand.

As the music of the day continued around them, an orchestra performing exclusively for their benefit, they sat looking at each other for a long moment. The sun drifted behind a cloud, then floated out again, altering the lighting and mood around them. A gentle breeze rippled over them, carrying the coolness of the lake water, soothing and refreshing.

A scream ruptured the harmony.

The fact that it came did not surprise Krishna. He had known it would happen sooner or later, but just not precisely when, where or how.

He knew now. It was here and now. It had begun, again.

Krishna was on his feet at once. Radha sat bolt upright, looking around.

'Krishna,' she cried, pointing. 'In the lake!'

'I see it,' he said grimly.

He sprinted downhill.

eight

Balarama was the first to see the beast appear. He was running along the bank, playing with the other gopas and gopis when he sensed a disturbance out of the corner of his eye. He turned and looked out at the lake and saw the water swirling darkly. He knew at once that it was no ordinary eddy or backwash. There was something under the surface, rising up fast, something big. Though he had been playing and enjoying himself as much as the others, he had developed a preternatural alertness. In a way, he considered himself Krishna's early warning bell.

He turned to shout to those nearest to it to get out of the water. But before he could open his mouth, a gopi stepping into the water, carrying her little son on her shoulders, happened to look down. She saw the dark water rising beneath her and screamed a blood-curdling scream.

'Out! Out of the water, everyone!' Balarama bellowed, running around the shore, pulling those to the banks to dry land, wading into the shallows to help others get out quicker.

He didn't need to glance around to see where Krishna was. It went without saying that he would be arriving as fast as his feet could carry him. Balarama's job was to get these innocents away from the new threat as quickly as possible without anyone coming to harm.

With a sinking heart, he saw that it would be quite

impossible. There were too many people in the water, many of them children and elders incapable of exiting quickly. And going by the swirling in the centre of the lake, the thing that was emerging was coming much too fast.

More than that, it was big. Bigger than any underwater creature had any right to be. How it had lain there all this while without anyone noticing, he could not fathom. Then again, the lake was extremely deep in some spots, perhaps even deep enough to contain a monster without anyone suspecting. So long as the creature stayed out of sight until the opportune moment, it was undetectable.

He cursed, wishing he had had the foresight to dive into the lake and delve as deep into its depths as possible before they began swimming. That way, he might have found something amiss and been quicker to alert everyone.

'Out! Everyone, hurry!' he shouted. But they were still moving too slowly, confused by the splashing and hampered by having to move through choppy water.

He splashed into the lake, helping an elderly couple to wade, gasping, to where their younger family members could help them ashore. He glanced back and saw that, still dripping from the lake, eager to move as far away as possible from the imminent threat, people were already climbing the hill. That was reassuring. After the last few encounters with demons, there was no telling how large this new creature might be or what form it might take. The larger the area left deserted, the better the chance of innocents staying safe.

He helped a pair of young children out of the water, grasping each by one hand and swinging them to their mothers on shore. He sensed movement beside him and knew without looking that it was Krishna.

'Took your time,' he said, grumbling. He had seen his brother on the hilltop, playing his flute and talking to Radha.

'What do we have?' Krishna asked, picking up an elderly gopi and carrying him like a babe to safety. He set the elder down carefully, nodded his head in acknowledgement of the profuse thanks and blessings, and splashed into the water again to assist the next person.

'Something big, mean and ugly would be my guess,' Balarama said, taking a young tyke off his father's shoulders as the father struggled to manage two other young children.

'Get everyone to the top of the hill first, make sure they're all safe, then head back to the village.'

Balarama picked up a hefty young boy who was too shocked to swim properly and all but hurled him to his parents' arms. They caught him and shouted their blessings to Balarama.

'I'm staying with you, Bhai. You may need my help!'

'They need your help more,' Krishna shouted back from several yards away. He was pulling a raft with a dozen-odd youngsters on board, all of whom were too terrified of the churning water to swim back to the shore. 'Top of the hill, then back home!'

Balarama gritted his teeth in frustration. He was tired of playing nursemaid. He could lift ten times what the strongest grown man in the village could lift, throw as many times as far as the best pitcher, and was stronger and faster and a better fighter than even the veterans. Yet, every time there was a crisis, all he seemed to do was carry little children on his shoulders and urge everyone to move 'faster, faster'.

But he knew better than to argue with Krishna at a time like this. So he busied himself with getting the last of the stragglers ashore. Then he turned and looked at the lake.

Krishna was in the lake, treading the water, and it was all he could do to keep from being pulled into the lake. It was no longer just a swirling, or even an eddy. This was a full-blown whirlpool, spinning madly around with great force and speed. It already covered more than half the surface of the lake, and kept growing, increasing in fury and force as if some enormous invisible butter churner were churning the lake. Children were sobbing and screaming as their elders led them away from the lake.

Krishna could hear Balarama's voice bellowing behind him, herding their people to safety. Then the sound of the whirlpool increased, the water whipping with a frenzy that could only be described as madness, frothing and bubbling and eddying in gouts that spouted unexpectedly like boils bursting upon the back of a great beast. The sound itself resembled some furious whirlwind trapped in the lake, as if a dervish was struggling to break free.

Krishna felt the whirlpool suck at his legs, drawing him in. He fought the current, but the force was prodigious, like a storm centred upon the lake. It was then that he realized that the beast that lay under the lake was not seeking to burst free. It was seeking to suck people *in*. Down to its depths. Into its natural habitat.

He glanced around and was relieved to see that there was

nobody left behind. Balarama had cleared everyone to safety. They were climbing the hill even now, struggling to reach the top. He heard the shouts and cries of those who had already reached the top, calling to those still climbing to hurry. He heard his own name called out time and again, and knew that every pair of eyes was seeking him out, every heart anxious for his well-being. That was what was at stake here: not merely the lives of those he loved and cared about, but the survival of mortalkind itself, and of the values and principles that made it worth saving. The concern for all loved ones, even if one happened to be invulnerable, indomitable, or, as in his case, God Incarnate.

Krishna knew how to deal with this attack. If the beast would not come up to face him, he would have to go down to meet it.

He relaxed his body, ceasing to fight the sucking claws of the whirlpool. Then he allowed the vortex to take him into the eye of the storm, into the lair of the underwater beast.

Krishna sucked in one last gasp of air, not because he needed it to survive but because he wanted to taste air before he went in to battle. The water engulfed him and the surface of the lake closed above him.

All sound changed. Gone was the music of the earth, the song of Bhoodevi.

Instead, he was left with only the ballad of the beast. A deep watery keening that was as sad as a dirge and as desperately hopeless and fatalistic as an end-of-the-world dance. It was a strange and terrible song and Krishna knew that this asura would be no easy opponent. This one was a singer of death.

He opened his mouth wide and swam down to meet it. He himself had a verse or two that he wished to sing to it.

ten

Radha watched with her heart in her mouth as Krishna plunged into the whirlpool. From her vantage point at the top of the hill, the maelstrom looked like a gigantic eye in the lake, as if some unimaginably huge monster was gawking through a hole in the earth to peer up at heaven. The water itself was swirling so swiftly and angrily, boiling and raging, that she could not understand how Krishna could withstand its pull. When he finally took a deep breath and plunged in, she reached out with one hand, suppressing a shout by covering her mouth with her other hand. She remained that way for several moments, willing Krishna to reappear … now … now … now …

He didn't.

The last of the stragglers reached the top of the hill. Those who had not been by the lake had arrived as well, and all the inhabitants of Vrindavan now stood atop the hill overlooking the lake. Balarama pushed the last of the young tykes up to the top before turning to look down. His fair features reflected his anxiety and frustration.

Radha knew Balarama was no less brave and strong than his brother and enjoyed fighting much more than Krishna; yet he was always the one handed the task of shepherding the flock while his dark-skinned brother fought the demons. She could guess how frustrating it must be for Balarama and admired his fortitude and loyalty. Even now, his attention was focussed on ensuring that everyone was present and accounted for, and only when he was certain his task was successfully accomplished did he turn to see how the battle fared.

There was not much they could see from where they stood. The water continued to churn furiously. From time to time, a spout would shoot up, sometimes rising several score yards in the air, topping even the tallest lakeside trees, before falling back in a plume of spray. But mostly, the maelstrom raged and bubbled and spun around as if it would never cease.

Finally, after several minutes had passed, Balarama began asking everyone to head home. Many protested weakly but gave in when Balarama firmly told them that it was Krishna's request. Every family had young ones or elders or both and everyone knew that if the battle came this way, there would be no time to get the slowpokes out of harm's way in time. As it is, they were lucky simply to have escaped without a single casualty. There were a few minor injuries and some broken limbs, including a pair of broken legs as a result of running away from the lake too fast while looking back over one's shoulder: that was little Samit who had a habit of running races that way as well, and had fallen before for the same reason, though never this badly.

Most were shaken and bruised but otherwise unharmed. Many praised Krishna for having saved them yet again and prayed for his speedy triumph. Radha thought of reminding them that it was Balarama who had first seen the disturbance and got everyone out, but realized there was no need. They all knew Balarama's contribution, but regarded the older brother as a part of Krishna. It was the way one said 'Thank God' – you didn't need to say 'Thank all the gods'.

They began the long trek back. Radha turned her head to watch as the procession wound its way towards the village. Balarama was the last one, bringing up the rear. He turned and saw Radha still on the hill and frowned, beckoning to her.

She folded her arms on her chest, firmly.

'I'm saying,' she said.

Balarama shook his head. 'Krishna said ...'

'You'll have to carry me kicking and screaming if you want me to go home,' she said. 'And I bite too.'

He looked at her for a long moment, sceptical.

She made two fists of her hands and raised them in a fighting stance.

He grinned. 'Don't be absurd.'

'Don't be stupid. I'm staying. Take the others and go home.'

He looked at her a moment longer. 'He will kill me if anything happens to you.'

She raised her fists higher. 'I will kill you if you try to make me leave.'

He thought about it for another moment, then shrugged. 'Remember to tell Krishna later that you said that.'

She lowered her fists. 'I'll tell him I fought and beat you and you cried for your mother and ran back all the way home.'

He grinned. 'That will do too.'

Radha turned back to look down at the lake. She had no intention of budging until she knew her Krishna was safe.

eleven

Krishna was being given the battle of his life. Putana had been no match for him. Her only real weapon had been her poisoned milk, and once he had consumed that and survived, she had nothing left. The other asuras each had some special power or unique ability. But this asura was remarkable.

For one thing, it was a serpent of mythic proportions. He could not tell exactly how long its body extended, but guessed it went on for at least a mile or two. That in itself was not unique: Aghasura had been far bigger in terms of sheer size. The difference here was that this demon was a water serpent. And its venom was lethal. Almost as toxic as Putana's poison. It was extraordinarily strong as well, and its multitude of heads was something he had never imagined possible. Each time he wrestled a new head away from himself, or prevented one from sinking its fangs into his body, beating it aside or crushing it with his hands or feet, a new one popped up, and another, and yet another. This had been going on ever since he had descended into the vortex.

That was the other thing: the demon was able to twist around at a speed that matched any tornado, except that it could do so underwater. In that way, it was as unique as Bakasura, whose special ability had been the manipulation of wind.

This asura combines the powers of all my previous attackers. Whoever sent it thought that even if I could defeat each of those asuras individually, I wouldn't be able to withstand this assault by a demon that packs all their abilities in itself.

It was an ingenious idea and one that Krishna couldn't discount as a failure. Not yet. Perhaps not at all.

For one thing, the serpent managed to strike home a few times. The sheer number of heads it possessed and the blinding speed with which they attacked from every side made it simply impossible for Krishna to deflect or destroy them all. Besides, the asura was shrewd, shrewder than most demons and better versed at battling gods. Every time he used a manoeuvre that would have bested a lesser demon, he found himself counterpointed and attacked again in a new way. Not only was the demon a worthy opponent, it was able to hurt him!

Krishna felt the places where the demon had sunk its fangs into his body, albeit briefly. Each point throbbed with pain. The poison was no ordinary toxin intended for creatures of the earth. It was a special Halahala type of venom that could slay gods. He didn't know how much it would take to kill him, but suspected that if he was struck enough times, it would succeed. After all, even he was subject to the limitations of his human form. His eternal being would survive, of course, but Krishna the mortal would perish. And Krishna was what he was in this life and at this time. Losing this body and being forced to take another rebirth or avatara or amsa would be a defeat, perhaps a decisive one. Certainly an unacceptable one. He could not let that come to pass.

The main purpose of this descent to earth was to rid the world of the last of the asuras. Those demons that had somehow managed to survive and stay upon the mortal realm despite the repeated cleansings he had inflicted upon this plane in previous incarnations.

That was why he had chosen to descend as Vishnu Incarnate. Not an avatar or an amsa but as God himself, albeit in a mortal identity. And that identity was Krishna, the closest he had come to replicating himself as he truly appeared, in his own image. Krishna was *He*. It was why he had maintained the black skin, the dark features, the facial similarity, and so many minute details.

He was Krishna in this life. He could not let an asura defeat Krishna. Not this asura or any other. He roared, the sound audible even deep under the water.

They were perhaps half a mile beneath the surface of the lake now, the serpent demon seeking to draw him in even deeper, to take him to the bowels of the earth, thence perhaps to transport him to some place where he could bite him to his heart's content until Krishna lost all resistance and succumbed to the lethal god-slaying venom. Already, the power of the vortex was enormous, the pressure immense. He roared to give himself courage and struck back.

Hitting at the serpent with renewed vigour while grasping hold of the slippery coils and drawing them upwards, he made for the surface, forcing the demon upwards, ever upwards, even as he fought and kicked and punched it.

The demon sensed what he was doing and fought back just as fiercely, striking with several heads at once now, not caring how many he destroyed so long as a few got past his defences and pierced his flesh with their fangs, sinking in a little more venom with each strike before he could react and rip out the offending head, twisting and crushing it.

Krishna felt his body surrender to the poison even as his wounds bled openly now, releasing his precious life fluid into the agitated waters that had turned dark with his own blood, as if night were falling inside the lake. He knew then that if he did not take this battle to the surface and turn his desperate defence into a powerful offence, he would lose.

And if he lost, the mortal realm itself would be lost.

twelve

Radha was relieved when Balarama relented and permitted her to stay. She couldn't bear the thought of being far away again while Krishna risked his life to battle another demon.

She knew he was probably not risking his life in the sense a normal human boy might, but he was still battling an unknown opponent, one that had been sent to kill him. And if he was truly invulnerable, why would demons try to kill him? Surely, each successive asura hoped to exploit some weakness in Krishna and succeed where others had failed.

She watched the lake for several moments after Balarama and the rear-enders had disappeared down the winding road that led homewards. The water continued to simmer and seethe, explode in plumes and geysers, spin furiously. But nothing else happened for a long while. She wondered how Krishna could hold his breath for so long. Clearly, he *did* breathe, so that meant his body required air to survive. How then could he survive underwater for so long?

She recalled the legend of Matsya, the fish incarnation of Lord Vishnu. She knew that fish breathed air but absorbed it through the water. Perhaps that was how Krishna could stay underwater for so long: by extracting air from the water. Next, she wondered about his skin and his bones: could they be cut, pierced or broken? She did not recall ever hearing of Krishna being hurt in any way, not so much as the smallest cut. Even after battling those terrible asuras, he had been unscathed. So he was invulnerable. Which begged the question again: why send asuras to try to kill an invulnerable God?

She knew she was ranting mentally, that the inability to know what was happening beneath the lake was driving her insane with worry. She tried to calm herself, to hum the song Krishna had been playing on the flute only a short while ago. It was so soothing, so calming, like the sound of wind, or water, or birds …

What was it Krishna had said?

The song belongs to those who listen.

He had meant her. *She* was the listener, he the singer. And so long as he sang, she was content to listen eternally.

Suddenly, she saw something change in the lake. It was still churning madly. But the colour of the water had altered subtly and continued to change.

She squinted, peering intently.

Yes, there was no doubt about it. The water looked darker now. She looked up. There were no clouds above the lake, nor any whose shadows could be darkening the surface of the water. No. The change in hue came from the water changing colour. She watched as the water grew steadily darker, changing from its usual bluish green to a more reddish brown.

Suddenly, she knew what that meant. The lake was filling with blood. Someone – or something – was bleeding.

She put her fist in her mouth, stifling a gasp. She prayed it wasn't Krishna. Even the thought of him being injured made her sick.

Surely he couldn't shed so much blood, enough to change the very colour of the lake itself? Then again, that was exactly what she had been ranting about just now: the fact that she had no idea what God Incarnate could or couldn't do. Perhaps he *could* bleed. And if so, then surely he could bleed sufficiently to make an entire lake change colour? After all, he was a god.

She clenched her fists tightly enough for her fingernails to dig into her palms. She began praying to Lord Vishnu to protect her beloved friend, then realized the redundancy of that prayer. She settled instead for praying to Lakshmi Devi, eternal companion and consort to Lord Vishnu. Somehow, it seemed more appropriate.

thirteen

The head of the long line was reaching the outskirts of the hamlet up ahead. Balarama had done as Krishna had asked: he had escorted all the people back to the village. Now he shouted to Nanda Maharaja and the other headmen of the clan that he was going back and turned.

He paused by his house for a moment to pick up something. His plough. The same one he had kept all these years and carried in his childhood as well. He liked the way it felt in his hands. It also made an excellent weapon.

He sprinted like the wind. Being heavyset, Balarama could not sustain a fast pace over long distances, but he could sprint short distances with greater power than other boys. The distance to the lake was a mere yojana, barely nine miles. He could sprint that distance and barely break a sweat. He put his back and shoulders into it, roaring up and over the hills and down the dales, leaving a dust cloud that was visible for miles in his wake. Back at the hamlet, his mother Rohini saw it from her threshold and knew at once that it was her son hurrying back to join Krishna.

Balarama reached the top of the hill just in time to see Krishna break through the surface. Radha was standing exactly where he had left her, staring down with her hands clasped in front, barely breathing. Her eyes were set intently on the lake below. Balarama fell to his knees, forcing himself to breathe steadily rather than gulp in great breaths. He had no trouble bringing his breathing under control in a moment. As he had expected, barely a few beads of sweat had popped out on his forehead and forearms.

He leaned on his plough and watched as the surface of the lake turned deep maroon from what could only be blood.

Something was emerging, something so huge, it was pushing great quantities of water above and ahead of it. Balarama held his breath as the water finally broke and the beast emerged.

Radha gasped and cupped both hands over her mouth in that peculiar way that girls had.

Why do they do that? Balarama wondered irritably. *Do they mean to stop themselves from crying out? Why not simply cry out then? It isn't as if there's anybody here to mind!*

He rose to his feet, stunned at the sight.

The asura was a gigantic water serpent, jet black in colour. Its scales were glistening and shiny, a diamond pattern breaking the glossy blackness every few yards. Though nowhere near as thick as Aghasura, its torso was huge.

The earlier asura had been massive enough to resemble a gigantic cavern. This asura, a water serpent, was barely as thick as a few dozen banyan trunks banded together. It could probably swallow a small hillock, but it was not a python or boa constrictor. Its neck was slender and shapely, the mouth widening to an immense flattened head some three score yards long and one score yards wide, if Balarama's assessment was correct.

The mouth opened to reveal a dark-red serpentine mouth with a long, forked tongue that slipped in and out, and great fangs, some three yards long apiece, dripping viscous, thick green venom.

But that was only the upper torso and main head.

As Balarama watched, the serpent continued to emerge from the water, the force of its momentum causing it to rise high in the air. As it rose, its upper body split into a myriad of heads, all identical to the first, all venomous serpent heads, but of varying sizes. Some were almost as large as the main head, others much smaller, probably no bigger than an asp, most comprising in-between sizes. And there were so *many* of them!

Balarama tried to assess how many heads there were in all and gave up at once: it was hopeless to even try to count. There were easily a hundred, perhaps several hundred. A thousand? Quite possibly.

He had never seen or heard of anything like it before. A giant water serpent with a thousand poisonous heads.

And riding atop the largest head was Krishna.

Balarama grinned proudly as he saw his brother – attacked constantly by the other heads of the beast that were lunging, striking, sinuously snaking around to attack from every side conceivable – standing on the hood of the great serpent's biggest head.

He lost the grin as he saw the wounds on Krishna's body, several bleeding quite profusely.

As he watched, another head struck home, sinking its fangs into his brother's foot.

Beside him, Radha screamed.

Krishna bent down, dodging a large head that was lunging to bite his neck from behind, grasped hold of the head that had attacked his foot, crushed its neck, and tossed it away. Balarama saw it hang limply now, dead, and was pleased to see that several dozen other heads were similarly crushed and killed. But how many had struck their fangs into his brother's precious flesh?

How many had injected their venom into Krishna's body? And how potent was that venom? Enough to do real harm to Krishna?

He saw now that the blood in the lake was all Krishna's. A copious amount of it. That could hardly be good. If Krishna had shed so much blood, he must have absorbed a great deal of venom as well. Whatever this asura was, it was no ordinary water serpent. Its venom must be highly toxic, perhaps even toxic enough to harm a god. And with such immense quantities being pushed into his body, Krishna would have weakened at the very least.

Balarama roared with fury, stamping his foot. He prepared to start downhill, intending to go to Krishna's aid at once, to leap into the water and start strangling the serpent's heads, killing them one by one. He didn't care what his brother had said. He would not simply stand by and watch his younger sibling being killed. He would die before he let that happen. Besides, Krishna was clearly outmatched and outnumbered right now. If they couldn't fight back with one thousand heads, then at least two were better than one!

He would battle, to the death, if need be.

But before he could start down the hill, Krishna began to dance.

fourteen

Krishna felt the venom coursing through his veins. Though his body was infused with Brahman at the most basic level, the flesh was mortal. Gods did not possess flesh, blood, bones … not in the human sense of the term. The humanoid forms they appeared in during the rare interfaces with mortal beings were the closest approximations possible: their true forms were beyond the ability of mortal beings to perceive. It would be like attempting to see Brahman itself, the force that pervaded, bonded and bound all Creation. Human eyes would only perceive a humanoid form, not the deva parts and processes which were beyond human ability.

So his divinity was unharmed by the venom but he still experienced the suffering of his mortal flesh. He knew that this body could not survive too many more injections of venom.

He was smashing and crushing and breaking Kaliya's heads – he had come to think of the serpent asura as Kaliya because, like Krishna himself, he was jet black in colour, an irony that was not lost on him – as fast as he could manage, but there were simply too many of them.

The more he killed the more appeared to take their place, lunging from every direction, lithely slipping in under his guard and striking home with lethal accuracy. Krishna felt his organs failing, his blood getting polluted, his heart pounding in agony, and knew that this asura had harmed him in ways that no other asura had been able to achieve until then. Kaliya, his namesake and brother in skin colour, had succeeded where all others had failed. The water-serpent asura was winning this battle, Krishna was losing.

So be it. Let me die. And dying, go out in a blaze of glory.

When all else is lost, one may as well sing, raise one's voice in defiant song, not merely to voice a protest, but to make a statement: *You have beaten down my body and crushed my flesh, you have destroyed my physical form, you have demolished my earthly presence … and yet I survive. My aatma lives on, eternally. My soul outlives all crises. My will overcomes all reversals. My essence triumphs regardless. Even as I stand here dying, I sing to show that this being, this individual, this unique bonding of spirit and flesh, skin and soul, still exists and remains bloody yet unbowed, beaten yet undefeated, broken yet spiritually whole. I am Krishna. I am evergreen. Hari! Hari! Hari!*

And he danced.

His feet found purchase even on the slippery, mobile hood of Kaliya. They drummed out a syncopation of their own.

He danced with frenzy, with fury, with the exultation of dwindling life, with the white hot fire of tapas.

Shiva in his Nataraja form, dancing the dance at the End of Days to uncreate Creation, could hardly have danced more passionately or ferociously.

Krishna danced even as the venom coursed through his veins, killing his mortal organs, destroying the fragile mortal bond he had with the earthly realm.

He danced, and the world seemed to realign itself to his rhythm, to rearrange its song to harmonize with his pattern, to provide accompaniment.

He danced, and the music of the spheres accompanied him, the songs of the earth, the sun, the moon, blazed out in harmony.

He danced and sang his defiance of mortal death.

He was Krishna.

He was infinite.

If he must die, he would die dancing and celebrating his own death and rebirth.

He would embrace the darkness that was ultimately his own shadow.

He danced.

fifteen

Watching him from the top of the hill, Balarama was stupefied, Radha stunned. Both watched in astounded silence as Krishna danced away atop the black snake's hood. The serpent itself swayed, the lunging attacks of its myriad heads stalling as it reacted to this astonishing behaviour.

It was obvious that the serpent could not make head nor tail of Krishna's dancing: was it a precursor to a new retaliatory attack? Was it itself meant to be an attack? Was it something godly incarnations did during battle? Its bewilderment was writ plainly as it swayed slowly, its frenzied movements ceasing until it resembled nothing so much as its earthly brethren, just a serpent swaying to the rhythm of a *been*-player, a snake-charming musician.

'Look,' Radha said, pointing. 'It's dancing with Krishna!'

Balarama watched closely.

She was right.

Whether knowingly or instinctively, the serpent was mimicking the rhythm of Krishna's pounding feet. It was likely the serpent had only paused to try and assess this new behaviour, not intending to move in rhythm with its enemy. But in observing Krishna's dance, it had fallen into the hypnotic pattern of his footfalls.

As Radha and Balarama watched, the swaying grew more and more pronounced, until Krishna's emphatic footfalls, marking the end of a bar or movement, were matched by noticeable jerks and sinuous shifts of the giant hood itself. What was more, even the other heads began to sway and dance in syncopation, the smaller ones moving faster to keep double time while the larger ones moved slowly in a half-beat rhythm.

The overall effect was mesmerizing.

A magician seeking to charm and hold a snake's attention could not have performed a more elaborate trick.

'He's hypnotized it,' Balarama said in wonderment. 'He's hypnotized the asura with the rhythm of his dance.'

And so he had.

Krishna's feet were the only thing making contact with the serpent's body. And snakes, lacking hearing, could only sense sounds through physical contact, usually through vibrations felt in the ground on which they lay. Krishna's dancing was a constant rhythmic series of vibrations, transmitted to Kaliya through his hood, passing through his entire body. Somehow, Kaliya was understanding what Krishna was 'saying' through his dance, and was listening intently. And in this manner, Krishna had succeeded in gaining control of the serpent asura through the means of rhythmic communication.

As they continued to watch, Krishna danced on.

Balarama realized that Krishna was doing more than simply controlling Kaliya. He was also ridding himself of the venom the serpent asura had injected into his body: the more he danced, the more his blood pumped through his veins, the more his wounds bled. His body was covered with gaping wounds, all oozing, dripping blood. The blood pooled on the hood of the serpent asura and dripped into the lake which was stained blackish red now.

Balarama's heart ached at the sight of so much blood, his brother's vital fluid, being shed. How could Krishna survive such a great amount of blood loss, let alone dance with such frenzied passion?

But that was the greatness of Krishna. That was why he was God Incarnate. While in this mortal form he might be subject to the limitations of the body to some extent, but his spirit was divine and indomitable. Even as his body died, his spirit drove it on relentlessly.

Krishna danced on.

Hours passed.
   Still Krishna danced on.
   The day became night.
Still Krishna danced.
Balarama and Radha sat down at last, exhausted from merely watching.
Slowly, the night went on, passing into day again.
Still, Krishna's dance continued unabated.

As the days passed and Krishna's dance went on, the villagers ventured back to the lakeside.

In time, the hillside was covered with Vrishnis watching their brightest son performing yet another miracle.

Many of these same people had watched as Krishna had taken his first steps, then broken into an impromptu dance upon the corpse of his first attacker, Putana. They had seen him grow and gain in strength and wisdom and love, and play mischief and get up to boyish pranks as well. Now they watched as he danced out every last drop of venom from his body and every last ounce of energy from the serpent that had come to slay him.

eighteen

Eight days and eight nights, Krishna danced. And with each passing day, despite the prodigious loss of blood, he seemed to grow stronger, healthier. It was miraculous to watch.

While with each passing night, the serpent grew visibly weaker, paler, sicker.

As the epic dance progressed, it was evident to all who watched that it would end only with Krishna triumphing and Kaliya dying of sheer exhaustion.

Somehow, yet again, Krishna had turned certain defeat into unmitigated triumph.

By the end of the seventh day itself, it was evident that the great serpent Kaliya was near death. Attempting to match Krishna's ferocious energy – *compelled* to match it – the asura had depleted its life force. It had nothing more to give. It barely survived now and was fast fading into oblivion.

Just as Krishna had grown stronger and healthier with each passing day, it had grown weaker, sicker. Now it was dying.

And Krishna danced on. It was no longer just a dance of death. It was a dance of life for himself – and death to Kaliya.

By the end of the eighth day, everyone knew the inevitable was coming. Kaliya would succumb at any moment. And Krishna would survive. But before that could happen, someone intervened.

nineteen

It happened on the eighth day.

Krishna was still dancing on Kaliya's hood. His wounds had healed completely, the bleeding had ceased, and he appeared whole and well again, even more vigorous than before. The blackness of his skin had always been tinged with a bluish aura, since birth; now, as he exerted himself and exuded sweat and energy, it was much more pronounced. He seemed to glow with a blue aura that pulsed and throbbed with his heartbeat. Everyone took it as yet another manifestation of his divinity and praised him as Hari in human form.

Kaliya, on the other hand, was drooping and wilting like a dying flower. The once powerful serpent asura, so energetic and seemingly capable of slaying gods, now appeared to be nearing its death. Its jet black scales had turned dull and lacklustre; grey wisps of dried skin peeling off to fall into the lake, its coat appeared to be shedding prematurely; most of its heads appeared to have died from sheer exhaustion. Even its main head hung much lower than before, almost touching the water.

It was evident that Krishna had the beast completely in his control. He could probably will it to drop dead any moment, but clearly, he was enjoying the dance as well as taking the time to heal himself. It was only a matter of hours now, Balarama suspected, before Kaliya bid adieu and Krishna stepped back onshore, triumphant.

That was when it happened.

The water around Krishna and Kaliya thrashed and seethed before erupting in sudden bursts.

People gasped and pointed. Balarama rose to his feet, as did a number of other watchers.

'Balarama Bhaiya, what is it?' Radha asked.

Balarama shook his head, silent. He didn't know. He wondered if he should move the people back home again, to avoid any person coming under danger once again. He decided to wait a moment or two before deciding.

It was logical for another asura allied to the first to attempt to attack the Vrishnis while Krishna was preoccupied fighting its compatriot. If that was the plan, it was better that the Vrishnis were there too, so that Balarama could protect them and Krishna could know at once.

The gouts of water hung in the air momentarily, then resolved themselves into a number of water serpents. They surrounded the drooping body of Kaliya in a cluster, like a ring attack formation in battle.

Balarama hefted his plough and began making his way downhill, turning only to shout briefly to his people. 'Everyone stay here!' He ran down to the lake shore.

As he ran, he saw the multitude of serpents raising their hoods, their malevolent tongues hissing. They were all much smaller than Kaliya, yet if they attacked together, they would probably be lethal. Like a pack of dogs attacking a lion.

This time, Balarama was determined that Krishna would not fight alone. Let him be angry with him later.

But before he reached the lake shore, he saw that the cluster of serpents surrounding Kaliya and Krishna were not attacking. They were praying.

Krishna looked down at the serpents surrounding him. Their hoods were half-raised yet bent, their stalks curved downwards. He recognized the stance. It was the closest a snake could come to bowing or showing obeisance. His own celestial ally Ananta Naga prostrated himself in exactly this fashion while greeting him whenever he returned home to vaikunthaloka.

But who were these serpents and why were they bowing to him? The answer came to him as the serpents called out to his mind.

Lord, we are the wives of the unfortunate one upon whose hood you stand.

Ah, the wives of Kaliya. Naturally. Even demons had families. What did they want?

Lord, you are infinite and eternal, all-powerful and all-dominating. You have proved your superiority over our lord and consort.

'I have no need to prove anything,' Krishna replied. 'He attacked me as an assassin. He sought to harm my people. He wounded me grievously. What I do, I do only in self-defence and retaliation.'

Yet he is no match for you. We see that now. He is at death's door. He will surely die if you continue your divine dance.

'As he sowed, so must he reap,' Krishna replied curtly. He had no doubt that before Kaliya set out on this assassination attempt, leaving his subterranean watery cavern, these same wives would have encouraged and praised him, praying to their deities for his success and triumph – namely, the death of Krishna and the destruction of the Vrishnis. He had no sympathy for them or their 'lord and consort'.

We beseech you, lord. Spare him. You are great and merciful. What purpose will it serve you to take his life? Look at his condition. He will never harm any living being again. At best, we could hope to nurse him back to a semblance of health and care for him the rest of his days. He is no threat to you or anyone else.

'No matter. He came to kill or be killed. He failed to take my life. Now he must die. That is how I must show my enemies that anyone who assaults me or my people will suffer the same fate.'

Still, the serpents wept and cried piteously. Their pleading continued for the rest of the day.

Kaliya's hood drooping lower and lower until it was evident that the serpent was facing his final hour, Krishna continued dancing relentlessly.

Finally, the lamentation of Kaliya's wives reached Krishna's heart. He thought of his mother's brother Kamsa and how cruelly he had dashed out the brains of the six newborn children that had preceded Balarama and Krishna into the world. That heartless taking of life was one of the things that distinguished an asura from a deva. For an asura cared nothing about creating or giving to the universe, only about taking and destroying. If he killed Kaliya, would he not be the same as any asura, as Kamsa himself?

The thought itself slowed his feet. Gradually, his dancing ceased. He came to a halt, took a moment, then sighed. After all, he was God Incarnate. Not Shiva, the Destroyer of Worlds. Or Brahma, Creator of the Universes. But Vishnu, Preserver and Protector.

His mission was to preserve, not kill.

Speaking with his mind, he urged Kaliya to lower him to the lake shore.

The great water serpent obeyed, its immense hood and torso trembling with weakness and fear as it stretched out to reach the lip of dry land around the lake.

Krishna stepped out on solid land for the first time in days.

He sent a greeting and blessing to Bhoodevi, spirit of the earth, expressing his gratitude at being back upon her soil once again. A flock of parrots flew screeching into the sky, their green plumes fluttering like coloured banners in the air, adding a festive touch. Trees showered petals. The wind blew soft and gentle fragrances.

Yes, Bhoodevi was clearly glad to see him back safe and sound.

Then he turned and regarded the nemesis that had come close to destroying him.

'Kaliya,' he said grimly. 'After the heinous manner in which you attacked my people and then myself, do you expect me to let you live? Speak!'

Krishna faced the black snake. Kaliya's hood shook, trembling as much from exhaustion and sickness as from fear. For it was truly terrified of Krishna now, he sensed. He took no satisfaction in this fact. If anything, he felt sad for it.

'NEVER BEFORE HAVE I FACED ANY MORTAL, ASURA OR DEVA SUCH AS YOU. THE LEGEND IS TRUE, THEN. YOU ARE HARI HIMSELF. SWAYAM BHAGWAN. PRAISE BE TO YOU, MIGHTY VISHNU IN KRISHNA FORM.'

'I have no desire to hear your praise. I only grant you this reprieve because your wives petitioned on your behalf and compelled me to feel pity for you. If you will not speak quickly and to the point, I will deny their petition and destroy you where you stand.'

'FORGIVE ME, LORD. CONFRONTED WITH YOUR EFFULGENCE, I COULD NOT BUT SHOW MY RESPECT FOR THIS DIVINE DARSHAN. I WILL WASTE NO MORE OF YOUR TIME.'

'Speak, then. How do you justify your assault on me?'

'I CANNOT JUSTIFY IT, LORD. I CAME TO ASSASSINATE YOU. HAD I BEEN ABLE TO DO SO, I WOULD HAVE KILLED YOU WITHOUT REMORSE OR REGRET.'

'And if my people cried out for mercy, or lamented my loss? Would that have brought you to care enough to spare me? Or to spare their innocent lives?'

Kaliya's great hood lurched sideways before balancing itself with some effort. '*NAY, MY LORD. I ADMIT I WOULD NOT HAVE CARED WHAT THEY SAID OR DID. I WOULD HAVE KILLED YOU AND ALL YOUR PEOPLE.*'

'Even the little children who could do you no harm?'

'*ESPECIALLY THE LITTLE CHILDREN. FOR THE ONE WHO SENT ME ON THIS MISSION IS HIMSELF KNOWN AS CHILDSLAYER. HE TAKES SPECIAL PLEASURE IN THE DESTRUCTION OF YOUNG LIVES.*'

Krishna clenched his fists. 'I should strike you down here and now as you stand. You are a brutal and heartless monster. You do not deserve to be spared.'

Kaliya's wives cried out shrilly, their serpentine shrieks harsh and cloying. But Kaliya's response was measured and without emotion. '*MY LORD, I KNOW NOW WHAT I DID NOT UNDERSTAND BEFORE. I HAVE TWO THOUSAND EYES, YET ONLY NOW HAVE I LEARNT TO SEE CLEARLY. I KNOW I WAS A FOOL EVEN TO TRY TO ATTACK YOU. IF YOU WISH TO SLAY ME, DO SO. IT SHALL BE MY GOOD FORTUNE TO DIE AT THE HANDS OF HARI INCARNATE.*'

Krishna raised his hands, feeling the power of his deva shakti coursing through them. Above the lake, the sky grew dark and stormy all of a sudden, and blue lightning blazed down through to centre upon Krishna's raised hands, taking the shape of a gleaming golden disk.

Krishna's eyes flared blue as well.

His voice boomed and gnashed like thunder in a closed chamber. 'It would be a pleasure to slay you, monster! I should cut every head off your body with a single flick of my weapon.'

Kaliya's wives were silenced. The great serpent himself stopped swaying and held still, sensing his imminent demise.

Suddenly, as abruptly as it had appeared, the lightning vanished, leaving only clear blue skies above. Krishna's eyes flickered with blue light but were normal mortal eyes again. And his hands were a normal boy's hands as well.

'I should slay you. But I will not,' he said. 'I will spare you instead. You are to leave the mortal realm forever and return to the watery cavern from whence you came, and spend the rest of your meagre life in the company of your wives and young ones.'

Kaliya bowed to him, hood swaying drunkenly. '*MY LORD, WHY DO YOU SPARE ME? THERE IS NO ARGUMENT THAT I AM AN EVIL CREATURE. THAT I SOUGHT TO DO YOU AND YOUR LOVED ONES IRREPARABLE HARM. IF I WERE IN YOUR POSITION, I WOULD NOT BE AS MERCIFUL AS YOU ARE BEING. WHY, THEN, DO YOU SHOW MERCY AND SPARE MY LIFE?*'

Krishna raised his hand, blessing Kaliya as well as bidding him farewell.

'Because I am not you,' he replied. 'I am Me.'

Balarama slapped Krishna on the back and hugged him hard. Krishna pretended to be panting and heaving when Balarama finally released him. 'Brother, even Kaliya did not crush me as hard!'

Balarama laughed and punched his brother's shoulder playfully. Then he hugged him again, squeezing him tight enough that Krishna could barely breathe.

Beside them, Radha smiled shyly and expressed her pleasure at Krishna's safe return. Balarama, who was on the other side of Krishna, waggled his eyebrows provocatively. Krishna elbowed him hard. Balarama pretended to gasp and stagger briefly.

'You spared your own would-be assassin,' Balarama said. 'Do you think it will make the next one merciful towards you or your loved ones?' He shook his head. 'You are too easy-going with these asuras, Bhraatr. They must be destroyed, exterminated from the earth.'

Krishna sighed. 'You are probably right, Bhaiya. Yet I do not see them as a species. I see them as individuals. Each is different.'

Radha nodded, agreeing with Krishna.

Balarama glanced at her and snorted. 'Nonsense. All demons are alike. They are evil and wish to destroy all that is good and righteous in the world.'

Krishna shook his head. 'I am not so sure. Some are merely forces of nature or tools manipulated by others. They are not evil in themselves, merely powerful means to some end.'

'And as long as that end is *our* destruction, they are evil!' Balarama retorted.

Krishna smiled. 'That is itself a fallacy. To assume that those who are against us are evil and we and the ones supporting us are good. What if it were the other way around?'

Radha's eyes widened. 'You cannot mean that, Krishna. How can you think of yourself as evil?'

Krishna sighed. 'That is not what I meant. I merely suggest that things are not always black and white and grey. Each individual is unique, like a shade of colour in a palette of infinite colours. We cannot dismiss all asuras as evil. Or assume all devas to be good. Sometimes, one force does a good deed while the other does a bad one, for reasons that seem logical at the time. But when viewed dispassionately, they can often be questionable.'

Balarama scratched his head. 'How is killing innocent people questionable? It's evil, that's all!'

Krishna sighed and slapped Balarama on his meaty back. 'Let me show you what I mean. Even as we speak, a new crisis confronts our people. We must rush to their aid.'

Radha and Balarama looked around, peering in the direction of the path that led back towards the hamlet. The last of the people had vanished from sight over the rise by this time.

'What new monstrosity seeks to attack them this time?' Balarama said. He looked around for his plough. 'Let me tackle this one, Bhraatr. I will dash its brains out on the ground with my plough.'

Krishna smiled again, wistfully. 'That is exactly what I have been trying to explain to you. It is no monster that threatens our people. It is not an evil force or a demon from the underworld. Our people are in grave danger nonetheless. Come now, we must hurry. Running will be too slow.'

He put an arm around Balarama and gestured to Radha. She shyly stepped into the circle of his other arm. He clasped her shoulders, drawing the tiniest of sighs from her. Then, with as little effort as drawing a breath, he rose up into the air.

They stood a brief moment as he tilted his head to point them in the right direction; then they were hurtling through the air, over the hilltop, down the next rise and up the next, following the undulating landscape over the few miles that separated them from the hamlet.

Before they could reach within sight of the hamlet, they came to a thick patch of woods. The path disappeared into the woods and the last of the people were visible on the path, approaching the shady overhang of the trees.

'Balarama, Radha,' Krishna said as they descended to earth, 'you must run and warn as many people as possible to turn back and come out of the woods, head for open ground. They will be safe there.'

Krishna set Balarama and Radha down on the ground as gently as possible, then shot away like a flash.

'What did he mean?' Radha asked anxiously. 'What threatens them in the woods? Another giant snake?'

Balarama hefted his plough. 'Whatever it is, we will take care of it. But first, let's do as Bhai said. Your shriek is louder than my loudest bellow, Radha, so run ahead and scream to everyone to turn back. I will guide the people towards open ground as Krishna instructed. Go on!'

Radha needed no further urging. Running up the path into the woods, she screamed as loudly as possible. The sound rang through the woods as clearly as a temple bell pealing at midnight.

Balarama winced and followed. What new demon was it this time, he wondered grimly.

twenty-three

Krishna was right. It was no demon. It was a forest fire.
Radha nodded and sprinted. From above, Krishna saw her lithe form race down the dirt road, catching up in moments with the stragglers, then going past them and running up the length of the procession.

She shouted as she went, and heads turned as people heard and reacted. Krishna was gratified to see them increase their pace at once and urge their cattle and yoked beasts on faster. Even so, he knew, they would not be able to get out of the wooded area in time. That was the whole point of the attack: to make it impossible for him to save every person. Like any general who was unable to eliminate his main enemy, Kamsa was now fighting a war of attrition. Kill as many Vrishnis as possible, harm Krishna indirectly. For he knew that even a single life lost was as painful to Krishna as losing a limb.

That was why Krishna could not let even a single life be lost.

He descended to earth, stepping on the forest floor. A pack of wolves fleeing the fire reacted in alarm to the unexpected sight of a human descending from the sky and ran even faster, dark fur blurring past.

He turned off the path and headed towards the forest. Dry leaves and twigs cracked and crunched underfoot. Several small creatures passed him, running swiftly, not the way the Vrishnis were heading but the other way, down to the pastureland and lake and brooks. There was water there and even the smallest living creature understood instinctively that water provided a natural break for a forest fire. He saw a wildcat and a deer running alongside each other, temporary companions during the hour of crisis.

He heard heavy footfalls approaching from behind, making far more noise than he did. That would be Balarama, following. He still had that ridiculous plough in his hand, carrying it like a mace warrior bearing his mace. Krishna shook his head at the thought. Balarama would always be Balarama!

By the time he reached the clearing he sought, the fire had grown rapidly. It already covered a substantial part of the woods and as he had expected, had leapt across the road to begin consuming the far side as well. The noise and smoke were increasing with every minute, and he felt the scorching heat singe his face and eyes even from where he was.

Balarama came up beside him, hefting the plough.

Krishna glanced sideways at it. 'What do you intend to do with that? Use it to put out the fire?'

Balarama looked down at the plough as if just remembering that he was still carrying it. 'Why not? I could use it to dig up the ground and bury the fire!'

Krishna snorted. 'Yes! That would work!'

Balarama squinted at him. 'You have a better idea?'

Krishna nodded. 'Watch.'

Krishna turned to the fire, leaned forward and, opening his mouth, began to inhale. He sucked in air slowly at first, then harder, increasing his intensity until he could feel the searing heat of the air from the fire enter his lungs. It burned. He ignored the pain and continued, exerting superhuman force.

Balarama exclaimed. 'It's working, Bhai! You're sucking the fire in! I can see it moving this way.'

Krishna continued, inhaling with enough force for flames engulfing entire trees to bend and swoop and fly towards him and enter his lungs. The pain was agonizing but he didn't stop. He could hear the screams of the Vrishnis as they raced to exit the woods before the fire consumed them and knew that he had only moments in which to work. He pulled in his breath with all the strength in his being, sucking the very air from the forest.

Several moments later, Balarama clapped him on his back. 'You did it, Bhai! You inhaled the forest fire. Everyone is safe and sound.'

Krishna coughed out a great puff of black smoke. Soot and ash settled in front of him.

Radha came running up, coughing and waving away the last vestiges of smoke. 'Krishna, are you all right?'

'What would happen to him?' Balarama said. 'I'm here, aren't I?'

Radha ignored Balarama's quip and looked at Krishna.

He coughed up another mouthful of black smoke.

'I'm all right, Radha,' he said. 'Is everyone safe?'

She nodded briskly, beaming. 'Every last man, woman, child, cow and calf.'

Krishna smiled. 'Time to go home, then.'

She slipped her hand into his and they headed home. Krishna heard Balarama mutter something behind them and then follow, his plough ready for whatever new threat that might present itself next.

twenty-four

Gargamuni beamed with pleasure as he sampled the first mouthful of food. 'Sadhu! Sadhu!' he exclaimed.

Nanda Maharaja smiled, then moved on to serve the next person seated cross-legged beside the preceptor. A line of servers followed him, each serving a different dish, piping hot and freshly prepared for the feast. The line stretched all the way to the end of the clearing and around to the other side. The feast day of Lord Indra was being held at the foot of Mount Govardhan, long considered a holy mountain and one sacred to Indra Dev. Brahmins, Chandalas, Kshatriyas, Vaishyas, all varnas sat together and ate in brotherhood, shoulder to shoulder, consuming the same food and engaging in pleasant conversation.

While it was true that varna was often used as an excuse for discrimination in some places, it was not in itself the basis for prejudice. People who were biased could find any reason to regard others as 'inferior': class, wealth, position, nationality, ethnicity, religion. But to the Vrishnis under Nanda Maharaja, varna was merely a convenient division of labour, made by choice and passed on by birth only if desired. But to acknowledge the existence of caste-based discrimination and combat it, Krishna had suggested that the Indra feast that year be dedicated to community sharing.

So everybody was eating together, not merely different castes, but different classes too – landowners and workers, farmers and herders, rich and poor. And, in the ultimate levelling of differences, even the cows and dogs were being fed at the same time!

That was true proof of non-discrimination, Krishna said. 'If we are agreed that all living beings are equal and entitled to equal rights, then why stop at varna, caste or class? Let us acknowledge the equality of even the four-footed, the furred, the winged and the voiceless. Let us acknowledge all life as precious.'

Radha took one look at the long line of dogs sitting and waiting for their meals, none barking or complaining about the other's portion, and Krishna knew she was sorely tempted to make a comment about the patience and discipline of their four-footed friends versus the two-footed ones. But credit to her, she kept the thought to herself.

After the meal, Gargamuni sought out Krishna and bent to touch his feet. Krishna stopped him at once. 'Swami, what are you doing? You are our preceptor and elder. It is I who must show respect to you.'

The acharya of Vrajbhoomi smiled in admiration, joining his hands together in supplication. 'Truly we are blessed to have your presence among us, lord. There has never been an avatar or amsa who displayed such power and humility both at once.'

Krishna affectionately clasped the guru's hands in his own. 'Be it power, wealth, strength or anything else, the more one possesses, the more humble one should be. For these are but gifts, not a birthright. One must be thankful for what one has been given, and enjoy it while it lasts. For nothing truly lasts.'

'Wisely spoken,' the aging Brahmin replied. 'Words to live by. And what you are doing today is a great example as well.

Encouraging unity and harmony among castes,' the acharya chuckled at the dogs who were hungrily wolfing down their food,'even among species.'

'We are all of the earth, all beneficiaries of the same resources. Only by living in harmony can we survive. It is sad that some who dwell on earth choose to ignore these basic truths.'

Gargamuni and Krishna walked awhile, speaking of many things, philosophical as well as material. They passed a pair of Brahmins who appeared agitated, lost in debate. They saw their preceptor and Krishna approaching and fell silent at once, rushing away.

Krishna noticed that the guru appeared perturbed.'What is it, swami? Is there some disagreement among your Brahmins?'

'It is impossible to conceal anything from your sight, Krishna. Some of my followers and colleagues fear that foregoing the usual sacrifice to Indra this year may result in the great lord of thunder and war taking offence.'

'But we are still performing the ritual ceremony,' Krishna pointed out.'All the oblations are being made and due procedure being followed.'

'That is so,' Gargamuni replied, his thin face drawn in long sad lines.'Yet, instead of feeding only Brahmins devoted to Indra, we are feeding Brahmins of all faiths. Indeed, we are feeding not only Brahmins but all varnas. And some have remarked that the feeding of cows and dogs may be construed as a deliberate affront to the great king of the devas.'

'It is not intended as such,' Krishna said. 'Merely a demonstration of communality and brotherhood of all living things. Surely, being a great and powerful god, Indra will understand and appreciate what we are attempting here.'

Gargamuni looked at him silently. 'Krishna, my child, my god. If only all gods could possess your wisdom and vision.'

A sound interrupted them.

Their eyes went to the skies at once.

It was the sound of thunder. A storm was brewing at the peak of Mount Govardhan.

One of the Brahmins who had been agitated spoke up: 'Perhaps Lord Indra does not share your sentiment, Gargacharya.'

The rain pelted down relentlessly. The wind was increasing in fury with every passing moment. Everyone was gathered together in the relative shelter of the thicket beside the clearing where the ashram of Indra's Brahmins was located. But Krishna could see that this meagre shelter would not serve as protection for much longer. Already, the boughs of the trees were shivering violently in the gusts of wind and the rain seemed to be seeking them out under the eaves, splashing cold icy water in their faces with deliberate malice.

The storm had come out of nowhere, bursting from a clear sky. Thunder, lightning and torrential rain, all out of season.

Everyone was silent. The Brahmins whom Krishna had seen arguing earlier looked vindicated, gazing proudly at the Chandalas and other lower castes huddled in common misery alongside the Vrishnis. Krishna felt sure that they blamed this storm on the feeding of low castes on Indra's feast day. He resented such attitudes and biases. It made him angry.

But he controlled his anger. The bigoted Brahmins were not the cause of this crisis. *He* was. It was he who had chosen to feed all castes, communities and species in a show of communality. The only mistake he had made was to do so on Indra's feast day. Clearly the god of wind, rain, thunder and war resented this appropriation of his day for such a purpose. And to have done so under the auspices of Indra's ashram in the shadow of his sacred mountain ... It was quite obvious that that the king of the gods had taken offence.

Krishna had always found Indra to be mean and spiteful, given to petty acts of vengeance and retaliation, not to mention his notorious philandering and penchant for launching military offensives at the slightest provocation. Had he not been upon the mortal realm right now, engaged in a mission of vital importance, he would have shed this incarnation and gone to Indraloka in his true form, as Vishnu, and given Indra a piece of his mind. Even the king of gods did not dare pick a fight with the Preserver himself, one of the holy Trimurti.

But that was not possible under current circumstances. He was Krishna. He had to stay and fulfil the purpose of this birth. And he had to do everything as Krishna, the child-god. And right now, that meant acting to save these people and creatures from Indra's wrath.

The storm was only increasing in fury. Bushes and smaller trees were being uprooted and carried away, as if by a hurricane. The sheer rage was evident in every aspect. This was no mere storm. It was an act of war.

Yet Krishna could not retaliate. How could one fight a storm? Wind? Rain? Lightning? No. He must put aside all thought of vengeance or retaliation and focus solely on protecting these innocents. He had a brief moment of pique when he thought perhaps he should leave those Brahmins to suffer the storm since they seemed to take great satisfaction in Indra's fury, but of course, he could not knowingly harm them or allow harm to come to them. Their only crime was ignorance and lack of true wisdom.

'Krishna!'

Balarama fought his way against the wind, reacting as lightning struck the ground only yards from where he bent over, struggling to make his way to the spot where Krishna stood, buffeted by the elements.

'We have to do something.'

Krishna nodded. 'Gather everyone and tell them to stay there. As close as possible.'

Balarama nodded and left.

Krishna stepped forward, looking for a foothold. He stamped his foot on the ground, searching. Yes, this seemed a good spot where the ground was packed. No layers of stone for several yards down. He looked around. The neighbouring area appeared much the same, none of the red veins or streaks that indicated igneous formations or rocks underground.

The storm was growing frenzied. He felt lightning strike him directly several times. It shook him, stopping his heart momentarily each time, and after the third or fourth time, he thought he heard Radha cry out in concern, but perhaps he was just imagining it. The noise was too deafening to hear her cry, although he had no doubt she must be beside herself with anxiety for his well-being.

He stamped his foot, settling for a relatively smooth flat patch of ground.

This will have to do.

He offered a brief prayer to Bhoodevi, asking her to lend him her support. 'These are your children I seek to preserve, Mother,' he said. The wind tore the words from his lips before they could reach his own ears. But he knew that Mother Earth did not need words spoken aloud in order to hear them. She would do what she could by way of offering him support. The rest was up to him.

He bent down and pushed his fingers into the earth, digging them deep inside, as deep as possible. Then, taking hold of the rocky base of Mount Govardhan, he pulled with a mighty effort, splitting the mountain from the ground on which it lay. To his surprise, it broke away with far less effort than required. He knew then that Bhoodevi had indeed heard his prayer, and was assisting and aiding him in his attempt.

With renewed hope and vigour, Krishna bent down again and picked up the mountain.

twenty-six

Radha gasped as she saw Krishna pick up Mount Govardhan. Everyone reacted. It was a sight to behold: a boy picking up a mountain. For a long moment, nobody knew what to say or do. Even the priests loyal to Indra, gloating with pride at their deity's vengeance, were stupefied.

As Krishna raised the entire mountain on his palms, Balarama shouted to the people and animals huddled in the ashram clearing. 'Come closer together! Everyone.'

They did as he asked, clustered together. The vain priests found themselves being pushed towards the group of Chandalas and reacted at once. 'We will not pollute ourselves by standing near them,' shouted one Brahmin. Balarama ignored them and concentrated his efforts on the rest. If the foolish Brahmins wished to endanger their lives by facing their own god's fury, it was their choice. He had to ensure that the rest were brought within the umbrella of safety quickly, before the storm began taking its toll.

Soon, he had every man, woman, child, cow and dog gathered in a rough circle that extended over a considerable area. He understood now why Krishna had given that instruction. The sheer number of people and animals made them a substantial mass. Even Mount Govardhan was not infinite in size. The mountain would just about provide this large gathering with sufficient overhead shelter. If they were spread out farther apart, they would be subjected to Indra's rage.

He heard shouts of wonderment and joy. Turning, he saw Krishna walking slowly towards them. His brother carried the entire mountain upon the palm of one hand.

'Look at the ground,' Radha shouted above the roar of the wind.

Balarama looked. With such an epic weight upon his hand, Krishna ought to have sunk deep into the ground. But he appeared to be walking normally, leaving only the usual footprints that any young boy would leave on such a surface. Others noticed this phenomenon and pointed it out to each other as well, marvelling at this new evidence of Krishna's divinity.

'It is Bhoodevi's blessing,' Balarama said to himself. 'She is supporting Krishna and aiding her children.'

As they watched, Krishna carried the mountain to where the villagers were grouped. When he reached the place he had chosen, he stopped.

Everyone gathered around him, except for the Indra Brahmins who were adamant in their refusal to be sheltered in the same space as low castes. Balarama saw Gargamuni attempting to appeal to their common sense and humanity but they would not be deterred. He watched as they – their bodies shuddering as they were pounded by the powerful screaming winds and tearing rain – stepped away from the shelter of the mountain held up by Krishna.

Balarama turned his attention to Krishna. As he watched, Krishna lifted the mountain upon a single finger, the smallest finger of his left hand.

He held it up with little effort, with only a faint semblance of a smile twitching his left cheek. He held it that way, taking up a position. Then, with his free hand, he fished out his flute from his waistband and placed it on his lips. A gentle melody began to waft forth from his flute, audible despite the torrent of the storm.

Here, within the shelter of Mount Govardhan, Krishna tended his flock.

twenty-seven

There was little rest for the Vrishnis and their deliverer that year. The assaults by Kamsa's assassins continued unabated.

A rakshasa named Pralamba – bearing no relation to Kamsa's chief advisor of the same name – attempted boldly to attack Krishna in broad daylight and was despatched easily.

Another snake beast named Vyoma attempted to swallow Nanda whole while on a trip to a nearby shrine. Nanda called to his son for help. Krishna arrived at once and tore the beast to pieces.

Balarama finally had his chance to play hero when an asura named Baka attacked him from behind while returning home and attempted to pick him up bodily to throw him. Not expecting Balarama to weigh as much as he did, the asura was nonplussed when Krishna's brother increased his weight to the point where the asura was suffocating under the unbearable burden. Descending to the ground, Balarama then roundly thrashed the villain and despatched him to the afterlife.

There was another attempt by fire, apparently a perennial favourite when large populations were to be decimated, and once again Krishna tackled the threat in exactly the same manner, by swallowing the fire whole and absorbing it into himself. If a method worked, there was no reason not to use it again, after all.

Eventually, the assassins and attacks slowed, then ceased altogether. A brief period of respite followed, expanding eventually into a whole season of rest, then a year, then several years.

Time passed.

The Vrishnis began to believe that perhaps, just perhaps, the gravest part of the danger had passed. Maybe the Usurper had finally decided to leave them in peace.

Krishna knew better, but said nothing. He made the most of the intervals between the bouts of violence by spreading merriment and hope with his heart-melting smile and languorous flute-songs.

He also knew what none of them did, that the worst still lay ahead. That the real battle was yet to begin. All this, after all, was merely a foretaste of the real war that lay ahead. The mother of all wars, a conflict so terrible, so awesome, that it would pit every living, able-bodied, civilized soldier against his fellow soldier, brother against brother, kin against kin, and would end only when the population of the civilized world was all but wiped out.

He could say none of this to his people. Besides, it would serve no purpose. This was not a storm that they could prepare for by taking shelter or securing hatches and fences and mending roofs. This was the end of the Yuga. And the cusp of the bloodiest, most violent age of all in human history.

The Age of Kali.

It would come no matter what they, or he, or anyone else did, or did not do.

So he played his flute and danced the ras-garbha with his fellow gopas and gopis and ate mangoes and swam in the lakes and ran through the fields, growing taller, broader, handsomer, as the weeks of peaceful respite turned to months, and the months into years, and the boy became a man, and the God became a mortal for just a short while.

Between battles.

Before the war.

Just for a breath's breadth, a pause between past and future.

And he played his lila.

twenty-eight

Radha laughed and splashed water on her fellow gopis. They whooped and laughed and threw water on each other until the riverside resembled a waterfall with water and spray flying every which way. The gopis were in a boisterous mood this season; it had been a long time in Vrindavan, in veritable exile. Idyllic as life was here, the awareness that they were perpetually under threat — a community hunted and condemned by the Usurper and his demoniac soldiers — had bred a stubborn anger within each one. They lived and worked and ate and slept happily enough, but beneath that veneer of normalcy there had begun to fester a sense of resentment and frustration, a desire to throw off the yoke of oppression and live free. To go back to Vrajbhoomi and walk the green grassy slopes of their homeland once again, to live free in Gokul, to travel, to meet their relatives and friends, to marry and love and procreate and proliferate. All the water and food and supplies in the world could not make up for the lack of freedom. They remained a people under siege.

All this translated into a lot of pent-up energy which came out in the roughhouse play of Balarama and the other gopas during the sports and other play. With the gopis, expected to be demure and well-behaved, it exploded on occasions such as this when they were on their own, away from prying eyes, playing in this secluded glen, bathing in the river.

They gambolled in the water until every last one of them was soaked through and through.

Finally, Radha said, 'We may as well spread our vastras to dry and bathe properly.'

The others chorused their approvals. Discarding their garments, the gopis laid them out on rocks and low-hanging branches to dry in the late morning sun, while they went back to frolic in the water. Even though it was late autumn, almost early winter, the day was unseasonably warm, and the river relatively cool, especially in the shade of the riverside trees.

They had come to the Kalindi River early that morning to offer ritual oblations to Devi Katyayani at the onset of the hemanta season. They had already bathed once in the water at sunrise, then made an image of the goddess with sand. The effigy still stood on the riverbank, lovingly shaped and carved, adorned with garlands, offerings of agarbattis, mud diyas, fresh fruits and newly grown shoots, rice and numerous other offerings, some glinting gold, others of lesser monetary value, but all equal in devotional worth.

It was only after they had offered their prayers to the goddess and eaten the ritual food prepared for the occasion that their talk had turned to more playful matters, leading to a little mild splashing of water, which quickly escalated into the all-out battle that drenched one and all.

The gopis played for a while, as happy as gandharvas and apsaras, and when they were tired, they lay in the water and talked about all manner of things.

A favourite topic of discussion was Krishna, of course. At some point, every single gopi mentioned him, always with a wistful look in her eye and a soft sigh.

'Katyayani Devi,' an attractive gopi with a well-endowed form said aloud, clasping her palms together and addressing the effigy of the goddess on the river shore. 'Great Maya, maha-yogini, mistress of the universe, I pray to thee: make the son of Nanda and Yashoda mine in marriage.'

Giggling at first, the other gopis remarked that on such an auspicious day, it was said that the devi actually granted the wishes of young unmarried girls such as they, provided the wishes were made with sincerity and devotion.

After mulling over this for barely a moment, the other gopis turned their attention to the goddess and began offering their own prayers.

It took Radha only a moment to realize that their prayers were all the same: each one of them was asking the goddess to grant them a husband. And the husband desired by every gopi was the same: *her* Krishna!

Radha began to grow jealous. It was one thing for the gopis to joke about Krishna, flirt with him, and even make coy advances on occasion. But this was serious. To pray to the goddess on her sacred day, that too in this manner, standing unclad in the devi's Kalindi River, and ask for Krishna as their husband ... it was too much!

What if the devi heard their prayers? What if she granted them? Naturally, she could not make Krishna husband to them all. But what if she granted the wish of any one girl here? What if slender, doe-eyed Chitralekha's wish was granted? Or if homely-looking but nicely plump Sudhasattwa were to have her prayer answered? Or buxom Balini?

No. This was intolerable. She could not bear the thought of her Krishna marrying another woman.

Fuming, she made her way to the edge of the water and reached for her clothes which she had left on a rock within reach so that she would not have to climb out without her clothes. Unlike some of these other girls, she was not bold about baring her body, even though this was a secluded glen where the gopis of Vrindavan were known to bathe and were therefore permitted their privacy.

She felt the cool smooth surface of the rock and patted it, stretching out as far as her arm could reach. She could not feel her garments and frowned and peered up the length of her arm. Her clothes were gone! She issued a sound of exasperation.

Must be those mischievous monkeys.

She looked around the trees, trying to spot the telltale red eyes twinkling in the shadows, or the flashing white teeth. It took her a moment to realize there were none in sight.

No monkeys.

And no clothes.

All their garments had vanished. Not just her own, but every single vastra belonging to every gopi, left hanging from tree branches or laid out on stones to dry, had disappeared!

Radha shrieked.

twenty-nine

At the sound of Radha's scream, the gopis left off their prayers and came to see what the matter was.

'Asuras!' Radha cried.

At the mention of the dreaded word, the other gopis began screaming as well. Pandemonium ensued. Once again, there was much thrashing about and panic as the girls looked about and splashed in the water, trying to decide where the demons might be and what to do next. It took several minutes before everyone realized that no danger was visible and that the only harm that had befallen them was the pilfering of their garments.

'Is that all?' said one of them scornfully. 'Radha, you would leap off a cliff to avoid a mosquito! I thought it was a real demon attacking. Like Aghasura. Or Kaliya!'

'The monkeys must have taken our clothes,' another gopi joined in. 'They took Saraswati's garments once when she was bathing, remember? Come on, everyone look in the trees, the rascals must be hiding there.'

Everyone began to look about for monkeys in the trees.

It was Radha herself who spotted the familiar face peering down from a fork in a kadamba tree. She gasped at first, unable to believe her eyes. Slowly, a smile played across her pretty features and soon became a blush.

'I found the rascal,' she said aloud.

The other gopis clustered around her. 'Where are the monkeys?' they asked.

'There,' she said, pointing.

Everyone looked where she pointed and saw the familiar face laughing from the kadamba tree.

'Krishna!' they exclaimed. 'It's Krishna!'

At once, the sound of catcalls and cries broke out from across the grove. Other gopas appeared, leaving their hiding places to come forward. They stood with their hands on their hips, grinning boldly.

The gopis blushed and screamed in embarrassment, covering themselves with their hands. 'You took our clothes!' they cried out. 'Give them back!'

Balarama shrugged. 'We had nothing to do with it. Krishna took them.'

Everyone turned to look at Krishna who grinned, dangling Radha's bright yellow upper garment. Radha blushed even deeper.

'They're telling the truth, dear gopis,' Krishna cried out. 'I have your garments. Don't you want them back?'

'Yes!' the gopis cried. 'Please return them.'

'Of course,' Krishna said with mock seriousness. 'They're of no use to me. You may have them all back at once.'

The gopis sighed in relief, staying low in the water to avoid being seen by the boys.

'But you must come and take them from me, one by one,' Krishna said.

The girls looked at each other, round-eyed. Radha lowered her eyes, blushing redder than a gulmohar flower in full bloom.

'Well, that is the only way you will get your clothes back,' Krishna said. 'By coming to me one by one and taking them from my hand.'

The gopis were struck dumb. None knew what to say.

It was Radha who spoke.

'Don't misbehave, Krishna,' she said, her cheeks still flaming red. 'Give us back our clothes. Otherwise we will tell Nanda Maharaja.'

Krishna raised his eyebrows. 'Tell him *what*, exactly? That you girls came to offer oblations to the goddess but decided to take off your clothes and prance around like gandharvas and apsaras in the water?'

Radha stared at Krishna, then turned to look at the other gopis. Krishna was right. It was they who had been caught red-handed, in a manner of speaking. As young girls, it was not exactly becoming for them to have frolicked unclothed in the river in this way.

'We are sorry for our mischief,' she said, 'but—'

'But *I* am not sorry for *my* behaviour!' Krishna cried out. 'In fact, I am only trying to teach you girls a lesson! The devi would be very displeased if she saw that you spent more time and energy in enjoying yourselves than in performing the rites to honour her. Balarama, the other gopas and I came to see if all was well with you. It was Nanda Maharaja himself who sent us, concerned about your welfare.'

The girls looked around uneasily. What Krishna said was quite true: this was the devi's sacred day. They had wasted a lot of time and energy in frolicking after the rituals and had lost all track of time.

'And after all,' Krishna went on in a gently chiding tone, 'were you not praying to the goddess to bring me to you?'

'They were,' said one of the gopas. 'Each one was praying to the devi to make you her husband!'

Now all the gopis blushed, embarrassed at being found out. But none denied the charge, for it was true.

Radha was silent. She did not know what to say.

'I will return your clothes,' Krishna said. 'All you have to do is walk up here, one by one, and claim them from me. That way, we may find out which one's prayers to the goddess will be answered.' He paused and looked at each one of the girls in turn, immersed up to their necks in water. 'You do want to know which one of you will have her wish come true, do you not?'

The gopis stared at him, transfixed. At once, their attitude changed. They began moving towards the shore, eager to come to Krishna and learn whether what he said was true. Indeed, none of them doubted that he spoke the truth, for Krishna never lied. Rather, they were eager to know the answer to the riddle he spoke of: who among them would be the lucky girl chosen by the devi to be Krishna's paramour.

But at the edge of the shore, they hesitated. For while all desired Krishna enough to be willing to walk unclad all the way to where he sat on the kadamba tree, they had no wish to be seen by the other gopas in this state of undress.

'Krishna,' they cried out plaintively, 'ask the other boys to go away. We cannot step out in front of them.'

'Why not?' Krishna asked. 'They have been watching you for a while.'

The gopis blushed. 'Watching us?'

'Yes,' Krishna said. 'We came here together, looking for you. We saw you frolicking in the water, then praying to the goddess for a suitable husband. At that time, you were too absorbed to even notice us. So I told the boys I would teach you a lesson in modesty by stealing your clothes. After all, if you were willing to bathe without your clothes for the whole world to see, then what need did you have of them anyway!'

'We are sorry for being so shameless,' the girls replied. 'We admit it was wrong of us. But we cannot step out when the other boys are looking!'

'Yes, you can,' Krishna said. 'If you wish to have your clothes back, it is the only way.' His eyes twinkled with mischief.

The gopis had no choice. The day had suddenly turned cool and after all this time in the water, they were beginning to feel a chill. The sky had become overcast in the past hour and as they were talking, a gentle wind had begun to blow from the north, making them shiver. They would catch a cold if they did not exit the water and wear their clothes soon.

Left with no alternative, the gopis did as Krishna bade.

One by one, they got out of the water, covering themselves with both hands as best as they could, and walked up to the foot of the kadamba tree where Krishna sat on the fork, his feet dangling.

Krishna handed each girl her garments. To take the garments, the girls had to raise their hands. As each girl took her clothes from Krishna, she bent forward and pressed her forehead against his dangling feet, sending up a prayer to the goddess again to grant her wish and make Krishna her mate for life.

Then she took the bundle of clothes and ran blushing into the woods to get herself dressed.

Radha was the last to emerge from the water. She took her clothes from Krishna without comment. But instead of touching his feet as the others had done, she looked up at him and said, 'Even the devi cannot answer the prayers of every gopi in Vrindavan. Only one of us can get the husband she desires. Who shall it be?'

Krishna looked down at Radha's beautiful face, even lovelier than usual after bathing in the river, her hair damp and open and spread out upon her bare shoulders, her complexion invigorated by the cool water and bracing wind.

'The devi is Arya, purity personified, and therefore goddess of chaste young girls. She grants every unmarried girl's wish. Each gopi desired to be able to make me her husband. Today, by touching my feet while in that state of undress, each of you has enjoyed touching me in a wifely manner. Your wishes have indeed been granted by Devi Katyayani. And as such, each one of you shall enjoy the lingering pleasure of my touch to the end of your days upon this earth. For if that is not the joy of being married to the person one loves, what is it?'

Radha had no answer. She stared up at her beloved. Then, doing as her fellow gopis had done, she bent her head and touched her forehead to Krishna's feet, clasping Achyuta's feet with her hands as well.

In addition, she kissed those feet of Damodara with affection, before clasping her garments to herself and walking away with dignity and pride.

thirty

Kamsa returned to Mathura in a red rage.

He descended from Haddi-Hathi in a single leap. Ignoring the nubile young women waiting with the ritual ceremonial greeting thalis and flower garlands, he stormed up the palace steps and strode to his throne room. The sabha was in session.

'Get out!' he roared.

The ministers and representatives left as quickly as their feet would carry them.

'Shut the doors and don't let anyone in,' he ordered his serving maids. 'And fetch me soma. Quickly!'

He was still drinking soma several hours later when a very nervous aide prostrated himself before the throne of Mathura. Kamsa threw the half-consumed goblet at the man's head, opening a cut on his temple that spilled blood on the marble floor. 'Fool! I said I was not to be disturbed.'

'Sire, it is your father-in-law,' the man blurted, certain his life would be ended any moment. He ignored the blood streaming from the cut on his forehead. 'He is coming to see you.'

Before Kamsa could throw something more lethal at the man, the great doors reopened and Jarasandha strode in, accompanied by his entourage of Hijra bodyguards and closest champions.

'Son,' Jarasandha said shortly, dispensing with the usual formalities. 'You took your time returning to Mathura. I arrived days before you did.'

'I took a detour,' Kamsa replied. 'I had some business to take care of.'

Jarasandha looked at him closely. It was evident the Magadhan expected to be told what that business was, but when Kamsa offered no further explanation, he shrugged and gestured towards the fallen goblet and splashed soma stain on the marble floor. 'I see you are not in the best of moods.'

Kamsa looked at him from beneath heavy lids, then slumped back in his throne, chin resting on his chest. 'You know why.'

Jarasandha nodded, climbing the rest of the way up the royal dais. He took the seat next to Kamsa, intended for a preceptor. 'The so-called Deliverer has survived all our attempts on his life; all our assassins have failed.'

'Yes,' Kamsa snarled. 'Even our appeal to Lord Indra was a failure.'

'In point of fact, our appeal was a success. Lord Indra believed the message we sent him, cleverly passed on through Narada-muni, that Krishna was attempting to convert Indra's Brahmins into Vaishnavites and raising a community of low castes in order to drive out the Indra worshippers. Indra reacted just as we hoped. He attacked Vrindavan with great storm and fury. But the Deliverer protected his people yet again.'

'And then he killed Baka, your great champion. And Shankhachuda whom we sent to kill Nanda Maharaja. And Vyoma. Our last three asura assassins. All your plans have failed, Jarasandha.'

Jarasandha glanced sharply at Kamsa. It was the first time his son-in-law had called him by his name, openly, to his face. It was obvious he wasn't pleased by the familiarity of usage. 'Then perhaps you should take matters into your own hands.'

In his inebriation, Kamsa's face took on an overly quizzical look. 'How?'

'Kill the Deliverer yourself.'

Kamsa stared at him. 'I thought you said I ought *not* to do that.'

'At that time, I thought one of these several methods would work: attempting to kill the children of Krishna's adoptive clan, or his adoptive father and mother, or to destroy the whole clan by fire or natural calamity. But nothing has worked, has it? So I think it is time you stepped up and did your own fighting.'

Jarasandha stood up and placed a hand on Kamsa's shoulder. 'The time has come for you to face the "Slayer of Kamsa" and prove the prophecy wrong.'

After Jarasandha had left, Kamsa sat for hours, pondering his father-in-law's words. He waved away courtiers, ministers, even Pralamba who had urgent matters to discuss with him, spurned more wine and drink, and even rejected the advances of his favourite women.

Hours passed, then days. He paced the corridors and halls of his palace.

Finally, he went down to the basement of the palace, down the winding stone stairways and walls dripping so freely with moisture that they had turned lichenous green, sprouting weeds in places. The doors here were made of iron and most had rusted solid over the years, opening only reluctantly, with a great deal of creaking and screeching. The guards were old and mostly lying drunk in stupor for they had no real work to do but merely stay on watch for the prescribed number of hours, day after day. It was so mind-numbing, they turned to drink or gambling to while away the hours. Kamsa ignored them. Many were former aides or guards who had been penalized for errors by being sent to these postings. There was little point in punishing them further. Besides, no prisoner had ever escaped these dungeons. In most cases, the prisoners had never even been seen by the guards. So long as the food was eaten and the slop trays filled each day, they assumed the wretched souls were still alive. Other than that, nobody knew or cared.

In the lowermost level of the deepest, darkest dungeon in the kingdom, he made his way to the farthest end of a long deserted corridor. Stone walls bounded each side and the ceiling sagged noticeably from the weight of the groundwater and rock pressing down. He had to duck his head in places to pass. Here, the doors were rusted shut. He tore them apart like paper with his strength, but normal human guards would not have been able to pass through. Indeed, none had: these deep dungeons were serviced by conduits on the upper levels. Food was placed in cloth bundles and thrown down from time to time. That was all the care these prisoners received. Whether they lived or died, nobody knew. In the ancient texts, it was said there were seven levels of naraka or the hellish realms. If there was an eighth, this dungeon would surely be it.

There were only two prisoners in this lowermost level of hell. As Kamsa reached the stone wall that marked the end of the passage, he stopped and looked up, holding the torch he had taken from a sconce on a higher level during his descent. The tip-tap of water dripping irregularly on stone was the only sound in this place. The crackling of the mashaal counterpointed it now.

High up on the wall were a few niches, cut into the stone. They were just sufficient to allow a little air to pass into the walled compartment beyond. These niches and the conduits down which food bundles were thrown were the only access to the cell. He found that the torch sucked up whatever little air existed in the corridor, leaving almost nothing to breathe. Already, his head felt faint from the lack of aerial sustenance. To survive in that enclosed cell, the prisoners must have to breathe only marginally, the way tapasvi sadhus breathed in high Himalayan grottos, drawing in just enough for survival. There was no more than that to be had.

He decided to put out the mashaal. He dropped it on the floor which had squelched underfoot as he approached. The torch fizzled out instantly, leaving him in pitch darkness.

After a moment, he raised his palms, touching them to the cold wall of the cell. He said nothing, did nothing else, just stood there. Finally, he turned and left the way he had come. The sound of his footsteps ascending the stairway echoed down in the deepest dungeon.

They could be heard inside the walled-in cell.

thirty-two

Akrur felt a peculiar mixture of sadness and anger as he approached the palace complex of Mathura. The towering stone towers of the old palace had long since been subsumed by the gleaming new facades of the new one raised by the Usurper. He felt worse as he rode his horse up the winding stone pathway – designed to make it harder for invaders to approach and easier to defend – that led uphill.

Once, he would have counted himself as being among the defenders, should Mathura ever happen to be attacked. Now, if such an event were to occur, he would almost certainly be on the opposite side of the great gates, leading a rebellious force of militia uphill to reclaim their stolen heritage and restore the Yadava nation to its former glory.

It had not been too long ago that he had come up this same winding path, accompanying his dear friend Vasudeva and so many other kith and kin. What hope had filled his heart that morning, what expectations he had carried aloft along with the cheerful krita-dhvaja banner of the Vrishnis that he had held up as he rode! The watching crowds that had thronged the walled streets had shared that hope and expectation, filling the crisp morning air with their shouts and roars of encouragement and support. And within those great ancient stone walls, as Vasudeva and his counterpart King Ugrasena had crossed rajtarus, how deafening had the cheers been! Loud enough to carry across all Bharatavarsha, this great land of Jambudwipa, subcontinent of the Jamun tree, where the Bharata tribe had coexisted in relative harmony since the seminal battle fought by Tritsu Bharata King Sudas on the banks of the Parusni, the battle that won the Bharata nation the right to continue to inhabit and proliferate across this great realm.

Surely their ancestors had heard those cheers and smiled at their optimism, just as they must have shaken their heads and sighed as the historic peace treaty had been shattered within hours by King Ugrasena's own son, the then Prince Kamsa.

Now that prince was king, usurper to his father's throne. Vasudeva and his wife Devaki were in veritable exile, preferring to call it a pilgrimage to reduce the political implications of their years-long absence. The Yadava nation was embroiled in the nastiest tribal politics and infighting since its inception by the great ancestor Yadu.

A semblance of peace hung over the nation like a reeking cloud of smoke over a cremation ghat, but beneath that obscurantist facade were the ugly faces of opportunists taking venal advantage of the atmosphere of exploitation and oppression. Those with capital in their fists and greed in their hearts thrived and grew richer and greedier. Those with only honest labour and the skills of craft, art or knowledge suffered and were misused by the holders of capital. It was the lowest a society could descend to morally and still appear to be prosperous and vital, and it was all the result of Kamsa's kingship, supported, encouraged and artfully designed by Jarasandha.

Akrur stood against all that Kamsa stood for: a far cry from that day of the peace treaty when he had stood beside the son of Ugrasena and prayed for peace. Today, he led the most widespread resistance movement against Kamsa's continuing oppression of the people, controlled a militia the size of a small army, and managed a network of refugees and migrants that moved across the Arya nations like a concourse of rivers and tributaries.

He represented the illegal, unofficial opposition faced by Kamsa and was responsible for more actions against the state and its governing head than any of the hundreds of criminals rotting in the city's deepest dungeons.

And yet, here he was, riding alone and unarmed up the last leg of the pathway that led to Kamsa's palace. In a moment, he would reach the great gates and pass through as he had that long-lost day of the peace treaty. Some time later, he would be taken to Kamsa and presented. And after that, it would be seen whether he was condemned and executed, tortured or torn apart.

His people had begged him not to go. They had pleaded, cajoled, urged, argued, fought and done everything else possible to make him stay.

Yet here he was. Riding into the demon's den. The asura's lair. The rakshasa's hellish homestead.

Why?

The reason was simple: Kamsa had summoned him. And he was curious.

Akrur reached the great gates of the palace in Mathura and passed through them unchallenged.

thirty-three

Kamsa grinned down at Akrur. Leaving his throne, he came down from the dais, surprising the entire court. At once, Akrur sensed people stepping back, cringing or wincing as they anticipated a bloody end to the royal visitor. He had heard tales of how Kamsa enjoyed using his new-found ability to despatch those who offended him in court, be they emissaries from foreign lands or his own people. He would crush a man's skull between his thumb and little finger with no more effort than an ordinary man would need to squash a grape, and with similar results.

Akrur held his ground, keeping his palms pressed together in the same namaskaram stance in which he had just greeted Kamsa. He maintained the same pleasant look on his face and kept his head slightly bowed as a show of respect. But inwardly, he thought that if Kamsa had planned this as a means of crippling the militia and the resistance, he had certainly played this hand with more finesse than Akrur had anticipated.

He did not tense visibly as Kamsa stretched out a hand towards him, a hand that appeared quite normal if a bit thickened at the wrist as befitted a swordsman and wrestler, but which he knew was capable of feats of strength that elephants could not hope to match. Even the legendary Haddi-Hathi, recently retired from active duty due to age and ill health, had never been feared as much as Kamsa's strength was now. If even a tenth of the rumours were to be believed, the Usurper was as close to being superhuman as it was possible without aspiring to godly status.

Akrur did not even need to credit rumours: he had himself watched more than one wrestling match where Kamsa had participated, observing incognito from the crowd as the Usurper had pounded and hammed opponent after opponent to bloody pulp. It had been a chilling sight and he had been filled with greater respect for Kamsa than he believed possible.

It appeared that as Kamsa had grown in strength and ability, he had gained in self-control and maturity. While the old Kamsa had wildly struck out at anyone and everyone, using his rakshasa size and power to kill randomly, this Kamsa picked his fights and opponents carefully and kept his considerably enhanced strength well curbed, unleashing it only in the wrestling akhada. That was impressive and also a sign of a dangerous opponent.

Now, as Kamsa's legendary hand reached out to Akrur, he tensed despite himself. One twist of those powerful fingers and the head of the resistance movement would be crushed, quite literally.

But the most feared fingers in the kingdom descended with surprising tenderness upon his shoulder, resting there with the weight of a normal man's hand.

'Bho! Bho!' Kamsa said. 'Well met, friend Akrur. Well met indeed.'

'The privilege is mine, my lord,' Akrur said mildly.

'You do yourself a disservice,' Kamsa said loudly, clearly speaking for the benefit of the court. He turned theatrically and continued addressing Akrur even though he faced a chamber filled with those who represented the considerable wealth and prestige and power of the nation. 'You are among the most respected Yadavas in the land today. Do not even bother to deny it!'

Akrur did not deny it. He listened, curious to see what new political manoeuvre was being unfurled.

Kamsa continued praising Akrur in language that sounded carefully rehearsed, perhaps even scripted. Akrur noted that the old minister Pralamba was present and appeared to be hanging on to every word spoken by Kamsa. Akrur resisted the impulse to smile openly. So Kamsa had asked Pralamba to prepare this eulogy for him and had memorized it word by word. Interesting. That was not typical Kamsa behaviour. Which raised the question: was this to be Akrur's last eulogy?

After several minutes of typical bombastic political wordage, Kamsa finally came to the nub. 'You are friend alike to the Bhoja and the Vrishni clans,' Kamsa said, now standing with one foot on the first level of the dais, knee bent, leaning with one arm on his own thigh. 'You act as spokesman for both clans, conveying delicate messages from one to the other with tact and diplomacy. Your neutrality is unquestioned, your wisdom and loyalty to the Yadava nation beyond dispute. Most of all, you are famous for always acting in the best interests of others, even when the outcome may not be in your own best interests.'

Kamsa put the raised foot down, straightened himself and came towards Akrur once again.

Now, he will finally spill his guts, Akrur thought, *or he will spill mine.* He had already listened to more praises from Kamsa's lips than he had heard spoken aloud from any of his dearest friends in his entire lifetime. Perhaps what the wise said was true: 'Nobody can praise you the way an enemy does ... right before he slips the knife between your ribs.' Now he waited for the knife to pierce his skin.

Instead, Kamsa paused in front of him and raised both hands in a gesture that could be interpreted as welcoming as well as pleading. 'Act now in the interests of all Yadavas everywhere,' Kamsa said. 'Do what is best for us all. Perform a small favour for this humble servant of our great nation.'

Humble servant of our great nation? Kamsa? Phuargh! Akrur was glad he had not eaten before coming to the court. For if he heard one more sentence like that last one, he was sure to regurgitate his stomach's contents.

'What is your desire, my lord?' Akrur asked aloud, speaking in as pleasant a tone as he could muster. This was a play being enacted for the benefit of Mathura, after all. He would play his part as well as Kamsa did. It was the reason why he had been tolerated and permitted to live in Mathura and stay alive all these years, while so many others, more patriotic than he, had been executed summarily or forced into exile.

Kamsa beamed a boyish smile, even though the first signs of grey were already visible at his temples. 'Most charitable Akrur. Giver of gifts and doer of deeds. I ask you a boon just as a tapasvi asks for a boon from the devas after decades of penance.'

Akrur's heart began to beat faster. Suddenly, he thought he knew what was coming next. Some sixth sense gained from a lifetime in politics warned him. Yet when the actual words were spoken aloud, they still came as a shock.

'Go to Nanda Maharaja, master of Vrajbhoomi, lord of the Vrishnis. He has two sons, Krishna and Balarama …'

Akrur heard his voice speak as if from a great height above his own body. 'Yes, my lord, what of them?'

'Bring them here to Mathura,' Kamsa said, smiling. 'Take my finest vahan. Return with them as fast as my horses will carry you there and back.'

Akrur swallowed to buy himself a moment, glanced around at the enraptured court. 'Forgive me, but may I ask why, my king?' he said, careful to make the question sound as innocuous and non-threatening as possible.

Kamsa grinned broadly. 'So that I may kill them both.'

'And then he said, after he had killed you both, he would slay every last one of your family members and relatives, even the most remote, distant of relatives by blood or marriage. And when he was done killing them, he would slay the entire Vrishni, Bhoja and Dasarha clans, followed by his father, the old King Ugrasena, his mother Padmavati, his uncle Devaka and all other Yadavas who could threaten his power, now or in future.'

Akrur stopped speaking and remained silent as the roomful of people absorbed his words. Outside the door of Nanda's house, the carriage in which Akrur had just arrived was still visible, for he had given instructions for the horses to not be unhitched as he would return within moments. The animals, flanks steaming from the heat of their long run, snorted and stamped their feet. Barely a few hours had passed since Akrur had stood in Kamsa's court and heard those terrible words, yet the world had changed entirely since then.

'It has come then,' Nanda said sombrely. 'The day we have long dreaded.'

'We knew it would, Father,' Krishna said. 'It is the only way this can finally end.'

Even at fifteen, Krishna was more than a young man. His face shone with the glow of a superior being. His pitch-dark face appeared almost deep blue, the blue of the sky at midnight in certain seasons. His crow-black eyes were soulful, intense, smouldering with a quality that was similar to human emotion yet transcended mortal feeling. A light gleamed deep within his eyes, like the promise of lightning in a thundercloud or the threat of a gharial lurking deep within still waters, capable of rushing up and wresting away life before thought could comprehend the action.

His voice had deepened a little, though not as much as Balarama's, whose voice matched his bulk and breadth. Krishna's voice was still a tenor, a flute-player's voice, soft and clear. Yet the authority in that gentle voice was impossible to ignore. Even the cows paused in their chewing to pay heed when Krishna spoke, as if they could understand his human words. Perhaps they could. Perhaps all creatures could.

Yashoda could not understand what he meant.

'You will not go,' she said, rising from the floor where she had been sitting cross-legged since Akrur's unexpected arrival moments earlier. Beside her, Rohini arose as well, but said nothing though her face spoke volumes. 'I will not let you go, neither of you,' Yashoda declared.

With age had come a greater dignity. Even as her features had thickened along with her waist, her maternal appearance had grown matriarchal. She moved and spoke with the authority of the legendary matrons who had founded the Arya clans in ancient ages, those great dames who had sired the famous princes and kings who were more often the subject of portraits and epic ballads. At this moment, Yashoda's face and manner matched the mythic power of those legendary kings.

'Mother,' Balarama said in his deeper voice, placing a large fair hand on her back. 'It was foretold even in the prophecy of yore.'

'Then untell it!' she cried. 'Cancel the prophecy. Erase destiny. Forget the foretelling. Ignore the summons. Remain here. Just for a while longer!'

'How long, Mother?' Balarama asked kindly. For Krishna and him, both Yashoda and Rohini were mothers, as was Devaki whom they had seen but once in their lives. 'How long will we bide our time and slay the asura assassins that come. First they only threatened Krishna. Now they come to harm all of us. Last time it was Father's turn. Next time—'

'Let the assassins come,' Yashoda said. 'We will fight them.'

Balarama shook his head. 'Sometimes, one has to take the fight to the enemy. One cannot simply wait.'

'But he has called you! You heard what Akrur said. This is his plan. To summon Krishna and you to Mathura and kill you both. After which he intends to kill everyone else.'

'Yes,' Balarama acknowledged. 'And now that he has issued a summons in this fashion, publicly, in front of the court of Mathura and in full hearing of all the clans, we must go, or we shall lose face.'

'But he is the demon of demons,' Yashoda said. 'A master of evil. What does it matter what he says or does? Ignore him. Stay home. You are safe here.'

'What good is it if we are safe when Mathura remains unsafe for our people, Mother?' Balarama asked gently. 'We must go.'

'It is a trap. His assassins have all failed, so now he is resorting to this last desperate effort. Because he lacks the courage to come himself and face the two of you. He seeks to lure you into his domain where he can attack you in devious, treacherous ways.'

'Perhaps,' Balarama agreed. 'But we must go still.'

'He has promised to kill you. He cannot go back on such a promise without losing face. He means to follow through this time. To destroy you both!'

'Then we must give him the opportunity to follow his promise through – or prove him wrong ourselves.'

Yashoda joined her hands together and beseeched Balarama, then turned and gestured towards Krishna as well, tears spilling freely down her lined cheeks, dampening the strands of hair that lay upon her face. 'I beg of you. If you love me, do not go!'

Krishna came forward and clasped Yashoda's hands in his own. 'We love you , Mother, just as we love our mother nation. For the sake of our mother, we must go. What Balarama has said is right. We cannot refuse this invitation. This is the very day for which we have both been waiting, for which we have prepared, for which we have been put upon this earth. This is our mission. This is the purpose for which we came. This is what we must do in order to rid the world of Kamsa's evil.'

'But you are still just two young boys, barely young men. He is a great and powerful rakshasa, surrounded by other rakshasas. He has laid a terrible trap for you. He will do everything possible to destroy you.'

'That is how it must be,' Krishna admitted. 'It is how it has always been. But we have one thing that he can never have, has never had, and will never have.'

Even Yashoda was silent, wondering what Krishna meant.

Then, in the dialect of a distant tribe, the Marathas who inhabited a region farther south and on the westward coast of the Bharata subcontinent, Krishna said, '*Aaichi punyaaii*' (Mother's good karma).

And he bent low and touched his forehead to Yashoda's feet. Balarama did the same. Both brothers prostrated before Yashoda and Rohini.

'Bless us, Mother,' they said together.

Yashoda cried as she blessed them.

thirty-five

'Krishna,' she cried out.

Krishna paused in the act of climbing aboard the vahan. Radha came running barefoot down the central road that ran the length of Vrindavan. She stopped several yards away, as if afraid to come closer.

'I will follow you, along with the rest of our people,' she said.

It had been agreed that all the families would go with their two best sons to witness the encounter and ensure that some fair balance was maintained, if such a thing were possible. Already, the hamlet was a bustling scene of chaos as people loaded uks wagons, dogs barked, children ran helter-skelter, and men and women alike cried openly as they contemplated the possible end of their community and the even more heart-rending thought of the possible cold-blooded murder of their two best-loved sons. After all, however remote the possibility, it could not simply be discounted. When a warrior went into battle, no matter how great a yoddha he might be, he could not presume himself invincible. He had to prove it so. That was the difference between a warrior and a trader of goods. A trader could promise anything and deliver another thing altogether and still get away with it; a warrior paid for overconfidence with his life and limbs. The atmosphere in Vrindavan was one of great alarm, as if a mighty disaster had befallen the Vrishnis.

Krishna turned and nodded to Radha. He waited for her to say more. She too waited for him to speak.

Finally, Balarama said, from atop the vahan. 'We are ready, Bhai.'

Krishna looked at Radha who remained standing where she was, yards away. Children ran between them, dogs scampered, and even a calf bounded past. The whole world seemed to have decided to come between them.

'Fight well,' she said.

He nodded. 'I shall do my best.'

She hesitated, then said, 'I understand now what you tried to tell me once, on the hill overlooking the lake.'

He waited for her to continue. Balarama waited on the vahan for Krishna. Akrur waited for them both. Around them, the Vrishnis hurried to make arrangements to leave.

'You came here for a reason,' she said, gesturing mildly, indicating towards the sky, the forest, the ground, the world. 'To fulfil a purpose. Today, you are leaving to complete that purpose. You belong to everyone, not just one person. I was wrong to want you only for myself. You cannot belong to just me or to any single person. You serve a higher purpose, a larger karma. You are everybody's Krishna.'

He looked at her for a long moment, then said softly, 'I am your Krishna too. I shall always be.' Then he turned, climbed aboard the vahan and nodded to Balarama.

Balarama nodded to Akrur who started the horse team moving.

The vahan began rolling away, down the pathway, up the long road to Mathura, away from Radha. Krishna stood with his back to the charioteer, looking at Radha as he was drawn away.

She remained standing in the middle of the road, goats and calves and dogs and children and people running to and fro and around her. She stood there, watching as the vehicle drew farther and farther away, taking Krishna away from her. *Her* Krishna.

When he had gone too far for her eyes to see any more, she followed him with her heart.

Kaand III

Kaand III

Twenty-three years had passed since Kamsa had usurped his father Ugrasena's throne, fifteen since the birth of Krishna.

In that period, tens of thousands of Mathurans had fled the city state and chosen voluntary exile over life under the yoke of tyranny. Others had joined the rebellion, either openly taking up arms against the Usurper and harrying his armies on the borders and other vulnerable areas, or choosing to join the forces of those who resisted Jarasandha's armies and the onslaught of the Magadhan imperial juggernaut; they preferred to die fighting against their mutual enemy rather than for a Mathuran Army led by Kamsa.

The internal campaign had been led by Akrur who functioned as a rebel commander as well as ambassador of sorts. Over time, politics makes bedfellows of everyone, and even Kamsa had dealings with Akrur, sometimes to resolve disputes, at other times to parley settlements. Over time, Kamsa had learnt the art of diplomacy from Jarasandha, knowing when to use words rather than swords and vice versa. He used Akrur when it was worth his while, never making the mistake of trusting the friend of Vasudeva, nor expecting trust in return.

Once Vasudeva and Devaki had embarked on their pilgrimage, it was easy enough to extend it indefinitely. There was no shortage of sacred sites to visit, and without labelling their absence 'exile', they managed to stay away from Mathura and out of their tormentor's reach. More than once, Devaki wished to return, if only to be within visiting distance of her beloved Krishna and his brother Balarama. But Akrur convinced her that it would be too dangerous. Not only might Kamsa harm her and Vasudeva directly, Jarasandha would certainly use them as pawns in his larger game of empire building. Besides, once the Vrishnis themselves went into exile, there was no way Krishna could risk leaving Vrindavan to meet her, nor could Vasudeva and she chance going to Vrindavan themselves. Kamsa's spasas were everywhere, watching and reporting back to Mathura, and so were Jarasandha's spasas, keeping an eye and relaying the information to Magadha. It was a dangerous era, and alliances were constantly being made and unmade.

Complicating matters further were the growing disputes over ascension in the great empire of the Kurus, the ancestral family home of Yadu, son of Yayati, forebear of the Yadava line. Hastinapura, the legendary capital, was the prized epicentre of a great game of thrones raging between two lines of the Kuru dynasty. Both lines claimed their own birthright over the throne and dynasty; both disputed the other's right. The issue was complex and required an understanding of Kuru history, but the basic facts were simple enough: one hundred and one Kurus or Kauravas as they were better known, versus five sons of Pandu, or Pandavas as they were better known. The great patriarch of the dynasty, Bhishma Pitamah and the ageing matron Satyavati were both said to be silent on the issue – although other rumours claimed that each had their own favourite and it was with their backing that the dispute was being fuelled. As with all such matters, rumours and gossip dominated over hard truths, and all news was to be instantly distrusted and preferably discarded.

The one thing that seemed certain was that war was inevitable. It was only a matter of time before the dispute spiralled into open civil war between the Pandavas and the Kauravas.

Vasudeva's relationship with the Kurus ranged back decades, stemming from the fact that his own sister Pritha, or Kunti, as she was known after marriage, had married the fair-skinned 'Pandu' the White, which made the five Pandava boys his nephews. Naturally, his loyalty lay with his sister's son, and if and when Vasudeva returned to the throne of Mathura as everyone assumed would happen eventually, there was little doubt that Yadava forces would fight on the side of the Pandavas.

Kamsa's resentment towards his sister's husband drove him to show hostility towards the Pandava cause and espouse the Kaurava claim instead. A warmonger to the core, Kamsa actively encouraged Duryodhana, the eldest Kaurava, and assured him of full military support in the event of a civil war. Interestingly, Jarasandha remained aloof in this matter, biding his time. Observers of politics compared his role to that of the carrion crow that waited for the battle to end to pick at the spoils. It mattered little to Jarasandha who won, only how it affected his own plans of expansion.

But on the day of the great wrestling tournament, even mighty Hastinapura was less concerned with its own internecine disputes than with the events unfolding in distant Mathura. Across the length and breadth of the civilized world, people debated the possible outcomes of the day. Many favoured Kamsa's chances of survival over all other options. Ugrasena's son had surprised many with his longevity and unexpected ability to change from a demoniac tyrant to a ruthless but efficient ruler. A rakshasa he was, no doubt, and tales of his legendary appetite for violence and cruelty sent shivers up everyone's spine, but many believed that sometimes it was better to have a rakshasa as ruler than a weakling. Besides, war was a way of life for most, and Kamsa never shied away from war or from settling his disputes through violence, as even his success and fame at the sport of Yadava-style wrestling demonstrated. Ugrasena had been old and too weak to go to war any more, and Vasudeva was regarded as too ineffectual to rule. People were loath to respect a person who permitted his own newborn infants to be slain rather than fight back.

But these were the politicians speaking. The people loved Vasudeva, missed Ugrasena, hated Kamsa and longed for Krishna to save them.

Krishna, the eighth child of the prophecy. The Deliverer of the Yadava people. Saviour of the Vrishnis. Slayer of Kamsa.

Every time a new wave of atrocities swept across the land, the people consoled themselves with the knowledge that one day the Deliverer would rise and avenge them.

And finally, after twenty-three long years of suffering and faith, that day had come at last.

two

Not since the day of the peace accord between Ugrasena and Vasudeva had Mathura seen such a turnout. Every citizen came out of doors to view the arrival of the Deliverer. People who had been in exile returned home, preferring to risk their lives rather than miss this once-in-a-lifetime opportunity. Wanted men, entire factions of banned political groups, armed militia and civil rebels, outlaws and fringe collectives – every imaginable group in the Yadava nation drifted into Mathura to watch the long-awaited conclusion of the Prophecy.

Kamsa enlisted the help of Jarasandha's Mohini Fauj to help maintain law and order. Their bald gleaming pates shone at every street corner and their wickedly curved weapons and armour warned against any attempt to turn the day's sporting event into a political uprising. The Mathuran Army was out in full force as well, the soldiers helmed and wearing protective gear as if for full battle. Armoured elephants and horses and vahans were arrayed at every square.

Mathura had grown accustomed to being a military state, but where there had been simmering resentment or outright hostility towards the oppressor's army before, today there was an atmosphere of ridicule and laughter. Even little children made funny faces and boldly knocked on armour plates, warning, 'The Deliverer is coming to get you!' Even more unusual, the soldiers themselves seemed reluctant to suppress this insolence and seemed willing to tolerate even the most humiliating insults and behaviour rather than resort to their usual crowd control methods.

Kamsa woke early that morning. He was in a good mood. He had slept well, better than he had slept in weeks. He was in excellent form physically, and he thought he might have reached the peak of his abilities.

He could not see how he could be more powerful or destructive. He was now able to turn himself into the human equivalent of a solid iron ramrod, and there was nothing made of flesh that could withstand his combination of power and technique. He was the undisputed master of the wrestling field and his team comprised the most dreaded champions across the civilized world.

He had spent the night enjoying the company of both his wives at once and felt confident that either or both would conceive from that joining. It was about time too. Jarasandha was impatient for a grandchild and Kamsa himself had begun feeling the need for an heir. Not because he desired a son or daughter but because it was politically useful. Such was the game of kings.

He was leaving his chambers when he noticed the old minister Pralamba waiting silently outside. The ageing mantri was keeping ill and seemed half decrepit already. He jerked to alertness as Kamsa emerged.

'Sire.'

'What is it?' Kamsa asked, less sharply than usual.

'My lord,' the minister said, somehow always managing to avoid using the word 'king' when addressing Kamsa, 'the old syce is dead.'

Kamsa frowned. 'Who?'

Pralamba looked startled. 'The old master of stables. I believe he was your friend and guru for a while. I thought you would want to be informed.'

Kamsa realized whom he meant. 'Oh, that old relic.'

'Aye, sire. His name was Yadu. Nobody seems to know exactly how old he was, and for some reason, nobody knows of any immediate family or relatives he left behind. The rumour is that he migrated here from another country a long time ago and outlived his immediate family.'

Kamsa shrugged. 'Why tell me all this?'

'Would you like to pay for his last rites, sire?' Pralamba asked nervously.

Kamsa laughed. 'Burn him and throw the ashes into the nearest ditch.'

He walked away without bothering to glance back at Pralamba. The nerve of the fellow, expecting him to care about some old idiot. Even if the man was *the* Yadu, actual forebear of the Yadava dynasty, Kamsa couldn't care less how he was cremated. As far as he was concerned, the Yadava line began with *his* reign and *he* would father a new dynasty, one that would take his people to supremacy over all others in Bharatavarsha, then the world.

three

Akrur drove the horse team the last few yards to the top of the rise and made it halt. The horses whinnied with relief, their flanks steaming, nostrils flared, dewlaps white with froth and foam. Akrur had driven them hard all night in order to reach Mathura by morning. Now he paused and leaned on the railing of the carriage, looking down at the view from the last hill on this side of the river.

Mother Yamuna was painted deep blue by the dim luminescence of dawn. The river flowed gently at this time of the year, swollen neither with the full burden of the monsoons nor with glacial melt. The scene was peaceful and calm, the road winding its way downhill to the ferry crossing, then continuing on the far bank up the sloping approach to Mathura.

Krishna stood beside Akrur, Balarama behind them. Together, they looked out at the sight of the capital city of their nation, admiring her towering structures and facades, the great house of the Yadava people built with the blood, sweat and tears of countless generations.

Finally, Akrur sighed and said, 'My lord, grant me leave to pause awhile and perform sandhya vandana in the river.'

Krishna said, 'We shall perform the morning ablutions together, good Akrur.'

Akrur egged the horses on to start the vahan. Already nuzzling at the grass growing by the roadside, they neighed

once in protest but trotted forward resignedly once they saw
that the path ahead went downhill. The royal vahan was heavy
and festooned with more precious ornamentation than required
in order to proclaim the king's ownership, and it was with great
relief that the weary team of horses slowed by the banks of the
river a few moments later. Akrur leapt off the vahan and was
about to tie the reins to a tree trunk when Krishna stopped
him.

'Free the horses,' Krishna said. 'They deserve a reprieve for
rest and refreshment as much as we do.'

Akrur looked at the horses, white-eyed and foaming with
exhaustion. 'My lord Vaasudeva, if I release them now, it will be
impossible to get them yoked and ready to ride again in time.'

'I understand,' Krishna agreed. 'That is why we shall walk
from this point on.'

Akrur stared at him, then looked towards the river, at the
distant roofs of Mathura. 'The palace grounds where I am to
take you are a good mile away, sire. They are on the far side of
the city, in the military cantonment.'

'A mile is a hop, skip and jump to a gopa, good Akrur. Fret
not, we shall walk and it shall be an enjoyable walk. Besides, it
will give Father and Mother and the rest of the entourage from
Vrindavan time to catch up with us. They cannot be far behind
but our broken-back uksan cannot ride as swiftly as your marut
steeds.'

Akrur shrugged. 'If you say so, my lord. But they are not my
steeds. They are Kamsa's horses.'

Krishna grinned as Balarama and he began removing the
elaborate and oppressive leather harnessing of the royal vahan's
horses. 'In that case, all the more reason to free them from the
Usurper's yoke!'

The horses stamped their feet and tossed their manes, turning their heads to look back down the length of their backs. It took them a moment to realize they were truly free. They whinnied with delight. Proud, magnificent creatures each of them, they looked around with unbridled joy at the lush green grass of the Yamuna riverbank, the fresh water collected in numerous ponds around, and neighed loudly to show their appreciation.

The leader, a beautiful, dark, chestnut-brown stallion, turned around once, then stopped before Krishna. Bowing his head, it dipped it to touch Krishna's feet and licked them once in gratitude.

Krishna rubbed the soft fur between the horse's eyes and scratched his mane affectionately. 'Go in peace, good marut. Give the ashwins my best regards.'

The stallion neighed meaningfully, then cantered off to lead its fellows to the nearest pond. They splashed in the water with such abandon, the water splashed tens of yards away, startling a clutch of black ducks that rose from a dense patch of grass and took to the air, complaining loudly.

Akrur, Krishna and Balarama performed the morning ritual standing chest-deep in a freshwater pool replenished by the flow of the Yamuna. Akrur's patron deity was Mitra and he performed his prayers to the great god with due diligence and all necessary ritual.

As they emerged from the water and came upon the grassy bank, Akrur began shedding tears freely. Balarama noticed it and caught hold of their elder friend's shoulder, steadying him. Balarama gestured to Krishna with his eyes and Krishna turned back to Akrur, steadying him from the other side. The trio sat on the grassy bank of the Yamuna. Birds flew overhead, a fisherman poled his boat upriver and a cluster of brahmacharis waited by the ferry stand to cross over to the Yamuna side. The first rays of the morning sun were slanting across the riverbank and there was a soft cool breeze blowing.

Krishna and Balarama waited for their elder to regain control of his emotions. Finally, Akrur managed to gain some hold of his senses and began to speak.

four

'Svaphalka my father and Gandini my mother, both great personages of the Satvata, saw fit to name me Akrur,' said the older man, still weeping quietly. 'Akrur means one who is not cruel. But in fact, I am the cruellest man alive today. For I am delivering you boys into the hands of your own murderous assassin, the wicked Childslayer himself.'

Balarama put a hand on Akrur's shoulder, comforting him. But Akrur was too greatly distressed to be easily comforted.

'By choosing to resist the Usurper rather than bow down to his dictatorial regime, I have sent brave men to their death. I have endangered entire villages and tribes through my leadership of the rebellion. I have even put my own family and loved ones in harm's way because it was required of me. But nothing I have done has made me feel this ashamed of myself. By taking you boys to certain death, I am condemning myself to eternal damnation,' he said.

Krishna said softly, 'Akrur, you are doing your duty. In this case, it happens to be your dharma. Your task was to inform us of Kamsa's invitation, *our* decision to accept it. No blame falls upon you.'

'How can you say that?' Akrur asked. 'It is all my fault. I should have refused to do as Kamsa bade.'

'Then he would have killed you,' Balarama said. 'On the very spot where you stood.'

Akrur nodded dumbly. 'Death would have been better than damnation.'

'You will not be damned, Akrur,' Krishna comforted him. 'You will ascend to swargaloka itself, the highest level of the heavenly realms. Your great deeds and actions will speak for themselves in earning you great merit. I am certain of it. What say you, Balarama?'

'I agree with Krishna. Heaven reserves a special place for those such as you,' Balarama seconded him.

Akrur shook his head, unwilling to be convinced. 'You do not understand. Kamsa invited you on a false pretext, to attend a bow ceremony or some such. In fact, he intends to challenge you before all Mathura to a wrestling bout.'

Krishna and Balarama raised their eyebrows and exchanged a glance.

'We enjoy a good wrestling match,' Krishna said. 'Don't we, Balarama?'

Interlacing his fingers, Balarama stretched out his meaty arms and cracked his knuckles loudly. The sound was loud enough to startle a nuzzling hare into scampering away into the woods. 'It would be my pleasure to wrestle Uncle Kamsa. I have some special moves I would like to show him.' He grinned, his teeth predatory in his handsome face.

'See? There is nothing to worry about, Akrur,' Krishna went on. 'Besides, you forget that we boys have a few tricks up our sleeves as well. We are not entirely without power. After all, that is how we have survived all the attacks by the assassins deputed by Kamsa over the past years. In a way, you could say we were *weaned* on assassins!'

Balarama grunted, catching the reference to Putana.

'You are boys yet,' Akrur said sombrely. 'You do not understand what awaits you in Mathura. Whatever assassins Kamsa may have sent to harry you all these years, they are no match for the man himself. He is more powerful than any being alive upon this earth now ... barring perhaps Jarasandha, his father-in-law. And he is surrounded by a coterie of other powerful men, each one of whom is a fighting force unto himself. I have myself witnessed the havoc these men can wreak upon a battlefield, facing contingents of armed and armoured soldiers. Kamsa makes mincemeat of hundreds of soldiers in a few moments. They are as ineffectual as ants when confronted with his power. No demoniac wet nurse with poisoned milk compares to the terror that is Kamsa unleashed.'

Akrur shook his head again. 'No, no. You do not understand. This is beyond your ability to survive. Even the great Deliverer cannot face up to Kamsa and his powerful demons in human form and survive. Perhaps once you are grown fully to manhood, it may be possible to wage a strategic battle and overcome them. But right now, you are still but boys. It is too much to expect of you. I am driving you to your certain deaths.'

Krishna and Balarama glanced at each other. Balarama shook his head once, pursing his lips as if to say, *The man is fixed in his opinion. What can we say that will change his mind?*

Krishna bent to Akrur. 'We will speak of this yet, if you wish. But first, go back to the river and wash your face, good Akrur. Then if you want to change your mind, we shall discuss the matter.'

Krishna rose to his feet and gestured to Balarama who followed his example. 'We shall stand here on the vahan and await your return. If necessary, we will harness the horses again and ride back to Vrindavan, if that is your wish. But first go and wash.'

Akrur took a deep breath, nodded, then rose to his feet. With heavy feet and a drooping back he walked to the river and immersed himself once again, this time only venturing knee deep. Bending over, he cupped water in his hands and splashed it on his face, refreshing himself. He wiped his face clean with the corner of his anga-vastra.

He glanced back and saw Krishna and Balarama standing on the empty vahan, waiting for him, limned by the light of the rising sun. They waved to him, smiling encouragingly, and he smiled back wistfully, impressed by their youthful maturity and clarity of thought. They were rare young men indeed. That was what made it all the more impossible for him to lead them to Kamsa.

A flicker of movement at the corner of his eye caught his attention and he turned back to see what it was.

five

Akrur looked at the river and saw two men standing there, immersed in the water, yet fully visible. He blinked rapidly and rubbed away any vestiges of tears or water from his eyes and peered. *Why, they look like Balarama and Krishna! What are they doing in the middle of the river?*

He turned back abruptly, splashing water as he sidestepped for the current was strong and he waist-deep, to look at the riverbank. There, beside the mound of grass where they had been comforting him only moments earlier, standing on the vahan were Krishna and Balarama. They saw him turning and raised their hands and smiled, waving gently. He raised a hand to wave back, then grew still.

He turned back to look out at the river once again. The two figures in the middle of the course were there still. He rubbed his eyes again and looked more intently. There was no doubt about it. The figures in the river were Krishna and Balarama.

Akrur was not a superstitious or overly religious man. He performed his rituals diligently, managed his darshan of the deities whenever possible, praised the appropriate gods at the appropriate time, propitiated those that required propitiation at the opportune moments, and did as prescribed by the sacred texts. He was a herder and a warrior and found himself more comfortable with a crook or a sword than a seer's staff.

This sight genuinely unnerved him. He did not know what

to make of it. Clearly, this was a supernatural phenomenon. In this age, there was no question of believing or not believing in such things: they existed, plain and simple. Things that could not be explained by rational means coexisted with the stones, the mud, the rain, the flowers, the solid and tangible. He knew this was one such event. He knew there was little point in trying to rationalize, explain or deny, or otherwise counter the vision he was witnessing.

Simpler therefore to attempt to understand it, to perceive whatever implications it had for him personally – he had heard enough about such things to know that if such a vision was being shown to his unschooled eyes, it must serve a purpose. Best to focus on that purpose and put the rest aside.

He steeled himself and looked out at the river. He was certain the figures were Krishna and Balarama and since he could not explain it, he accepted the fact. Never mind how the boys could be in the river as well as on the vahan on the riverbank at the same time. They simply were.

But as he continued to look at the boys in the river, he grew aware of the differences. Not in appearance or substance but in the other details. It was as if, when he first caught sight of them, they had been just as they were on the vahan, but the more he stared, the more details he saw … or the more details *appeared* around them. He could not say which. But there was no doubt that with each passing moment, he saw new things that he felt had not been there a moment earlier. This continued for he knew not how long, until at last the vision resolved into some form of solidity. At that point, it settled into a steady panorama of detail.

This is what he saw: the river was no longer a river. Instead, its entire sinuous length, traversing the length of the subcontinent all the way up to its Himalayan glacial point of origin, was self-evidently a serpent. The greatest serpent of all, its length unimaginable, exceeding even the hundreds of yojanas visible upon the mortal realm, continuing up to the heavenly levels and beyond into the infinite ocean of milk.

This great serpent had a thousand heads, each of which ended in a serpentine hood, proud, bejewelled, magnificent, eyes glinting like dark rubies. Upon each hood rested a golden crown. Its length was clad in deep blue vastra, contrasting beautifully with its fair scales which were the exact shade and texture of the fibrous substance of the lotus flower. It sat coiled, surrounded by countless asuras, gandharvas, charanas, and siddhas. All bowed in humility before the great Ananta.

Seated upon the lap of Ananta the great serpent was Krishna. Yet this was not the Krishna who stood upon the vahan on the riverbank waving gaily to Akrur. This Krishna was a being beyond easy description. He was no mere mortal. He was a god who possessed four mighty arms, each holding an object or weapon. His colour was the shade of a dark monsoon cloud, ghanashyam, so darkly pitch-black as to appear almost bluish. Setting off his black complexion were resplendent yellow silk vastras. His eyes were red as lotus petals, half shut in an aspect of ecstatic relaxation, the unmitigated calm of eternal nidra.

He was Vishnu embodied.

Akrur found himself unable to stop admiring the ethereal beauty of Vishnu. Although ostensibly in the form of a human male, it was evident that the resemblance to mortal man was more a result of perception than the inherent reality. What he might in fact look like when viewed by other, alien senses, Akrur could not imagine. Yet with his limited human vision, this was all he could see – and it was still breathtakingly beautiful.

Those eyes, those eyebrows, the line of that nose, the earlobes, the cheeks, the lips, the chin, his flowing throat, his low navel, his flat stomach, his powerful thighs, slender hips, shapely feet and calves … His toenails were as red as his eyes, and the reflection of celestial light cast a reddish glow on his entire lower body. He was adorned with bracelets on the arms and wrists and feet. A crown encrusted with large precious gems sat upon his head, and he had on earrings, the sacred thread, and a belt.

In his hands were a lotus, a conch, a disc and a club. Upon his chest was the Kaustubha jewel as also the tuft of hair known as Srivatsa. Around his neck was a garland of flowers taken from deep within a sacred grove.

Every detail was infused with beauty and perfection. Even in his state of nidra, he appeared to be laughing, at supreme ease, beyond all worldly anxieties or considerations. His eyes, lips and entire face seemed engaged in a smile that was infectious. Akrur felt his own heart lighten. It was an intoxication no soma could induce, a releasing of worldly cares. A dissolving of the calcified accumulation of a lifetime of emotional baggage, all melted away as easily as a grimy frozen crust in a warm current.

Resting upon Vishnu's broad chest was Sri, the goddess of fortune, bracketed between his long arms. She lay at his disposal yet possessed a dignity and pride of her own. She was a goddess in her own right. But the details of her appearance were not as clearly visible to Akrur. He could not understand why this should be so, but it did not matter. It was Vishnu/Krishna on whom his attention was fixated, as it was meant to be.

Then, as Akrur continued to pay darshan to the Lord of Lords, he saw that there were attendants close by, each paying homage to Vishnu depending on his mood. Sunanda and Nanda were posited near his head. Then there was Sanaka and a few others. Brahma was there. Rudra anyata Shiva was present too. The nine twice-born Brahmins who were sometimes seven were in attendance; here in the heavenly realms they were nine, headed by Prahlada, Narada and Vasu. There were others too, Akrur saw, as his mortal brain began to absorb more of the infinite detail being portioned out.

Apart from Sri herself who represented affluence, there was Pusti, nourishment; Gir, speech; Kanti, beauty; Kirti, fame; Tusti, satisfaction; Ila, earth; Urja, vitality; Vidya, knowledge; Avidya, ignorance; Shakti, power; and Maya, illusion.

After this, Akrur could absorb no more. His mere mortal mind was filled to the brim with devotional ecstasy and wonder. The hair on his body was standing on end, his eyes were shedding copious tears. He was perspiring from every pore. He felt as if his heart were filled with more love and devotion than it could possibly contain. It poured out like the river itself, an endless current of ecstasy that could wash away all cares, worries, anxieties, doubt …

With a supreme effort, he regained his presence of mind, joined his hands in supplication, bowed his head and offered obeisance to the Lord.

six

Akrur emerged from the river a different man from the one who had entered only moments earlier. To him, the vision appeared to have lasted an aeon, infinite and timeless, just as the devotional ecstasy that filled his being seemed sufficient to fill the entire universe; yet he had spent only a few scant moments in the waters of Mother Yamuna. His eyes shone with joy, his face and body were moist, his complexion clear and aspect rejuvenated. He appeared invigorated and ten years younger, as if infused with new energy and strength. All the gunas shone forth from his being.

He walked up the riverbank to where the vahan still stood. He folded his hands as he approached, bowing his head as if in devotion to Vishnu again – as indeed, he *was* bowing to Vishnu.

Krishna and Balarama exchanged a knowing glance, then Balarama spoke. 'What is it, Akrur? You seem altered.'

Akrur nodded. 'I have seen a revelation in the river.'

Krishna smiled. 'It must have been a wonderful revelation, judging by your aspect.'

Akrur turned his eyes up to Krishna, bowing before him in humility. 'It was yourself I was privileged to be shown, my lord. In your true aspect.'

Balarama glanced at his brother, smiling, and said nothing.

Akrur went on. 'Indeed, I see that it was both of you together, for while here upon earth you appear as separate beings, in your true state of existence, you are both one, the Lord and the Serpent who is his constant companion and mate. If Krishna is Vishnu then you Balarama are Ananta himself, as much a part of the Lord's being as a brother is to a brother.'

Akrur continued speaking. 'Until now, I had only known from afar of the deeds and exploits of the Deliverer. And like all such things, they appear as distant dreams viewed by another. However fantastical one's own dreams are, they are nevertheless linked to oneself intimately, intricately, and one clings to them as an infant to sensations and sights and sounds it can experience but never wholly comprehend. True miracles are like another person's dreams. They can never be wholly accepted because they lack the personal details and interweaving of experience and memory that makes one's own dreams intimate. Thus I heard and acknowledged but never truly accepted the stories of your exploits. It was not that I doubted them, merely that I regarded them as perhaps exaggerated in detail, possibly even wholly made up. I did not doubt their veracity, merely their detail and substance. There was no doubt that you slew those demons, merely a question of how you did so, and whether the demons were indeed as fantastical as described. We of this earth are compelled to live among the dirt and grime of everyday reality. We are not built to easily accept that which we cannot touch, feel, see or hear with our senses first-hand. Therefore we doubt. Therefore, when I was bringing you to Kamsa, I believed I was carrying you to certain death. Now, having seen your true aspect, I know how foolish I was being. For you are Infinite, Incomparable, Invincible. Whatever struggles you have upon this mortal realm are struggles of flesh and blood, limitations of the physical form you inhabit. Yet in the end, you will triumph. For what can resist your power? I see that now. And I see how foolish and impetuous I was to want to turn back. This is destined. This is the prophecy of the Slayer. It must be fulfilled.'

Akrur went on in this tone for a while, praising Krishna in more detail than could be summarized quickly. The gist of it came to his acceptance of Krishna's divinity and invincibility. In the end, he prostrated himself upon the grassy field and paid homage to his Lord God.

Finally, Krishna bent down and raised Akrur to his feet.

'Good Akrur, you served my father Anakadundubhi and mother Devaki well, you serve your people honourably, and now you serve me well too. It shall be rewarded. Come now, the time approaches for my encounter with the Childslayer. We must continue to Mathura.'

Akrur wiped his eyes clear of tears. 'I shall harness the team and hitch the vahan at once.'

'There is no need,' Krishna said. 'I meant what I said. We must go by foot from this point. You may proceed in the vahan. We shall aid you in hitching and harnessing, then you can ride ahead and inform all of our impending arrival. We shall come on foot after you by and by.'

Akrur glanced at Balarama who was already harnessing the team using his powerful muscles to compel them to return to their duty. Knowing they could not resist his strength and will, the horses submitted meekly.

'But, Lord, how can I ride when you walk? I was blind before, but now my eyes have been washed clean. Permit me to take you to my house. Blessed shall we be by your presence. I shall wash your feet clean of the dust of the road and serve you refreshment and we shall be eternally graced.'

'I shall come to your house,' Krishna said, 'and to every house in Mathura, but only after I have performed my dharma by killing the Childslayer and fulfilling the prophecy.'

Akrur found it hard to accept Krishna's instructions but he did not argue further. Finally, somewhat dejected and sad, he bowed his head and joined his hands in acceptance.

'I shall do as you say, Lord,' he said.

With these words, Akrur mounted the ready vahan and turned the head of the team leader, riding back to the road and then down to the ferry. He looked back dolefully at the two figures on the riverbank; his desire that they ride with him was palpable. But under the Lord's command, he continued on his way.

seven

Vasudeva reached the top of the hill overlooking the Yamuna and made the uks wagon pause. Beside him, Devaki clutched his arm. Both gazed down at the vista, enraptured.

Vasudeva was seeing the Yamuna for the first time since the night of his son Krishna's birth. Yet he recalled her colour, her fragrance and the sound of her voice as only a child can recall his mother.

He recalled the parting of the waters and the peculiar fish smell of the riverbed as he had carried his newborn infant across. He remembered the sight of fish and crustaceans trapped in the parted waters, still alive and swimming and gawking at the sight of Vishnu Incarnate in human form.

He recalled wishing his newborn son could stay in Mathura, grow old enough to stand on his own two feet, and run, play and swim like other Yadava children. He recalled thinking sadly that he would never be able to watch his Krishna do all those things and many more.

He remembered hearing from his friend Akrur about Krishna's first days in Gokul, how green and blue and beautiful the trees and sky were and how happy the little boy had been; how much he had loved this new world and wanted nothing more than to frolic and play and explore it. He had taken satisfaction in the knowledge that at least Krishna was safe and well and happy. If he and Devaki had to sacrifice the joy of parenting him in order to keep him from harm, so be it.

Yet he missed the years he had never spent as a father. And he knew that Devaki, seated beside him on the wagon, missed them too.

Not only had they had their first six children taken from them and destroyed by the heartless rakshasa Kamsa, they had lost the seventh and eighth voluntarily. Saved, yes. But lost as children to Vasudeva and Devaki.

The joys of parenting; the heartache of nursing a sick child; the sweet—sad pain of watching the changes of growth and knowing that that stage, that age, would be gone forever and would never come again, of knowing that with each passing day, this being was becoming an independent person who would one day leave home and go about his life and that the intimacy of those early years of childhood and parenting would then be gone forever. The thousand aches and joys, cares and pleasures of being a father, a mother, a guardian. He had been deprived the opportunity to experience those feelings forever. As had Devaki.

That was one of many things Kamsa had to answer for today, apart from the reign of terror he had brought to Mathura from the very first day of his rule. Those atrocities against the people inspired great anger in Vasudeva as well. He thought he had left that anger behind when Devaki and he had departed from Mathura and gone on their years-long pilgrimage, a veritable exile of sorts. But now, looking down upon the great city of the Yadava nation, he found it rising in his breast again.

Yet in the end, it was not vengeance he craved but peace.

He had never truly stopped feeling those emotions and a part of him still wished the fighting and warring and crises could just end, once and for all, and all beings live in peace, enjoying the benefits of their shared world. Why was it so hard for living beings to understand that together they were one whole being symbiotically interlinked through food, weather, biology and a thousand other intricate interdependent systems, while individually they were nothing but strays, incapable of sustaining or surviving? Why did beings like Kamsa even exist? Why had they been created? Why was it necessary for the Slayer to be born at all? Why could the creator not avoid creating cruelty and pain and violence and war? Why could the gods, in which category he knew his own eighth child was included, not rid the world of such things forever?

But these were questions for gods and seers, prophets and pundits. He was merely Vasudeva of Vraj. Once King Vasudeva. Now merely husband to Devaki. And birth father to Krishna.

Today, here, he was present in his capacity as father to Krishna, Slayer of Kamsa, who had come to face his nemesis at last; he had returned with Devaki as soon as they had received the news brought by one of Akrur's trusted associates.

Today, the history of the Yadava nation would change forever, thanks to their son Krishna.

An entire nation looked to his son to deliver it from evil. A world watched, holding its breath as it waited to see if the devas still held sway over the mortal realm or if they had finally surrendered it to the asuras, abandoning their creation and children.

Finally, it was Devaki who wiped her face clean of tears and looked at him.

'Come, Vasu,' she said, touching his arm. 'Let us go meet the Usurper and witness the end of this tale. I am impatient to meet our little Ghanashyam after this long while.'

Vasudeva wiped his face roughly in the manner of a man who is not accustomed to crying openly or showing much emotion. He nodded silently and urged the uks wagon on, down the long trundling raj-marg.

eight

'Senapati Bana, the Vrishnis are entering Mathura,' cried the captain of the outer gate.

General Bana of the imperial Mathuran Army already knew that the Vrishnis had entered the city. He could hear the roaring of the crowds. It was so immense, it seemed to come from everywhere, from around the world. Even on this narrow street, people had filled the houses overlooking the way that the procession would pass, crowded the rooftops and were leaning out of windows, eager for a glimpse. He had never seen Mathura so excited and happy in all his years. Not even the day of the peace accord had witnessed such a turnout or such adulation.

The Deliverer was here.

The same child who had been born in this very city, under lock and guard, heavy sentry watch, and surrounded by a hostile army and a demoniac king who had killed his earlier-born siblings.

He had returned now to wreak his vengeance and fulfil the prophecy.

Bana felt the stirring of emotion in his own heart as well. He had never failed to feel it each time he heard the people speak of the Deliverer. He had felt it when a condemned man prayed to the Deliverer at the moment before his execution, when a child had died of yellow fever with the name 'Krishna' on her

lips, when he saw the misery and suffering and pain inflicted by
Kamsa and all those who served him these past twenty-three
years.

The day the Deliverer had escaped Kamsa's grasp was as
fresh in Bana's memory as if it had happened this very day. For
that was also the day that Kamsa had compelled Bana to put
his own newborn twin sons to death, in front of his pleading,
sobbing wife.

And then, because he knew she would never forgive him and,
more importantly, he would never forgive himself so long as she
lived to remind him of his unpardonable crime, he had killed
her as well. Slaughtered his own family with the same sword he
still carried in his sheath even today.

All for what? To serve a master who was more rakshasa
than human? Who cared for nobody, respected nothing? For
dharma? He could almost spit into the dust of the street at
the thought of that word. Dharma! It was not his dharma to
slay his own loved ones. If it was, then the concept of dharma
itself was wrong, twisted, depraved. No act of violence could
be justified or condoned by any religious precept, however
rigorous the argument. Murder was murder, plain and simple.
No exceptions. And he had murdered his family just because
he feared Kamsa's wrath.

And it had all been for nothing. All those newborns slain,
other children slaughtered, so many more innocents killed …
for what? To slake the bloodlust of a demon king. To protect a
powerful rakshasa from the divine vengeance that was due to
him. To try to delay the judgement the gods had pronounced
on Kamsa for his many, many crimes on earth.

And he, Bana, was a part of those crimes. He deserved the
punishment of the gods almost as much as Kamsa did. For he

had done the evil overlord's bidding. And in doing so, he shared equal blame and responsibility.

But perhaps today, he would find some way to put right that long history of wrongdoing. If not redeem himself entirely, at least he might seek to balance the scales a little.

He turned his horse into a side alley. The roaring of the crowds was muffled by the close walls of the two houses that stood next to each other. Waiting in the alley was a man with his face cloaked despite the warmth of the day. He watched as Bana approached and dismounted at the point where the houses stood too close together to ride through.

Bana walked the rest of the way, admiring the choice of location for this tryst. Only one man could pass through at a time, that too slowly so as to ensure he didn't dislocate his shoulders. But then, Akrur was a clever man. Years of leading the Yadava rebellion against the Usurper had seasoned him into a shrewd and effective leader. In a way, Bana understood men like Akrur better than those like Vasudeva. He could never fathom Vasudeva's principles of self-denial and pacificism. How could you fight beings like Kamsa and Jarasandha without resorting to violence? He respected Vasudeva greatly, but felt that such times demanded men like Akrur.

He stopped at the place where the houses grew too close together to pass through. Akrur stood on the other side. Between them was a narrow gap large enough to see the other person, but not enough for a grown man to pass through, even slipping sideways. Bana wondered idly if the house builders had deliberately designed these residences to serve this very purpose. Why else would these walls curve this way?

'It is arranged,' he said curtly. 'All the men loyal to me in the Mathuran Army will lay down their arms and surrender to

Krishna if he defeats Kamsa in the tournament. It will be up to you and your supporters to ask for Krishna to be declared king.'

Akrur nodded. 'We will take care of our part. You take care of yours. What of those not loyal to you?'

Bana shrugged. 'Who can say? There may be some fighting. I'm sure you have the stomach for that.'

Akrur was silent a moment. 'If it is the only way, yes. How will my people know which soldiers are loyal to Krishna and which are not?'

'They will not. You will just have to wait and see the outcome.'

'What of the Mohini Fauj? There are very few of them but they are each deadlier than a dozen of your men.'

Bana bristled at the comparison but knew he could not argue the point. 'I cannot speak for them. Or for the Magadhan forces encamped within a day's ride from Mathura. If Jarasandha chooses to make his move and assert his claim on the city as an imperial holding, even our army and your militia combined will not be able to hold him back.'

Akrur frowned. It was his turn to bristle at the comparison. 'I think you overestimate the power of Magadha—'

'I think you underestimate it,' Bana cut him short curtly. He glanced back. 'I must return to my post. The procession will soon come this way. May our great ancestor Yadu look over you.'

Akrur said something that Bana ignored as he sidled carefully through the narrow gap, then strode back more confidently to where he had left his horse. He mounted the animal and turned its head, riding back to the street. From the approaching cacophony of dhol drums and trumpets and singing and chanting, he estimated that the procession would reach this place shortly.

It was then that he registered what Akrur had said in the end. *Yadu is dead.*

What had he meant by that? Yadu, their ancestor, founder of the Yadava nation, was dead? But surely he had died long ago, centuries earlier? Perhaps Bana was referring to the legend that Yadu was immortal, cursed with immortality, in fact, because he had refused his suffering father Yayati's request to exchange bodies with him. And that he could choose the day and time and place of his death. Did Bana mean that the real Yadu was here somewhere in Mathura and had chosen today itself to die? How ... strange! That was the only word that came to mind. He did not know if it could be called auspicious, for Yadu was a Pitr. But the choosing of this day and time suggested a larger meaning. Perhaps it was auspicious after all, or ominous. Only by the end of the day would he know for sure.

Bana sighed and returned the way he had come for the assignation, using his thighs to urge the horse up the sloping street.

It was time to ring in the Age of Krishna and ring out the Age of Kamsa. No matter what that transition might cost.

He gritted his teeth, remembering the sweet gurgling incomprehension on his sons' faces when he had killed them ... and the look on his beloved wife's face. He hoped to see a look akin to that when Kamsa died today.

For Kamsa would die, *must* die.

Or else all Mathura would die.

nine

They came walking at a steady pace up the avenue. Soldiers in full battle armour lined both sides of the raj-marg, keeping back the swelling crowds. At first, nobody recognized the two young men on foot. Nobody in Mathura knew what the Deliverer looked like in person. And the citizens of Mathura had been expecting a grand procession, a great vahan or carriage drawn by a magnificent horse team, festooned with jewels and bearing the colourful krita-dhvaja, not two adolescent boys walking briskly barefoot on the dusty road, clad in the simple vastras of Gokul govindas!

For this reason, they entered the city without any fanfare. It was only after they passed that the word rippled through the crowd. 'Akrur said they were coming on foot. That must be them!'

At once, the crowds ahead were alerted: 'Krishna and Balarama have entered Mathura! They are coming up the king's avenue!'

The crowd was enormous, the mood jubilant, the atmosphere electric with anticipation.

As Krishna and Balarama came around a curve in the road and were seen by the first groups of people who actually understood them to be the Deliverer and his brother, the response was immediate. A great roar went up, heard all across the city.

'*Krishna!*' shouted the people.

The soldiers fought to keep back the crowds. Only the presence of the elephants, horses, and an unwavering line of cruelly pointed spears and shields prevented the populace from surging forward. But for once, there was no eager wielding of spears or clubbing of heads as was usual: General Bana's instructions had been clear. The day would in all probability witness a regime change. The imperial army needed to prove that it was not hostile to this change. Or civil war would be a certainty and the army itself the first casualty.

Krishna and Balarama continued up the broad avenue, dust flying in their wake as they walked faster, not anxious about the crowds, merely eager to reach their destination and face their nemesis. They had come to settle a score and were eager to get to it.

Out of the press of people, a young man with a hunchbacked older woman came forward, clearly eager to have closer contact with Krishna. The bent woman was too stooped over to even look over the heads of the people in front. She might never have even seen Krishna, let alone come close to him, had someone in the crowd not started a scuffle with a guard which caused a horse to panic and the beast to lash out and kick at a soldier, knocking him down and injuring another soldier's shoulder. The guards next to them were forced to move aside to help in securing the panicked horse before it ran amok and excited the other animals.

As a result, for a few scant moments, a small gap in the line of spears was left unguarded. Just enough for an old woman to slip through – and she did.

She ran out onto the road, raising her hands in supplication. At once, an officer on horseback spotted her and barked an order. Immediately, half a dozen ready soldiers raised their weapons, prepared to wound the woman in order to force her to return to the crowd.

The old lady sensed the danger and cried out in alarm, raising her withered hands in despair. 'Krishna, help me!'

Krishna saw her plight and changed his direction. He strode to where the lady stood crouching and took her by the shoulders gently.

'Maa,' he said. 'You called for me?'

The soldiers on foot and the officer on horseback approached at once, ready to do whatever was needed to punish the woman for breaking the ranks of the crowd and to set an example. But Krishna raised a hand, not even bothering to look up, and they hesitated at once.

The legend of the Deliverer was a powerful one. And Kamsa's orders had been clear too: the young visitors were not to be touched or harmed in any way. They were to be brought directly to him, unmolested.

The officer barked a curt order and the soldiers kept their distance, watchful but making no further aggressive moves.

Krishna took the old woman's shoulders and raised her up gently.

Slowly, by degrees, the woman straightened up, up, up until she was standing normally, her back upright, her hunch dissipated. She looked around, feeling for her hunch with her hands by reaching around.

From behind her in the crowd, the young man who had been accompanying her exclaimed and reacted. 'It is a miracle! My mother's crooked back is cured!' Others around him agreed and shouted their amazement.

A cry rose from the crowd. 'Krishna cured the old woman's hunchback.'

Tears were streaming down the woman's face. 'My life's ambition is fulfilled,' she said. 'I have seen Hari with my own eyes.'

Krishna embraced her warmly. 'And he has embraced you, Mother. Go in peace.'

A great roar of approval rose from the crowd. The news travelled through the city: 'The Deliverer has performed his first miracle at Mathura!'

Suddenly, the mood changed. From ecstatic joy and cheering, the shouts of the crowd died away momentarily as everyone grew aware of some significant change or imminent threat.

Slowly, a new sound replaced the cheers: the pounding of heavy feet, approaching at a relentless pace.

It was accompanied by a shrill shrieking that only vaguely resembled an elephant's trumpeting.

An officer of the guard came galloping down the avenue, shouting to his fellow soldiers as he came. 'Airavata!' he cried. 'He is on the rampage.'

A loud cry of dismay rose from the crowd. 'Haddi-Hathi! He has gone mad at last. He will kill us all.'

People began to look at each other in confusion, unable to decide what to do. None wished to leave the sight of the Deliverer, yet all feared the dreaded mount of Kamsa, the bloodthirsty killer of so many of their brethren over the years. The battle elephant's kill score was only matched by that of his master, Kamsa.

Krishna raised his arms and spoke to the crowd, projecting his voice: 'Stay where you are. I shall deal with this threat.'

The crowd subsided at once. Everyone grew quiet as the loud pounding increased in volume and the mad elephant approached. Even the guards and their command officers stayed as far back as possible, one with the crowd in their fear of the dreaded elephant. For once maddened, Airavata did not care whether he crushed friendly or enemy skulls and bones. It was all the same to him.

Krishna spoke softly to Balarama who sighed but nodded and stepped aside.

Krishna stood alone in the centre of the wide open avenue in the morning sunshine, awaiting the arrival of his first challenger in Mathura.

ten

Radha was running alongside Nanda Maharaja's wagon when she saw Krishna standing in the middle of the avenue. She had been too excited to ride once they entered Mathura and had run from wagon to wagon, greeting each family and passing on messages. The crowds and buildings were overwhelming. Nothing in her rustic life in Gokuldham or Vrindavan had prepared her for such an experience. So many people gathered together in one place! Such magnificent buildings! She had been certain that the very first building she saw was the palace itself; she had been shocked to learn that it was only the gatehouse of the city! Since then, she had been seeing one extraordinary sight after the other.

But the only thing she truly longed to see was the sight of Krishna. She had been aching for him ever since he had gone away on Akrur's vahan. Every yard of the way, she had hoped they would catch up, even though she knew that a vahan travelled much too quickly for an uks cart to match, and they had started off hours later in any case. Still, she had hoped and prayed. After all, her heart did not care for the difference between the speed of an uks cart and a horse vahan. It only knew that it longed for Krishna.

She saw him now. And was overjoyed.

'*Krishna!*' she shouted. But her voice was drowned in the sudden roar of the crowd. The roaring had a peculiar tone to it.

It was not the overjoyed happy cheering to greet the arrival of the Deliverer that she had heard until now. This was ominous, frightened almost.

Then she realized that the crowd wasn't cheering Krishna's arrival, it was cheering him on.

He was about to face some enemy.

Radha had seen enough of Krishna's fights with asuras to know when Krishna was under attack again. The only difference was that this time it was taking place in Mathura city, not the hamlet of Vrindavan. And there were great numbers of people standing by and watching.

Good, she thought, *they will see the strength and wit of my beloved as he faces this new challenge.*

But another part of her, the same part that could not tell the difference between an uks cart and a vahan, cried out silently. *Krishna! Take care, my love!*

Both parts of Radha collided, even as Krishna and Haddi-Hathi rammed into each other.

It was a giant among elephants, he saw, a great white beast.

It was old too, its eyes rheumy and heavily wrinkled. Its hide was scored in a hundred places with scars of old battles in which it had fought: spear marks, lance scratches, sword cuts, javelin holes, arrow punctures … it was impressive that the beast still lived, let alone the fact that it had such energy and strength.

It moved with the ponderous gait of a heavy beast, and Krishna estimated it must weigh twice or thrice as much as most local bull elephants. Its enormous ears flapped like the fans held by royal servants serving a king. Its eyes were red and blazing with feverish rage, its mouth slobbering, its enormous tusks yellowed with age but still whole, still sharp enough to gore and kill.

Several Mathuran imperial guards followed in its wake, trying to subjugate it but failed, and as he watched, the beast turned its head disdainfully and gored another one, the poor man crying out as he was impaled on one deadly tusk, then trampled underfoot as the elephant freed itself of his body. He lay in the dust of the avenue, bleeding out pitifully.

It had already killed several others, he saw. Their blood was smeared on its tusks and armour. The shield itself was designed to drive fear into the hearts of the enemy and bristled with sharp jagged metal points and edges. Clearly, even friendly soldiers must stay far from this beast during battle, or else they risked inadvertently being cut to ribbons thanks to its armour. Krishna could easily imagine Kamsa riding atop this monster, matching its destructive power with his own killing rage. And being Krishna, in a flash, he saw the entire life history of the beast pass through his consciousness, every act it had committed since leaving its mother cow elephant's womb decades ago.

Airavata raised his trunk and trumpeted at the sight of Krishna approaching. The sound rang out across the city like a war horn announcing the start of battle. The immense crowds that had thronged the streets to greet the procession had fallen silent as news of the mad elephant travelled through the city. Krishna knew that people were watching from behind him, and would pass on every detail of what happened next, to be spread by word of mouth like wildfire.

Haddi-Hathi reared up and thudded back to earth with a force that even Krishna felt, dozens of yards away. It made the ground underfoot shake, and plaster dust fall from the walls of the buildings on either side of the avenue. With the crowds on either side, he could not afford to tempt the animal into turning head, for it would then rampage through the people and cause terrible casualties.

Krishna had to either come forward and face the elephant or turn back and be seen retreating.

There was no question of retreating.

He came forward slowly, walking as if he were walking in Vrindavan by the lake, along the pastures, overseeing his father's herd.

The elephant trumpeted its displeasure at this insolence, lowered its head, and charged.

Krishna paused and faced the elephant. Behind him, he could hear Radha's cry, as well as the voices of Yashoda and his aunts and uncles all voicing their concern. He had known they had arrived long before Radha had set eyes on him. He knew their concern was not entirely misplaced.

After all, even if he was a god and would eventually triumph, he did feel pain and trauma, and more than once in his battles with asuras had he come close to having his mortal form destroyed. Everyone understood this now and knew that 'invulnerable' was only a word used by those ignorant of the laws of nature. All that is born must die. All that is created can be destroyed.

Haddi-Hathi bellowed like a bull as it charged, head lowered, to aim its deadly tusks at man-level. Its feet pounded the dirt road, raising a cloud of dust. Its fury was prodigious. It meant to kill or be killed; there was no mistaking that fact.

Krishna did not budge. He stood his ground and let the elephant charge directly at him. Every pair of eyes in Mathura was watching. It was important to send a message loud and clear: Krishna would not be intimidated or turn away from threat. He was here to take a stand.

The elephant's pounding caused the ground to shudder as if in the grip of an earthquake. The great white body loomed in front of him, moving at the speed of a horse's fastest gallop, and those massive deadly tusks were pointed straight at his belly and vitals.

Man and beast met in a head-on collision.

eleven

Radha suppressed a scream by stuffing her fist into her open mouth. She bit down on the knuckle hard enough to draw blood. In the wagon beside her, Yashoda and Krishna's aunts reacted in similar ways. All down the road, those watching reacted as well, shaken by the sight of a man standing still before a charging elephant – then at the sight of that elephant colliding with the man.

She watched as the great white bull elephant rammed straight into Krishna with all the strength and power it could muster.

And nothing happened.

Krishna remained standing exactly where he was. He did not budge an inch, not even when one of the elephant's tusks struck his abdomen with force enough to punch through a solid brick wall. Instead, the tusk broke off with a resounding crack that could be heard several streets away. People exclaimed in astonishment.

The elephant's body shuddered at the impact, as if it had indeed struck a brick wall, but one so thick that even its formidable weight and power in that headlong rush could not overcome. It uttered a bleating sound, almost like a dog's yelp, and backed away, shaking its head and rolling its eyes. It was stunned by the collision. Nothing in its long life had prepared it for such an experience. To charge at a mere man and to meet resistance greater than a stone wall was not something it had expected or knew how to deal with.

After a moment, it turned around on its four legs, clearly too stunned to walk straight, then sat down on its hind legs as it bleated again. The loss of its tusk had evidently caused it some distress for it kept rolling its head and waving its trunk around, seeking out the missing trunk.

The trunk itself was in Krishna's hands. He held it up for the elephant to see. It had snapped off cleanly almost at the point where the root emerged from the elephant's body. Barely a few inches of its base were left on the animal. The entire length of it, all one dozen or more feet of ivory tusk as thick as a wrestler's thigh, lay in Krishna's hands.

Krishna waved the tusk, showing the elephant that he now possessed a part of its body.

The elephant remained seated on its hind legs, resembling a dog that had received a sudden blow to the tip of its nose. Its eyes watered profusely, issuing a whitish gummy substance that Radha thought might be masth or something similar.

Krishna stepped forward, walking over to where the elephant sat. Radha held her breath as she watched. The elephant reacted at once. Seeing its intended prey still alive, still hale and hearty, approaching, it rose up, shaking off the stupefaction that had overcome it, trumpeted once again, although nowhere near as confidently as before, and reared up on its hind legs, bringing the mighty forelegs and the weight of its upper body down on Krishna with bone-powdering force.

Krishna raised a hand and took the weight of one elephant foot entirely on that hand.

The elephant's foot bent and broke.

The sound was unmistakable, the sight awe-inspiring.

The elephant bleated in distress, then fell back at once, breathing heavily.

It hobbled on three feet, trying to put the fourth foot down and bleating at the pain.

Krishna looked up at the elephant and spoke. Radha was too far away to hear what he said clearly, but it sounded more like a gentle conversation rather than an angry threat. What could Krishna possibly be saying to the elephant?

After a moment, the elephant trumpeted at Krishna, clearly rejecting his offer. It attempted to use its trunk to strike at him, then waved its head to try to stab him with the other whole tusk.

Krishna stood his ground, neither avoiding nor fending off the blows. This went on for several more moments, during which the elephant forced itself to overcome the agony of the injured foot and stomped about on all fours again, trying its best to smash, crush, gore and harm Krishna in every way possible.

Krishna smelt the madness in the Haddi-Hathi's blood and sweat and knew that the creature was in great torment. He reached out a hand, not actually touching its hide but making a stroking movement to show he meant no harm.

'I know you,' he said softly. 'Your true name is Kuvalayapida. You were reborn in this form to serve Kamsa against your will. Your rage and violent temperament stem from your desire to be killed quickly and be rid of this chore you did not desire.'

The elephant listened with suspicion in its eyes.

'He treats you cruelly, so that you may treat his enemies cruelly as well. That is a tyrant's way, the asura way. Even though you are an asura now, you were not one always. You resent being forced to enact this violent behaviour. You seek to return to your old peaceful way of life. Like an elephant in the wild, you are not violent in spirit, and seek only to feed and love and live out your life in serenity. I can free you from this cycle of misery. I can liberate your soul so you will return to the great grasslands of your true home. Is this what you desire?'

The elephant had raised his trunk and curled it, reaching out with it to sniff at Krishna's face. He poked at Krishna, letting out a blast of rancid breath. Krishna didn't wince or grimace, though the smell was awful. He knew this was Haddi-Hathi's way of replying in the affirmative.

'Then rise up and attack me one last time so that you may die with honour in this life. Attack me with all your might and prepare to be liberated from the cycle of birth, death and rebirth forever.'

At once, the great white bull rose up, standing on all fours as if his injury did not matter, and attacked again.

As he had done before, Krishna permitted the beast to strike at him several times, then, when the opportune moment came, he raised the elephant's own broken tusk and stabbed it beneath the forelegs, hard enough to punch through the tough hide and formidable breastplate, piercing its ageing heart. The animal released a sigh of deep relief, then sank to the ground, blood spreading from its fatal wound and dampening the dust. It lay down on its side and died in moments, eyes turned to Krishna in baleful apology.

'I understand,' Krishna said. 'You are forgiven for all the lives you destroyed. Now go. Get moksha and be free eternally.'

The elephant's trunk curled weakly around Krishna's wrist, releasing one final puff of rancid air. Then it lay still.

Krishna turned and raised his hands in the universal gesture of triumph. He did so with no desire for self-aggrandizement or glory. It was necessary to let the people see and know that the Deliverer they had awaited so long was real and effective. That he was here and ready to fight. And that they had a chance at last to free themselves of tyranny. If nothing else, it would compel them to focus their energy on letting him deal with the day's challenges rather than take matters into their own hands. The situation in Mathura was volatile and could explode into civil violence at any instant. Krishna wanted to let the citizens know that he could and would resolve the problem of Kamsa on his own.

The immense roar of jubilation and support he received told him that he had accomplished one part of the challenge. He had won the people's approbation and trust.

Now all he had to do was kill Kamsa.

twelve

Mathura held its breath as Krishna entered the wrestling grounds on foot. Even now, after the news of Haddi-Hathi's defeat, the miraculous cure of old Ambavati the hunchback and numerous other stories of his fantastical feats in Vrindavan, Vraj and even earlier, there were many who wondered if this slight, short, dark-skinned cowherd could in fact be the Slayer of Kamsa. How was it possible? This slip of a boy who had never held anything but a govinda's crook was weaned on curds and buttermilk, and had spent his youthful years idling in the hills and fields, romancing gopis and playing at ras-lila … could he truly be the Deliverer? The one to end Kamsa's tyranny and free Mathura of the yoke of formidable foreign powers like Jarasandha? It seemed unlikely and the sceptical could be forgiven for doubting.

Yet there was no mistaking the easy, confident gait with which the boy from Gokuldham walked into the wrestling field. He did not have the overconfident muscled swagger of the typical mud wrestler, nor the cocky belligerence of the soldier bully accustomed to using his strength and force to get his way. In fact, he was a type never seen before: a young slender lover with a sweet smile that he flashed readily, even directing it at the royal tent where Jarasandha and Kamsa and their allies and champions sat in shaded luxury. He sauntered in as if he were there for a game of marbles rather than a champion bout with the most fearsome demon lord of this part of the world.

The lad even had the audacity to raise his hand, wave and grin at Kamsa's tent! Titters of nervous laughter broke out when he did this, some within the royal tent itself. Nobody had ever seen a wrestler with such a carefree attitude. It was unheard of. And clearly, it was no act, for the boy continued to wave and grin at all assembled in the field, the cream of Mathuran nobility and power brokers, the rich, beautiful, powerful and privileged. This ill-clad boy with little dusty feet, waving at them as if he were their prince returned to claim this crown!

And what was that tucked into the waistband of his dhoti? Could it possibly be what it looked like? A flute?

Yes. A shepherd's flute. The kind that govindas played in the wide sprawling meadows of Vraj so that their herds would not stray too far away, the sound itself shepherding them homewards at dusk.

What sort of wrestler carried a flute?

The crowd assembled in the arena did not know what to make of this purported Deliverer, the legendary Slayer of Kamsa, the alleged eighth child of Devaki and Vasudeva, raised in secret in the distant village of Gokul by Nanda and Yashoda. But in their hearts, each and every one of them hoped and prayed that they were wrong, that this flute-playing, slender-hipped cowherd was everything the prophecy said he would be, that he would be able to somehow face and fight Kamsa, and by some miraculous means, overcome him. For the alternative was too terrible to contemplate.

To the Vrishnis, assembling now in the large roped pavilion reserved for them, the mood was more sombre. They did not doubt or question Krishna's ability, merely that of his opponent.

For Kamsa's great powers were well known. And those who had witnessed first-hand the encounters between Krishna and some of the deadlier asuras knew that while his spirit was certainly divine, his body was still flesh and blood and subject to the vagaries of mortal failings. He could be destroyed, perhaps even defeated.

And today, if he died, he would not die alone. The whole clan would die as well. Nobody doubted that. The very manner in which they were placed – seated prominently with an excellent view of the wrestling akhada, but surrounded on all sides by enemy champions, wrestlers and the Mohini Fauj Hijras – seemed pre-planned. They were cleverly hemmed in.

They knew that the instant the fight ended, if the outcome was against their interests, they would be massacred without hesitation. They had been compelled to leave all weapons and potential weapons outside the gates of the city on the pretext that it was a friendly match. But the simple village folk saw now that everyone else appeared to be carrying arms, some discreetly, others openly. No doubt, the pretext was that Magadhans had to carry arms to protect themselves from potential attackers, and that Kamsa's guards had to bear arms to defend their king in case of assault.

Whatever the flimsy reasons, the fact was that the Vrishnis were boxed in, unarmed, and defenceless against attack. Even knowing that the imperial army would aid them if they had to flee was no comfort. For the imperial army was spread throughout the city, while they were alone in the arena. If they were attacked by Kamsa and his allies, even General Bana and his soldiers could not reach in time to save them.

To add fuel to the fire, the leaders and chiefs of all the main tribes and clans in the Vrishni line were present, including

several who had been banished, banned or exiled. There were
Vasudeva and Devaki who were seated beside Nanda and
Yashoda in the front row, as were Akrur and the rest of his
captains of the once secret rebellion: Brihadbala, now the
spitting image of his father; Chitraketu, chief of the Kannars;
Uddhava; Satvata; and even the old and decrepit Kratha,
leaning heavily on his crook and peering through rheumy eyes,
determined to be present with the rest of the sangha to witness
the most fateful event in the history of their race to date.

The only chance they had lay with Krishna and Balarama.
Only those boys could save them now. By fighting and laying
down their own lives, or by triumphing and defeating Kamsa
and his champions.

The conch shells sounded, announcing the imminent start of
the first bout. Soon, the judgement would be pronounced on all
Vrishnis. Live. Or die. It was out of their hands now.

thirteen

Kamsa laughed as Krishna strolled about the field, smiling and waving at everyone. 'I will crush him before he knows what has happened,' he said to Jarasandha conversationally as his aides massaged his body with oil.

Jarasandha affected a hint of a smile. 'I wish you would,' he said. 'But do not underestimate him. He did despatch all our assassins, starting with your great hope, Putana.'

At the mention of Putana in such a tone, Kamsa's smile vanished. Had it been anyone else, he would have killed the man instantly for daring to speak thus of his lost friend. But since it was Jarasandha, he only let his pique show in the tartness of his response: 'I think it's you who underestimate me, Father dearest. As you always have.'

Jarasandha turned and glanced at Kamsa. He had a gleam in his eye. The tip of his tongue flickered briefly between his lips. 'That, I do not deny. But you've mostly given me cause to do so. I am hoping that today you will prove me wrong once and for all. Defeat the great Deliverer of the Vrishnis, and I will declare you emperor-in-waiting of all my domains.'

Kamsa was struck silent. He had not expected such an offer. Jarasandha was not a generous man. For him to offer such a proposal meant that he was deadly serious. It also meant that he wanted Kamsa to win very badly, or he would not dangle such an enticing reward. 'Emperor-in-waiting,' he said slowly. 'That means that after you die …'

Jarasandha chuckled. 'In the *event*, unlikely as it may be, of my demise, yes, you will be crowned emperor in my stead. That is precisely what it means.'

Kamsa stared at Jarasandha. Nobody had ever showed such generosity to him. He took hold of Jarasandha's hand and kissed it. 'I will not fail you today, Father. You will be proud of me.'

Jarasandha nodded. 'It would give me great pleasure to see you break the back of that little cowherd. Nothing else would give me such great pleasure, I have to admit.' He hesitated, glancing across the field at the slight figure still making its way around the pavilions. 'Something about the very sight of him turns my stomach. For the first time in my life, I find I have no appetite. He makes me sick, this so-called Deliverer! Crush him, break him, twist him like a rope, tear him apart into shreds, crack him open like a betel nut, grind him like a whetstone, cut him like a rusty blade … do what you will, but do not let him walk off that akhada alive. And in return, you will have of me whatever you desire, for as long as you desire it. And all that I possess shall be yours.'

Kamsa nodded grimly. 'It shall be done.'

He was about to say something else when suddenly all those assembled in his pavilion began to mutter and laugh.

'What is it?' he asked, looking around. He saw Jarasandha staring too, his thin eyes narrowing to slits as he saw something that did not please him.

Then he heard the sound of the music. A simple reed instrument.

Krishna was playing his flute.

Akrur shook his head in delight as Krishna played his flute, walking around the field as if he owned it, then took up a stance with one foot crossed over the other one, arms crossed as well, head tilted just so, flute applied to the side of his mouth, a perpetual smile playing on his handsome dark face, and played a song sweeter than any that had been heard before.

'Truly he is the Lord of Lords,' he said to himself. 'Who else would dare come to a house of swords armed with a flute!'

He saw the reaction in the royal pavilion, saw Jarasandha and Kamsa glaring, exchanging words that left no doubt about their agitation.

Devaki leaned forward, speaking across Vasudeva who sat between them. 'My lord Akrur, why do you laugh and mutter to yourself?'

Akrur smiled sheepishly. 'My lady Devaki, I confess that until this morning, I did not truly understand the power of your son. But a vision was unveiled to me that showed me how little I knew. Now I gape in wonderment at his every gesture, see mischief in his every action. It is a great delight to watch him toy thus with the demon Usurper before they fight. Never before have Kamsa and Jarasandha been treated in this fashion by even their most powerful opponents and enemies. Yet there is Krishna, a mere cowherd boy, embarrassing them in front of all of Mathura. It is a sight to behold!'

Devaki smiled faintly, her eyes filled with tears of an unnameable emotion. She looked at Vasudeva who took her hand and squeezed it comfortingly. Vasudeva turned to Akrur. 'I hope he knows what he is doing.'

Akrur nodded. 'I am quite certain he does.'

He saw an aide leave the royal pavilion and walk towards the Vrishni pavilion, clearly despatched with a message to deliver. The man seemed somewhat confused about whom to approach. Unlike his masters, the Vrishnis did not have a simple hierarchy: every chieftain was king in a manner of speaking. Technically, Vasudeva was still king and representative of the sangha, but it had been so long since he had been able to represent his people at any formal event that the very courtiers of Mathura, like this aide, had all but forgotten him. Akrur stood up and motioned the man forward. He came with evident relief and spoke his message to Akrur.

Akrur turned to the others, who were wide-eyed and expectant. 'The matches for the tournament have been announced,' he said. 'The team for the royals versus our best champions.'

They had been asked to submit the names of their fighters earlier.

As the names were declared, many anxious looks were exchanged. Old Kratha began to rise, trying to raise his crook to wave it in protest, but Brihadbala stopped him and calmed him down.

'It is an outrage,' Kratha still managed to blurt out, his words slurred by age and palsy. 'They have pitted their strongest, most experienced and renowned fighters against two young boys. How can Krishna and Balarama alone fight so many champions at once?'

Akrur shrugged. 'It is how it must be, they say. They have the right to call the draw. And to be quite fair, it was we who put forth just two names.'

'Why?' asked someone else. 'Why not a whole team?'

'Because we chose to make it so,' Balarama said, coming up to the pavilion. 'Even our greatest wrestlers do not stand a chance against their fighters. They are not human any more; they possess supernatural shakti. To fight them will require superhuman skill as well. Therefore Krishna insisted that he and I alone represent our side.'

Everyone was silent. Nobody knew what to say. There was little to be said.

The conch shell announcing the start of the tournament sounded. It was time for the Slayer of Kamsa and the Childslayer to face each other.

fourteen

Kamsa slapped his thighs and rubbed his palms over his well-oiled body. He raised his hand, rubbing the excess oil on his finely twirled moustache, stroking the ends till they extended far outwards from his face. The crowd had been roaring like an ocean near a rocky shore, then had suddenly fallen silent. A deathly quiet had come over the arena. Nobody spoke a word. Even Jarasandha, watching from the front row on Kamsa's side, did not smile his usual half-smile. The Hijras flanking him on either side were as impassive as ever.

On the Vrishni side, though, there were visible emotions on display. Kamsa was pleased to see the obvious concern and anxiety on the faces of Krishna's adoptive mother and father and other relatives. And there was that young girl who had shown unsisterly affection for him earlier, fussing and cooing around him. Who was she? A pretty young thing, she was. She almost made him wish they were playing for spoils as was often the case in Jarasandha's wrestling tournaments. Winner takes all: wealth, women, wine, wheat. Then again, he remembered, he was Lord of Mathura. If he won, he would take everything the Vrishnis possessed, beginning with the lives of Krishna's entire extended family, down to the last remote cousin and his dogs and dogs' whelps. Not one would be spared. So that pretty young girl was as good as his, if he desired her.

But that was a matter for later.

Right now, he had a fight to win. And a Slayer to slay.

Kamsa slapped his own chest and stood up in his corner of the wrestling rectangle, taking up a stance, legs apart, arms open wide, welcoming. He felt better than he had in his entire life. He was stronger than he had ever imagined he could become. He felt indomitable, indestructible, invulnerable. He was certain of victory. What remained were the details: how he would maim and make his opponent suffer before finally killing him, how he would deliver the ultimate killing blow. He had thought of a myriad ways, any one of which would be agonizing and cause the strongest-willed men to die screaming and voiding their bowels as they departed this world. He had used every one of those holds and blows umpteen times. This would be the first occasion when he did so to a god.

He imagined it would not be very different. After all he was not much less than a god himself, Jarasandha had repeatedly assured him. Nobody could withstand him now. Certainly not this slip of a boy, his body so slender, his arms and legs so lean, no visible slabs of muscle, no excess padding, nothing to cushion the opponent's blows or provide strength for the powerful holds and grips and blows that were essential to victory in this rectangle.

Krishna looked so out of place in this wrestling ring, it was difficult to believe that this was the purported Slayer. The one Kamsa had been dreading for twenty-three years. The foretold Deliverer of the Yadava people!

He moved forward, ready to prove the prophecy wrong.

Radha watched wide-eyed as Kamsa and his team took the field. 'Dear Sri in vaikuntha,' she said softly, pressing her hand to her mouth, 'they are not men, they are giants made of stone and iron!'

As Chanura, Mustika, Kamsa and the others entered the akhara, their captain gave them terse instructions. 'Let's make this quick and brutal. Mustika, you go for Balarama. Chanura, you take care of Krishna.'

Mustika, who was not known for his agility of thought, frowned at the two boys at the far side of the playing field, his famous crooked jaw which had earned him his nickname jerking to and fro as he tried to guess. 'Which is which?'

Chanura slapped him on the shoulder. The impact was loud enough to rival a small thunderclap. 'The fair one's Balarama, the dark-skinned lad's Krishna.'

'Don't worry, Crooked Jaw,' Sala called out. 'If you have difficulty grabbing hold of the slippery bugger, I'll trip him over and sit on him till you come get him.'

Tosalaka snorted. 'Sala, if you sit on him, there won't be anything left for Mustika to get.'

'Childslayer,' said Kuta scornfully, 'I thought you said this would be a fun fight. From the look of these children, it'll be over before I have time to fart.'

Kamsa shook his head at the widest man imaginable, almost a full yard wide at the chest – and almost as wide the rest of his body. 'Kuta, your farts alone are enough to kill them both. Maybe we should all retire and leave you to it, huh?'

Everyone laughed.

'All right, now. Let's warm up,' Kamsa said.

'What's the point?' Mustika asked. 'This fight will be over in less time than the warm-up!'

'Tradition,' Kamsa said. 'We have to give the crowd what it expects. We are champions of the sport.'

Mustika shrugged. In the centre of their side of the field, aides had set up chopping blocks. Each block was a solid yard-thick chunk of lohit wood, the famed ironwood that grew in the forested region between Ayodhya and Mithila. Sharp axes could barely drive a dent in lohit wood. The aides had set three chopping blocks on top of each other.

Mustika raised a hand and brought it down in a chopping action on the topmost block. With a sound like a twig snapping, all three blocks lay cracked and broken into pieces.

Mustika raised the hand he had used, waving it sideways to show it was empty. The crowd roared with approval, cheering him on.

While the rest of the city might have been filled with citizens eager to sight the Deliverer, there was little doubt about the composition of the crowd in the playing field itself – apart from the Vrishni contingent, they were all loyal to Kamsa.

There were many other items ready for the display of strength by Kamsa's team. The Vrishni fighters had declined to give any such demonstration.

Radha had heard most of the banter between Kamsa and his men and it chilled her heart. Still, she could have dismissed it as mere bragging. But when she saw the demonstrations, she knew that it was much more than just talk.

She leapt over the side of the pavilion that kept spectators from the playing field and ran to the sidelines. Nobody bothered to stop her. Kamsa had seen no reason to place security around what was essentially a field of battle now. He had no reason to fear any attack on himself or his team – and if anyone wished

to harm Krishna and Balarama in the brief time they had left
before dying, they were quite welcome to do so!

Radha came to a halt near Krishna. He was standing in a
relaxed posture, waiting for the match to begin.

'Krishna,' she said, trying to attract his attention.

He turned and frowned at her. 'Radhey? You should not be
here. It is not safe for you.'

'You must stop this fight. It is not a fair fight. Those men
are super beings of some sort. They mean to crush you and
Balarama the way they are crushing those wooden blocks and
metal bars and other things.'

Krishna nodded. 'What you say is true.'

'Then stop the fight. You have ample grounds for objection.'

'Such as?'

'There are only two of you against so many of them.'

'They have said that they will ensure that only one of their
fighters engages one of our fighters in each round. It will be a
man-to-man bout.'

Radha shook her head impatiently. 'Even so, you are only
boys. They are great big men, experienced fighters.'

Krishna smiled. 'Balarama and I are grown men in terms of
age. We are entitled to the same rights as any of them. Besides,
Radha, we have fought our share of opponents too, remember?
We can hardly claim lack of experience!'

'Then say the truth: they are not merely men. They are
demons. Beasts!'

Krishna shook his head. 'All of Mathura saw me fighting
and slaying one of the most feared animals in the land. The
dreaded Haddi-Hathi himself. Single-handedly, unarmed. On
what grounds can I make such a claim? Besides, this is what
it is, Radha. Ever since time immemorial, this is how it has

always been. Many against few. Strong against the apparently weak. Powerful against the disempowered. Rich against poor. High caste against low caste. Upper class against the masses. That is what society has always done: separated, divided, put us into different categories and ranks. I wish to end that. And the only way is to do it by proving that even I, a boy, a cowherd, a Vrishni, can confront and best the most powerful demon king of our age. Go back to the pavilion, Radha. I have work to do. This is my dharma.'

Radha stared at him for a long moment.

The conch shells blew again, announcing the imminent bout.

She backed away wordlessly, then ran back to the pavilion and resumed her seat. Krishna had said everything there was to be said. All she could do now was watch and pray.

fifteen

The tournament began with the tossing of a dice to decide who would start first. Kamsa's team won the toss and chose to defend.

'All right, Chanura,' Kamsa said, 'now remember, you are to take him alone. The rest of us have to stay out of the way. Those are the rules. Man-to-man.'

Chanura snorted. 'You mean man-to-child! This isn't a fight. It's a massacre!'

The final conch shell sounded. A hushed silence fell across the vast field. Outside the arena, across Mathura, the crowds that still thronged the streets, filled the houses and courtyards and even camped by the riverbank waiting for word, all fell silent, waiting to hear what happened next. Even the birds hovered overhead, watching the field below, like carrion birds over a battlefield. The animals in the woods, the insects of the earth, the fish in the river, all seemed alert and expectant, awaiting the next several moments.

Krishna started forward, crossing the line even as he said aloud, 'Gokula!' Then he turned the word into a chant recited constantly in order to show that he was not taking a second breath. 'Gokula-Gokula-Gokula-Gokula-Gokula,' he muttered as he entered the enemy side of the field.

The quadrant was guarded by a team of sixteen men. But as per the rules agreed upon, only one man could engage Krishna at a time. Therefore Krishna entered the chalk-marked rectangle in which Chanura stood waiting. The others could engage him only if and when Krishna got past Chanura. Mustika was guarding the rectangle right behind Chanura's, and from the snarl on his disjointed face, he looked as if he wished Krishna would somehow slip past and come to him.

Chanura was wearing a garland of flowers that some woman had hung around his neck. He was enjoying the cloying sweet scent of the flowers and thinking of the woman and how he could put his arms around her neck afterwards and make himself a garland for her! He watched Krishna approach with derision, unable to believe that this stripling of a boy even had the temerity to stand face-to-face with him.

Krishna approached Chanura, making no effort to sidestep, dodge, avoid, or any of the usual tactics employed by players in the sport. It was obvious that he had either never played the game before or did not care for its rules. All he did was walk right up to Chanura, muttering his chant softly.

Under the rules of man-to-man, the players could stop chanting when they were physically engaged with each other: this was to permit the man-to-man bouts to continue until defeat, not merely out of consideration for depletion of breath. But until Krishna touched or otherwise engaged an opponent, he had to keep chanting or he would be disqualified.

Chanura hoped the boy wasn't careless enough to make such a mistake. He wanted to beat the boy, but not by a technical fault.

He wanted to break him into two halves over his knee!

As Krishna came within reach, Chanura spread his arms and grabbed hold of him. He had once uprooted a lohit wood tree this way, by grasping it and yanking it upwards in a single motion. Then he had thrown it two score yards away, at an oncoming enemy battalion, wiping out most of the battalion in one blow. After that, he had used the uprooted tree as a club to smash the rest of the enemy.

He grasped hold of Krishna and squeezed.

'Ho, boy,' he said, grinning. 'I hope you drank plenty of your mother's breast milk this morning, for I mean to squeeze every last drop out of you and drink it myself now!'

Krishna stared back at him impassively. 'Really? In that case, you need to use more strength. The force you're using wouldn't squeeze milk out of a pregnant cow's teat!'

Chanura lost his smile. It was true he was exerting just a little force, barely sufficient to crush a body and break the bones. That was because he wanted Krishna to suffer, to cry out in agony and scream as he died, not simply burst like a crushed grape.

But Krishna's body wasn't yielding as most others did. This much force should have shattered even the most powerfully muscled man's backbone and ribs and caused blood to spurt out of his mouth and other orifices.

Krishna was merely standing there, arms spread apart, a disdain writ large on this face, as if wanting a smelly hug to get over.

'That's a pretty garland you have there,' he said conversationally. 'Did you mean to give it to me after you're done hugging?'

Chanura roared with anger and squeezed with all his force. He forgot about his intention to squeeze slowly and make Krishna cry out in agony. He squeezed hard enough to crush a tree trunk into powder.

Still, Krishna just stood there, looking unimpressed.

Chanura blinked and released his hold. He opened his mouth, taking in a fresh breath himself. He stared at Krishna in disbelief. 'I used all my strength. You can't still be standing! That's impossible.'

Krishna cocked an eyebrow, then waggled both brows. 'Really? Maybe you didn't do it right. Here, let me show you how it's done.'

He sang out gaily, 'My turn!' and took hold of Chanura in the exact same grip, squeezing hard.

Chanura gasped, then screamed. Then he felt as if his spine were melding with his ribs, and his ribs being forced inwards to pierce his lungs, and his arms getting bent in a way that they could touch each other – through his torso. It was excruciating. He had never felt anything like this before. Was this how his opponents felt when he crushed them in his grip? Was this what it felt like for a tree to be crushed? It was unbelievably painful. He blacked out and lost consciousness for a moment.

When he regained his senses, he was lying on the ground, in the dust, the afternoon sun piercing his eyes, a thumping pain battering his chest.

Krishna was grinning down at him. 'Enough?' he asked, chuckling. 'Or would you like me to show you again?'

Chanura roared with rage and kicked out at Krishna's lower abdomen, striking his enemy's softest part with the hardest part of his own body, his heel. He felt the heel strike home, and expected it to rip through Krishna's body and emerge from out of his back as usually happened.

Instead, he felt his own heel shatter, the bone get crushed and fragmented, and the shards being sent back into his own flesh. His roar of rage turned to a whimper of agony. He yowled again.

Krishna pounced on him, grabbing him with both hands. The boy's teeth suddenly flashed bright white in his dark face, predatory and menacing.

'I like your garland, my friend,' he said. 'Let me pick some of the flowers.' Krishna reached out and snatched a flower from the garland, tearing it out of the string and holding it up. He pressed it between his fingers and smelt the pressed petals. Even Chanura could smell the fragrant scent of the marigold blossom. 'So refreshing, isn't it?' Krishna asked. 'And so soft and gentle and easy to take apart, petal by petal. The way you took apart hundreds of opponents, using your superior shakti to cheat them of a fair fight, using superhuman strength against ordinary brave warriors.'

Chanura snarled and struck hard at Krishna's elbows with the strength of desperation. He hoped to crack the bone and cartilage there, disabling his opponent. It had worked on another strongman who was as empowered as himself. With both hands broken and dangling from the elbows, the man had hardly fought back. Chanura had then proceeded to make mincemeat of him.

Krishna reached up and rubbed his elbows at once, making a face in reaction.

Chanura grinned, pleased at his own presence of mind. So! The invulnerable Deliverer had a weak spot after all. Two of them, in fact! Now it would be easy to turn the tables. Even with a shattered heel, he could take care of this slip of a lad on his own.

Krishna dropped his arms and grinned. 'Just fooling you!' he said, moving his arms to show that his elbows were fine. 'Now where were we?' he said, frowning, then remembered. 'Ah, yes, flowers.'

He reached down. 'I was saying, it would be quite fitting, given the way you made so many of your opponents suffer in the past, to treat you like this garland of flowers and take you apart, piece by piece. What do you think?'

Chanura kicked out and struck out blindly, roaring and fighting as hard as he could, knowing now that this was his last chance, that he was indeed fighting for his life.

His blows battered a body as hard and invulnerable as he had once believed his own to be. They had no effect. Or if they did – for he did see Krishna grimace once or twice – then his opponent must possess the ability to knit broken bones together at once, or some such miracle. For Krishna took everything Chanura had and more.

Finally, it was Chanura himself who gave up, ceasing his rain of blows and kicks, sobbing with exhaustion and fear. 'Spare me,' he cried out, weeping openly, not caring that everyone was witness to his humiliation. 'Mercy, Lord, mercy!'

'Of course,' Krishna replied, 'the same mercy you showed all those who begged you for it. Once for each life you destroyed.'

And Krishna reached out and plucked the flowers of Chanura's life, one by one, piece by separate piece, tearing them out as easily as he had plucked the marigold blossom from the garland around Chanura's neck.

sixteen

Balarama felt each blow that fell on Krishna's body as if it had struck his own. He felt the pain of impact, the agony of tearing tissue, muscle, tendon, the excruciating pain of broken bone, cracked cartilage, everything. It was no less than if Chanura had been striking him. In a sense, it was worse because while Krishna could feel anger in response and act on that anger, Balarama was standing on the field and was forced to watch without acting. He could not violate the rules of the game. It was vital that they played this out exactly as Kamsa dictated and still triumphed. It was not enough merely to win, but to win fair and square. That was dharma.

But when Chanura lashed out mercilessly at Krishna, Balarama was hard-pressed to keep dharma aside and go to his brother's aid. For the sheer agony of the blows was unbearable. How was Krishna tolerating it? The same way he had tolerated the attacks and blows and bites of asuras in the past. By enduring, knowing that his super-mortal divinity would repair his mortal flesh and bone, restore it in moments to its former state of perfect vigour and health. It was only the pain he must endure and survive. Although to call it 'only' the pain was wrong. For there were times in battle when the pain of the wound was worse than the wound itself. If Balarama felt such pain, how much worse must Krishna himself be feeling?

Still, Balarama had no choice. He stood his ground and

gritted his teeth discreetly as he watched his brother take the blows of his opponent despite having the ability to despatch the man in the first strike or two. He knew that Krishna was deliberately giving him fair chance to fight back so that all would see and know that the game had been played fairly and squarely. Such was dharma, such its demands.

Now he watched as Krishna finally struck back and went for the kill. As promised, he all but tore Chanura apart into pieces. It was a horrifying sight, mitigated no less by the fact that the man being torn apart was a demon in human form, a rakshasa among mortals who had wreaked havoc on numerous innocents as well as other warriors by taking advantage of his unfairly produced strength, the result of Jarasandha's arcane potions and sorcery.

Balarama wondered if anyone who had been related to or had cared about any of Chanura's former victims was present to watch the man's brutal end. He hoped so.

For his part, he watched the proceedings to the very end, dispassionate and calm. The reactions he had to Krishna's injuries had dissipated instantly, as quickly as his wounds had healed.

He saw a flicker of movement to one side and saw one of Kamsa's team rush towards Krishna who had his back to that side.

It was the tall, powerfully built giant with the oddly shaped face, the one they called Crooked Jaw. Mustika. Apparently, he could not bear to see his mate torn apart by Krishna and with a roar of fury, flung himself at him.

Kamsa watched in utter disbelief as the Deliverer took one of his best men and dearest friends apart, piece by piece, quite literally. He could not believe that this slender boy possessed such shakti. How was it possible?

Because he's Vishnu Incarnate, you fool! said a voice in his head. It was the voice of Yadu, his old stablehand, royal syce, and sometime trainer. The man who had become his guru and transformed Kamsa into the most formidable man-to-man fighter in the entire kingdom.

Suddenly, Kamsa wished Yadu were with him, telling him what to do, how to handle this, what moves he might use to counter this brutal attack by the Slayer.

But Yadu was dead, of course. Dead only recently. And he, Kamsa, hadn't bothered to grant him so much as a decent cremation.

Kamsa was jolted out of his stupor when Mustika roared in fury and charged forward. Either Crooked Jaw had forgotten that this was a strictly man-to-man bout, or he did not care. He had been a dear friend of Chanura, and apparently he couldn't bear the sight of his teammate torn to pieces by this young cowherd. He knew and cared nothing about the prophecy or the Deliverer. To him, Krishna was an opponent who had killed a teammate and friend, and was therefore a person who had to be destroyed.

Kamsa watched hopefully as Mustika threw himself at Krishna. Perhaps Mustika would fare better than Chanura. And that would mean the end of Krishna.

But as he watched, Krishna did not defend himself against Mustika's assault. He merely sidestepped smartly, letting Mustika's own weight and momentum carry him forward.

That was the amazing thing. How could Krishna be so thin-limbed and slender-bodied, yet so agile and athletic as well as capable of withstanding the full force of Chanura's blows? It was beyond Kamsa's comprehension. All he knew was that a person could make himself denser, packing his cells closer and tighter together even as they expanded, until they were as hard as iron itself, or harder. Or he could loosen them, allowing himself flexibility. Like a scale ranging from black to white, Kamsa could range across the various shades of grey, choosing to make his body denser and less flexible in movement or less dense and more flexible. The same held true for all his teammates who had been empowered by Jarasandha's potions.

But Krishna was not subject to the same limitations. He was apparently stronger and denser than any of them – or more than Chanura at any rate – while remaining as agile and flexible as any normal man.

Kamsa watched as Mustika turned around with some difficulty, trying to charge at Krishna again. But Krishna danced around behind Mustika, managing effortlessly to keep himself behind Crooked Jaw as the giant turned round and round, seeking his vanished opponent. Krishna even waggled his eyebrows and made faces at Mustika's back as they circled together, sending the crowd into splits of laughter and dissipating the tension that had followed the slaying of Chanura.

Then Balarama entered the field. Since Mustika had joined the fray, it was within Balarama's rights to do so. Kamsa thought of protesting, then stopped himself. Instead, he turned to Sala.

'Sala, you take Krishna. Go on.'

Sala glanced at him sideways, then flexed his powerfully muscled arms and moved forward, building up speed as he reduced his body density for the attack.

Meanwhile, Balarama stood facing Mustika who stopped trying to turn around and grab hold of Krishna and directed his fury at Krishna's brother instead.

Sala came running fast at Krishna, so fast that even Krishna, who was briefly distracted by Balarama's arrival, failed to notice him until the last moment.

Balarama saw Sala bearing down on Krishna, and called out, 'Bhai!'

Even as Balarama took the instant to call out, Mustika swung his upper body and struck at Balarama as hard as he was capable.

Both Balarama and Krishna were struck by Mustika and Sala at the same moment. The sounds of impact were like explosions of lightning striking tree trunks.

The crowd gasped in response, the Vrishnis rising to their feet.

Kamsa grinned and laughed aloud.

seventeen

Balarama felt Mustika's blow like the kick he had once received from the donkey asura. Mustika's blow spun him around and off-balance, and he felt as if his skull and every bone in his face and neck had shattered into fragments. In a sense, they had. But due to his divine essence, they knitted together almost immediately. Even so, for the fraction of a second when the bones *were* shattered, the sensation was indescribable.

At the same instant, Krishna was struck from behind by the charging Sala. The wrestler's rock-solid head was lowered and it struck Krishna's spine with the force of a giant battering ram striking a castle gate. It broke Krishna's spine into two halves, and each half into splinters, and Sala's head ought to have continued through Krishna's body, tearing a hole in it the way a flung javelin tears through stretched canvas. But Krishna's divinity caused his body to heal instantly, preventing Sala's skull from doing further damage.

These two attacks, brought simultaneously, almost ended the fight that day for the brothers. Nobody would ever know for certain how close they had come to defeat in that particular instant. Radha, who was watching intently, suspected, but she was reacting emotionally, fearing so much that she thought every blow that struck Krishna would harm him beyond recovery. So she could not tell that this one was the very blow that almost killed her beloved. Because she was watching only Krishna, she did not realize that Balarama was being struck as grievously at exactly the same instant.

What caused the crisis were not the blows themselves, but the fact that they came at the same time, and that both brothers were looking at each other when they came.

Krishna was so preoccupied with warning Balarama and Balarama with warning Krishna that both forgot about their own selves for an instant. Even though their bodies healed of their own accord, they continued to watch each other out of concern, in case the other should require help.

In that instant, had Kamsa also attacked them, either one of them, he would have had an upper hand. He might even have injured one sufficiently to cause him serious harm. Permanent harm. Or worse.

But Kamsa was afraid by then. Afraid of the Slayer's power. Of the prophecy. Of even the infant Krishna who had slain each of the assassins sent to kill him.

And so he remained where he was and watched instead.

And thus the brothers both got a moment to recover and each had only one opponent to fight. Each one saw that the other was hurt but could survive and fight back. And the moment of vulnerability passed. And then both were back in the fray.

Balarama was furious at being caught unawares by Mustika and struck back with his open palm, literally slapping the giant. Because of the considerable difference in their heights, he could not slap the giant's face or shoulders or back. Instead, his slaps landed on Mustika's backside. He smacked the giant again and again and again, relentlessly, intending to show that his open palm alone was sufficient to fight this opponent.

Krishna in turn was angry that he had almost let himself be bested in that moment of defencelessness. As a result, he struck out with a single kick at Sala's head. Krishna's foot struck Sala's forehead. In fact, only the tips of two of Krishna's toes struck Sala's head. They were sufficient to decapitate the giant. The crown of his head was smashed to a pulp and was torn from his head and body. It splattered across the dust of the field.

Sala's body stood swaying for a moment, then collapsed like a sala tree chopped at the trunk. It fell, spewing brains and blood into the dirt.

Balarama's slaps shattered Mustika's thighbone, hip, ribs and legs. The giant roared with pain and fell to his knees. Balarama continued slapping him relentlessly. Mustika's shoulders were shattered, his collarbone broken, his chest punctured and reduced to a pulp. Then Balarama slapped his jaw, smashing the legendary Crooked Jaw to smithereens. That was the end of Crooked Jaw Mustika.

Krishna and Balarama turned and looked at the remaining opponents.

Tosalaka stood in the next rectangle, facing Krishna directly. Krishna charged at him.

Kuta was confronting Balarama and filled with foolish fury. He saw Balarama charging and charged back at him.

All four fighters met in an explosive collision on the field.

Balarama struck Kuta with his left fist and dealt him a single blow. It tore through Kuta's body, shattering the petrified flesh to pieces. Kuta's corpse sprawled on the ground.

Krishna caught hold of Tosalaka by the waist in a wrestler's hug, moved his hands so that one was gripping the opponent's upper body and the other held the lower part, and literally tore the man into two halves.

Made unimaginably dense by his unnatural abilities, Tosalaka's body broke rather than tore. Krishna threw both pieces aside disdainfully. Then he looked at the rest of the fighters on the field.

One by one, they turned and looked at each other, unable to believe what they had just witnessed.

Some looked to Kamsa, others to Jarasandha. But there was no help to be had from either one.

They made their decision instantly. They decided they would rather be labelled cowards for the rest of their lives than die in the present. They turned and ran, heavy feet pounding thunderously as they left the field. They sounded and looked like a herd of baby elephants fleeing a pair of angry lions.

In moments, only the dust of their passing remained to mark where they had stood. Slowly, the dust cleared.

Only Krishna and Balarama remained on the field now.

And Kamsa.

eighteen

Balarama looked at the wrestlers fleeing the arena and laughed. 'I thought they were fighters. It seems they are runners as well, Bhai.'

Krishna grinned. 'So it seems. Who would have thought elephants could run that fast!'

Both brothers laughed, relieved at their narrow escape as well as pleased at their victory. Sensing the change of mood, the crowd began to titter as well. The giggle spread across the field until it burst forth as full-blown laughter. Even the supporters of Kamsa laughed, embarrassed at how easily two cowherd boys had defeated Kamsa's greatest champions.

Far too many had watched these same champions strut arrogantly in the arena as well as in the field of battle, killing and maiming indiscriminately. They took satisfaction now in watching the haughty giants paid back in their own coin.

As one, the crowd rose to its feet, cheering the winners and shouting and celebrating. Assuming that the tournament was at an end, the royal musicians began playing a merry tune which in turn led the crowd to dancing. Court dancers, groomed to dance for the audience's pleasure the instant the game was over, came out and danced, adding to the festive mood.

The news of Krishna's and Balarama's success spread throughout the city. But those who waited in the streets, like the Vrishni contingent, did not rise to their feet to celebrate. Not yet.

The Usurper was still alive. The Childslayer. The demon king of Mathura.

Kamsa still stood on the field, very much alive, seething with rage and impotent fury.

As the merriment continued, he roared. At once, his aides passed on his commands, and in another instant, the music stopped, the dancing ceased and everyone resumed their seats nervously, for nobody dared ignore Kamsa himself. Not so long as he lived.

'Enough!' he thundered. 'Enough of this despicable spectacle.'

He stepped forward. 'Seize those two murderers. They have violated the law of the land. I want them arrested and executed within the hour.'

He waited for the army to do as he commanded. But no soldiers came forward. Nobody saluted or barked orders, following through on his command.

Instead, General Bana stepped forward, almost casually. 'Apologies, my lord,' he said, loudly enough to be heard by everyone in the arena and for the word to be passed on to those too distant to hear him directly, 'but the imperial army has chosen to join the movement to restore the rightful king to his throne. King Ugrasena, your father.'

Kamsa raised both fists in anger. Had Bana been close enough to strike, he would have smashed him to pulp with a single blow for his impudence. 'I demand that Ugrasena be executed at once as well. He is clearly siding with these rebels against the empire!'

Akrur stepped forward, showing himself. 'Ugrasena has no part in this. We the citizens of the land support his cause of our own accord. It is we who wish that he be released and restored to the throne as is his right.'

Kamsa pointed an accusing finger at Akrur. 'You traitor. I will see to you afterwards. Right now, I will show you what it means to oppose the might of Kamsa and the Magadhan Empire.'

Kamsa turned to face the royal pavilion. 'Emperor Jarasandha,' he called out, 'my father-in-law and father in truth, I ask that you unleash your Mohini Fauj upon the ungrateful citizenry of Mathura and teach them a lesson. Even my own army has turned against me, clearly seduced by the Vrishni rebellion. Wipe them all out! Kill every last Vrishni man, woman and child. Exterminate the clan from this earth. Do all this and Mathura is yours, a part of your great Magadhan Empire!'

Jarasandha rose from his seat and turned to go. His aides and advisors followed him without so much as a backward glance at Kamsa.

Kamsa's face crumpled. 'Father!' he cried. 'Where are you going? I have need of you! Please stay. Help me quell this rebellion. We shall achieve all your plans!'

Jarasandha's vahan, clearly readied and kept waiting for just this moment, came briskly to a halt in front of the royal pavilion. The Magadhan paused and glanced scornfully at his son-in-law. 'Mathura's troubles are not Magadha's problem. You have made your bed here. Now lie in it.'

Kamsa's bewilderment showed that he had never expected such treatment from Jarasandha, not in a thousand years of imagining. 'But you *want* Mathura! I know you do! It is the jewel in the crown of your empire. You said so yourself just last night.'

Jarasandha nodded. 'So it shall be. And I shall have it. But in my own way, at my own time. Soon. Very soon. But first, I shall leave you to sort out your internal disagreements on your own. My daughters, your wives, have already been sent ahead to their summer palace. They shall await you there, in case you are still able to visit them after this issue is resolved. If not, I shall return soon enough to continue my plans with Mathura.'

Jarasandha mounted the vahan.

Kamsa lost all sense of dignity. He ran after the carriage, crying out. 'But I am your son-in-law. You love me as a son!'

'And now, I leave you to stand on your own two feet, my son,' Jarasandha said. Then with one sharp crack of his whip, he spurred his horses forward and raced the vahan away, leaving Mathura through the deserted army cantonments, the only route not crowded by citizens and militia and Mathuran troops who were on duty throughout the city for the match.

Kamsa watched Jarasandha leave and by the slump of his back, Krishna knew that his uncle's strength had left him.

By the time Kamsa turned, he was already a broken man. But he was a broken man with the power of a super-mortal and the strength and fury of a rakshasa.

'You,' he cried out in a voice that rent the air. 'You are the source of all that ails me ... Preserver of mortalkind. Hah! So you are God Incarnate? Now let us see if you can face a veritable god among asuras.'

And as Mathura watched with horrified astonishment, Kamsa began to grow larger, larger, and still bigger, until he once again stood with his head high among the clouds, bigger than he had ever been in his earlier transformations but still as dense and powerful as he had learnt to make himself with the help of Jarasandha's potions and Putana's Halahala poison.

'COME NOW, VISHNU,' he roared as he raised his foot and stamped down hard upon the royal pavilion, crushing every last one of his own entourage without caring if they were loyal to him or not. 'LET US SEE IF YOU CAN FULFIL YOUR PROPHECY BEFORE I FINISH DESTROYING MATHURA AND KILLING EVERY LAST YADAVA IN THE CITY!'

nineteen

Mathura was in chaos. Kamsa towered above the city, enlarged to such an enormous size, his head could barely be seen from the ground. He stamped about the cantonment area, smashing and killing everyone within reach. For some reason, his anger was directed at his own supporters and followers – perhaps because of their betrayal.

'Bhai,' Balarama said, 'we should move the people to safety before he turns his attention to them. I shall do it.'

Krishna turned to thank Balarama for taking the initiative without argument, but Balarama was already racing to the pavilion, shouting instructions. Krishna knew there was not much he could do there. His presence was better put to use against that tower of destruction on the rampage.

He needed no more than an instant to think the situation through. Kamsa's enlargement had come as a surprise, but not a shock. After all, Krishna had known that his uncle had once possessed the ability to expand and reduce in size. He had also known that Kamsa had acquired the ability to use the same power to make his body denser while remaining the same size. Somehow, Kamsa had found a way to combine both in secret and had waited until this day to reveal his talents.

If he lived up to his word, as he was likely to, all of Mathura would be destroyed by his running amok. The only way to avoid further casualties was to remove him from Mathura. And in order to do that, Krishna would have to make him take the fight elsewhere. Which left only one place to go to.

Krishna flew up, rising until he hovered high enough to be noticed by Kamsa. Then, using his power to project his own voice, he addressed his uncle. 'Uncle Kamsa!'

Kamsa had just finished pounding most of the court's nobility and aristocracy to bloody pulp. Krishna had no sympathy for the rich and overbearing overlords who had aided and abetted Kamsa during his reign of atrocities and abuse all these years, but it was still sickening to see people trampled thus mercilessly. Tearing apart a super-mortal wrestling champion in a bout was one thing, this, on the other hand, was simple murder.

Kamsa turned at the sound of Krishna's voice. He grinned down at the tiny figure hovering in mid-air. '*NEPHEW! DID I SURPRISE YOU? YOU DIDN'T KNOW ABOUT MY ABILITY TO DO THIS, DID YOU? HOW UNEXPECTED! IT SEEMS THE GREAT DELIVERER IS NOT OMNISCIENT, AFTER ALL!*'

Krishna ignored the taunt. 'Uncle. I shall give you one final chance to surrender and live. Only because we are related by blood. Yield now and I shall have you arrested and imprisoned for life. It is more than you deserve, and you know it.'

Kamsa chuckled. With his enormous size, it sounded like a thousand waterfalls crashing down cascades after the monsoons, echoing off a deep ravine's walls. '*LIFE IMPRISONMENT? WHY BOTHER. LET'S SETTLE THIS RIGHT HERE AND NOW. IT'S ABOUT TIME. I'VE BEEN WANTING TO FACE YOU, VISHNU, EVER SINCE MY MOTHER RAISED ME ON STORIES OF YOU TAKING REBIRTH TO DESTROY EVIL ON EARTH. MY MOTHER WAS THE SISTER OF THE GREAT LORD RAVANA, DID*

YOU KNOW THAT? THAT WAS WHEN MY NAME WAS KALA-NEMI, AND YOURS RAMACHANDRA. I ALSO REGRETTED THE FACT THAT WE NEVER GOT TO CONFRONT EACH OTHER. FINALLY, I HAVE MY CHANCE AND I INTEND TO MAKE THE BEST OF IT. COME ON, FACE ME NOW. OR STAND ASIDE AND WATCH ME DESTROY YOUR PRECIOUS CITY AND PEOPLE!

'So your plan is to fight me and in the process destroy Mathura as well?'

'*YES. BRILLIANT, IS IT NOT? EVEN IF YOU WIN, THE FIGHT WITH ME WILL CAUSE SO MUCH DESTRUCTION THAT I WILL HAVE TRIUMPHED BY DEFAULT. FOR I DON'T CARE A WHIT FOR THESE WRETCHED MORTALS. BUT YOU DO. SO WIN OR LOSE, THEY WILL DIE ANYWAY.*'

Krishna sighed. 'Then you leave me no choice.'

He flew directly at Kamsa.

twenty

Kamsa cried out in anger as he staggered, the back of his heels crushing a line of heavily laden carts loaded with weapons for the imperial army. Spears and swords snapped and crackled under his giant feet. He snarled and slapped at his own head, swatting at Krishna like a man might swipe at a troublesome mosquito. But before he could get hold of him, Krishna had taken hold of Kamsa's hair and was flying upwards. Kamsa had expected him to attack and fight, but instead, Krishna took hold of the giant rakshasa and flew in the one direction where nobody would be injured by Kamsa's gargantuan size and wicked intent: upwards.

Kamsa roared with fury as he realized what was happening. But Krishna was already lifting him bodily up in the air, rising higher and higher. Kamsa's feet flailed as they left the ground, narrowly missing striking a building. Crowds shrieked below as tens of thousands of Mathurans turned their faces upwards, watching the battle with rapt attention, less afraid for their own lives than eager to witness the fight for which they had waited twenty-three long years.

Kamsa continued to flail his hands. But it is near impossible for any man, or giant, to strike the top of his own head while being carried upwards. Still, he struggled and thrashed around mightily. It was only when he was several hundred yards up in the air and still rising that he stopped waving his arms about and froze.

Krishna sensed understanding flood through his uncle's giant brain.

'I SEE NOW WHAT YOU MEAN TO DO! BUT YOU CANNOT. YOU MUST NOT. I WILL NOT LET YOU DO IT. I WANT A FIGHT. I WANT THE BATTLE I DESERVE. I WILL NOT BE DROPPED DOWN LIKE A RAW EGG TO BREAK ON THE EARTH. I WANT MY FAIR DUE IN BATTLE. FIGHT ME, VISHNU. PUT ME BACK DOWN AND FIGHT ME FACE-TO-FACE.'

Krishna said grimly, 'Uncle, you lost your right to a fair fight when you slew newborns by dashing their brains out. You lost it when you ordered the execution of thousands more innocent children. You gained the right to be denied a fair fight when you committed a hundred thousand other atrocities over the past twenty-three years, not to mention those you had committed even before revealing your true rakshasa nature. Back on the field, there was a moment when you could have attacked me and had your chance at a fair fight. You failed to take it. Now, this is the only fight you get. It is the only one you deserve.'

'NO, KRISHNA, NO,' Kamsa cried, bellowing loud enough to be heard by the whole of Mathura. 'YOU CANNOT DO THIS TO ME. I AM A WARRIOR AND SO ARE YOU. FIGHT ME LIKE A WARRIOR. IT IS MY RIGHT. AND IT IS YOUR DHARMA.'

'I am a warrior, yes,' Krishna said sadly. 'That is the only reason why I had to wait this long and allow so many innocents to suffer and die before facing you today. If I was not a warrior and not bound by Kshatriya dharma, I would have crept into your palace as a babe and slaughtered you as you slept. But this is as far as my dharma will allow me to bring you. To this certain death. It is the only end for one such as you. Just as a mad elephant or beast must be put down instantly, without hesitation or thought, so must your life be ended now. If you have any last words, speak them now, before I release my hold on your body and let it fall to its death on the earth below.'

Kamsa made begging and pleading sounds to no avail. Finally, seeing that he could negotiate no further, he snarled. 'RELEASE ME, THEN. BUT KNOW THIS BEFORE I DIE. YOUR REAL STRUGGLE ON EARTH HAS NOT EVEN BEGUN YET, VISHNU. YOU HAVE FAR MORE SUFFERING TO ENDURE AND FAR GREATER BATTLES AND STRUGGLES TO OVERCOME BEFORE YOU ACCOMPLISH YOUR TASK IN THIS INCARNATION. THIS IS NOT THE END, IT IS ONLY THE BEGINNING.'

Krishna replied sadly, 'This too I know.'

And then he released Kamsa, letting the giant fall.

He took several moments, during which time the watching multitudes held their breath. Krishna had been careful to carry Kamsa's massive form farther north of the city, to the wastelands where nobody resided, the sprawling wadis and ravines of uninhabited desolation where Kamsa had once come to practise the use of his new-found abilities. Where he had pounded his fists and body time and again against rocks and boulders, testing his new shakti on inanimate objects and innocent animals, taking pride in it.

He fell into that wasteland. And the earth itself seemed to harden to receive him. As if Bhoodevi, Mother Prithvi, whatever you choose to call her, suffering for so long under the cruel yoke of Kamsa's tyranny, resolved that this time, she would be harder than Kamsa's dense muscled body and sinew and bone. And so, as the giant Kamsa struck the ground, his body was shattered into a thousand pieces, fragmented and fragmented again, until even the smallest fragment broke apart into dust.

A wind rose from nowhere and carried this dust away into oblivion.

And across Mathura, a million liberated souls cheered, only one word on their lips.

'KRISHNA!'

Krishna confronts Jarasandha and his
unimaginable powers in

RAGE OF JARASANDHA

Book 5 of the Krishna Coriolis Series

At a bookstore near you!

acknowledgements

R. Sabarish, my first reader, who read the first drafts of this version back in 2005 when it was still a part of my larger Mba (Mahabharata) retelling, and who shall probably be reading this published version on a different continent now – an achievement that suggests that perhaps I have managed in some way to keep the flame of our epics burning brightly after all. Thank you, Sabs!

Tapas Sadasivan Nair, who read through the final draft of the first two books in the Krishna Coriolis Series years before publication and suggested many valuable corrections and amendments. If not the first, certainly one of my best readers and whose feedback I value greatly. Read on, Kanjisheikh!

For the members of my erstwhile Epic India Group, Forums and the 40,000+ (and counting) readers who have left their wonderful reviews, comments and feedback on my blog at ashokbanker.com over the years. Too many now to name, so I'll settle for ululating without the benefit of a vuvuzela: 'EI! EI! YO!' Proud 2B an Epicindian. Always hamesha forever!

V.K. Karthika, who has turned out to be the editor and publisher who has shown the most faith and support for my work in my entire career, readily buying more books from me, trusting my instincts and giving me whatever was needed to enable the completion of this massively ambitious work. The interesting thing is that Karthika and I first connected not as author and editor, even though we knew each other as acquaintances for years, but as readers sharing a common interest in fantasy, romance and historical sagas. I think that's what makes her such a great editor to work with: she actually reads and enjoys the books she publishes, which is not something I can say for all editors working in publishing today. I am truly grateful for her enduring support and enthusiasm for my work. Karthika, I hope to continue publishing with you for decades to come.

Prema Govindan, whom I didn't even know by name when she turned in the first set of edits on the first Krishna Coriolis book, but whose great love for the subject of this book, Krishna, coupled with an intense professional drive to bring out the best book possible and the rare ability to appreciate an author's individual (and very quirky) 'voice' or style – including my penchant for mixing languages, cultures, et al. in an epic khichdi – resulted in the best editing of my career. And since I have now had the pleasure of working with her on four books, I must say, Prema, it has been a great pleasure and I hope to have your eagle eye and keen mind on every single book in this series and possibly many more as well.

The entire team at HarperCollins India – too many to name, yet each one a star in his or her own right – that is responsible for bringing this book to you, the reader holding this copy in your hands, aided and abetted by the distributors, stockists, retailers and other book trade professionals across the country who are helping the book publishing business defy recessions and break global records. Thank you, all!

As always, my family, starting with my beloved wife Bithika, my daughter Yashka, my son Ayush, and my constant companion Willow, whose love and support are the fountainhead of my life and work. Our story is the one story that I can never hope to better! Love, always.

And finally, you, dear reader, whether you're new to my work or a long-time familiar. If you've never read anything by me before, you should know that I approach every book as if it's my first and only book – never expect the same thing twice because I don't write the same book twice. And if you've read every single thing I've written to date, you probably know that already, in which case, you won't be surprised when you turn the page and find that this book and series is quite unlike everything else I've written before. But what really matters is that you like reading it as much as I loved writing it.

Because I really did. That, and that alone, is the reason why I wrote it. Because I love writing.

And love, like most communicable viruses, is extremely contagious, though thankfully not as harmful to your health.

ASHOK KUMAR BANKER
www.ashokbanker.com
Andheri, Mumbai
www.akbebooks.com
July 2012
www.facebook.com/ashokkbanker
www.twitter.com/ashokbanker

Govinda has been weaving his magic since before
he was born in ...

SLAYER OF KAMSA

Book 1 of The Krishna Coriolis

Cowherd, lover, warrior, god incarnate. The youthful superhero of ancient India is here ...

Forewarned by a prophecy, the demonic Prince Kamsa orders every male newborn to be put to the sword. But even in the womb, Krishna uses powerful magic to cast a spell across the entire kingdom on the night of his birth. Now, the stage is set for the epic clash of the child-god and the terrible forces of evil with the birth of Krishna, the slayer of Kamsa ...

The fantastic adventures of the Hindu god Krishna have entertained and inspired people for millennia. Playful cowherd, mischievous lover, feared demon-slayer – the legendary exploits of this super-being in human form rival the most rousing fantasy epics. Now, the author of the Ramayana Series®, the hugely successful epic retelling of the ancient Sanskrit poem, works his magic once again with the tales of Krishna. All the pomp, splendour and majesty of ancient India come alive in this extraordinary eight-book series.

Govinda has been dancing on, through many more action-packed adventures in …

DANCE OF GOVINDA

Book 2 of The Krishna Coriolis

Govinda, god-child, redeemer of the world, takes on the might of Kamsa

As we move into the second instalment of Ashok K. Banker's Krishna tales, the prophesied Slayer of Kamsa has been born and smuggled out of Mathura in the dead of night. Kamsa finds that his nephew has escaped and flies into a demoniac rage. Meanwhile, his ally Jarasandha of Magadha arrives in Mathura with his coterie of powerful supporters to ensure that Kamsa stays loyal to him. But Kamsa is not to be crushed. With the help of Putana, a powerful demoness living incognito among humans, he slowly regains his strength and acquires new powers.

Packed with surprising insights into the characters of Kamsa and Putana, *Dance of Govinda* is a brilliant interpretation of the nature of evil in a world that teeters on the edge of violence.

FLUTE OF VRINDAVAN

Book 3 of The Krishna Coriolis

The mischievous god-child wields the flute to make evil dance to his tune

Infant Krishna and his half-brother Balarama are the most mischievous children in all of Gokuldham, getting up to all sorts of pranks, raiding neighbours' dahi handis and letting the calves run free. But disciplining God Incarnate is no easy task. It slowly dawns on Mother Yashoda that the babe she is trying to protect is in fact the protector of the entire world! As Krishna survives one horrific asura attack after the other, she comes to terms with the true identity of her adopted son.

Meanwhile, Kamsa despatches a team of other-worldly assassins to slay his nemesis. Harried by Kamsa's forces, Krishna's adoptive father, the peace-loving Nanda Maharaja, is forced to lead his people into exile. They find safe haven in idyllic Vrindavan. But even in this paradise, deadly demons lurk …

The Preserver will rid the world of evil in the other books to come in the Krishna Coriolis Series ...

RAGE OF JARASANDHA

Book 5 of the Krishna Coriolis Series

His days as a flirtatious cowherd behind him, the new Lord of Mathura's powers are tested to the limit when a new enemy, perhaps his deadliest yet, threatens the city of his birth ...

Krishna has fulfilled the prophecy and the Usurper has been slain. But barely has old King Ugrasena been restored to the throne when a new threat rears its head. Jarasandha of Magadha encircles Mathura with a great army. Even the combined might of Krishna and Balarama cannot save the citizens of Mathura. Or can it?

In an instalment that ramps up the thrill and excitement, discover how the young Preserver realizes that the protection of dharma entails the heartache of collateral damage.